Tales of the Home Folks
in
Peace and War

HE WALKED OFF . . . AND LEANED AGAINST A TREE (Page 68)

Tales of the Home Folks
in
Peace and War

BY

JOEL CHANDLER HARRIS

Short Story Index Reprint Series

BOOKS FOR LIBRARIES PRESS
FREEPORT, NEW YORK

First Published 1898
Reprinted 1969

STANDARD BOOK NUMBER:
8369-3147-5

LIBRARY OF CONGRESS CATALOG CARD NUMBER:
75-98573

PRINTED IN THE UNITED STATES OF AMERICA

TO MY DAUGHTER LILLIAN
Who will know why I have included in Tales
of the Home Folks the little skit about
our friends in St. Valerien

CONTENTS

	Page
How Whalebone caused a Wedding . . .	1
The Colonel's "Nigger Dog"	34
A Run of Luck	71
The Late Mr. Watkins of Georgia . .	97
A Belle of St. Valerien	114
The Comedy of War	148
A Bold Deserter	184
A Baby in the Siege	215
The Baby's Fortune	253
An Ambuscade	293
The Cause of the Difficulty	345
The Baby's Christmas	377

LIST OF ILLUSTRATIONS

PAGE

HE WALKED OFF . . . AND LEANED AGAINST A TREE

   (Page 68) . . . . . *Frontispiece.*

"GO!" THE MARISTE REPEATED 144

LITTLE BILLY TROTTED BY HIS SIDE . . . 210

"GOD BLESS YOU, ME B'Y!" 336

TALES OF THE HOME FOLK IN PEACE AND WAR

HOW WHALEBONE CAUSED A WEDDING

Matt Kilpatrick of Putnam used to laugh and say that his famous foxhound Whalebone was responsible for a very brilliant wedding in Jasper. When Harvey Dennis and Tom Collingsworth were among his listeners (which was pretty much all the time, for the three were inseparable), they had a way of shaking their heads dubiously over this statement. Mr. Dennis thought that his dog Rowan (pronounced Ro-ann) ought to have some of the credit, while Mr. Collingsworth was equally sure that Music had as much to do with the happy event as any of the rest. The Collingsworth argument — and it was a sound one — was that where a lady dog is skipping along and performing to the queen's taste all the work that is cut out for her, she ought to come ahead of the gentlemen dogs in any historical statement or reminiscence.

When I first heard the story, considerations of local pride led me to feel that Rowan had been unjustly robbed of the credit that belonged to him; but time cools the ardor of youth, and mellows and sweetens the sources of partisanship. I can say now that Rowan had small advantage over his two famous rivals, when the scent was as high as the saddle-skirts and the pace the kind that kills.

Mr. Kilpatrick used to tell the story as a joke, and frequently he repeated it merely to tease those who were interested in the results of Whalebone's exploit, or to worry his fox-hunting rivals, who were his dearest friends. But the story was true. In repeating it I shall have to include details that Mr. Kilpatrick found it unnecessary to burden himself with, for they were as familiar to his neighborhood audience as any of their own personal affairs.

The way of it was this: One day in the beginning of December, 1860, Colonel Elmore Rivers, of Jasper County, put a negro

boy on a mule and sent him around with an
invitation to certain of his friends, requesting them to do him the honor of eating their
Christmas dinner with him. This invitation
was prepared with great care by Mrs. Rivers,
who was a schoolma'am from Connecticut
when the colonel married her. It was beautifully written on the inside of a sheet of fools-
cap, and this sheet was tacked to a piece of
card-board, by means of a deftly made true-
lover's-knot of blue ribbon. The card-board
was placed in a satchel, and the satchel was
arranged to swing over the shoulders of the
negro, so that there was no danger of losing
it. There was only one invitation, and it
was to be carried from one of the colonel's
friends to the other until all had been noti-
fied of his hospitable desires.

The colonel added an oral postscript as
he gave the negro a stiff dram. " Ding 'em,"
he exclaimed, " tell 'em to bring their dogs.
Mind now! tell 'em to bring their dogs."

Mrs. Rivers enjoyed Christmas as heartily
as anybody, but in beginning preparations
for the festival she always had her misgiv-
ings. Her father, Dr. Joshua Penniman, had
been a Puritan among Puritans, and some-

how she had got the idea from him that there was a good deal of popery concealed in the Christmas ceremonials. But when once the necessity for preparation was upon her she cast her scruples aside, and her Christmas dinners were famous in that whole region. By catering to the colonel's social instincts in this and other particulars, she managed, at a later period of his life, to lead him triumphantly into the fold of the Baptist Church. It was a great victory for Miss Lou, as everybody called her, and she lived long to enjoy the distinction it conferred upon her.

The day after the invitation had been sent around, a couple of weanling pigs were caught and penned, and, until the day before Christmas, they were fed and fattened on nubbins and roasted white-oak acorns. Three young gobblers were also caught and put upon such diet as, according to the colonel's theory, would add to their toothsomeness, and give them a more delicate flavor. These are merely hints of the extensive preparations for the Christmas festival on the Rivers plantation.

What the colonel always wanted was a merry Christmas, and there could be no mer-

riment where good-humor and good-cheer
were lacking. He had said to his wife years
before, when she was somewhat doubtful
about introducing her New England holiday,
" Go ahead, honey! Cut just as big a dash
as you please with your Thanksgiving. I 'll
enjoy it as much as you will, maybe more.
The Lord knows we 've got a heap to be
thankful for. We 'll cut a big dash and
be thankful, and then when Christmas comes
we 'll cut a big dash and be happy."

Thenceforward they had both Thanksgiving and Christmas on that plantation, and
Miss Lou was as anxious to satisfy the colonel with her Christmas arrangements as he
had been to please her with his zeal for
Thanksgiving. Indeed, one Christmas-day,
a year or two after their marriage, Miss Lou
went so far as to present her husband with a
daughter, and ever after that Christmas had
a new significance in that household: Miss
Lou satisfied her Puritan scruples by pretending to herself that she was engaged in
celebrating her daughter's birthday, and the
colonel was glad that two of the most important days in the calendar were merged into
one.

When the child was born, a poor lonely old woman, named Betsey Cole, who lived in the woods between the Rivers plantation and town, sent the colonel word that the little lass would grow up to be both good and beautiful. Nothing would do after that but the colonel must send the fortune-teller a wagon-load of provisions, and he kept it up every Christmas as long as Betsey Cole lived.

The fortune-teller certainly made no mistake in her prediction. The child grew to be the most beautiful young woman in all that region. The colonel named her Mary after his mother, and the name seemed to fit her, for her character was as lovely as her face. Even the women and little children loved her, and when this kind of manifestation is made over a girl, it is needless to inquire about her character or disposition.

It might be supposed that Mary had a lover, but if so, no one knew it but her own sweet self. Her father, the colonel, declared she was as cool as a cucumber when the boys were around, and the young men who raved over her thought she was even cooler than a cucumber. And yet she had her father's ardent temperament and good-nature, and her mother's prudence and sound discretion. It was a happy combination in all respects, and it had its climax in a piquant individuality that impressed old and young with its charm.

There were two young men, among the many that were smitten, who made it a point to pay particular attention to the young lady. One was Jack Preston, and the other was Andy Colston. Both were handsome and ambitious, and both had good prospects. Colston already had the advantage of a fortune, but Preston was as hopeful and as cheerful as if he possessed a dozen plantations and a thousand negroes. Mentally they were about evenly matched, but Preston had been compelled by circumstances to cultivate an energy in the matter of steady application that Colston never knew the necessity of.

These young men were intimate friends, and they did not attempt to conceal from each other their attitude toward Mary Rivers. It was perhaps well that this was so. Both were high-strung and high-tempered, and if they had been anything but intimate with each other, the slightest cause or provocation would have precipitated trouble between

them. And this would have been very un-
fortunate indeed ; for, if the name of Mary
Rivers had been even remotely hinted as the
cause of such trouble, the colonel would have
locked himself in his library, read a chapter
in the family Bible, called for his saddle-
horse and shot-gun, and gone cantering up
the big road on business connected with the
plantation.

But these rival lovers were bosom friends.
There were points about each that attracted
the other. When Preston was with Miss
Mary he lost no opportunity of praising the
good qualities of Colston, and Colston made
no concealment of the fact that he considered
Preston the salt of the earth, as we say in
Georgia.

All this was very pleasant and very confus-
ing. Mary was in love with one of them,
but she never admitted the fact, even to herself, until a curious episode compelled her to
acknowledge it. Even her mother confessed
that she had been unable to discover Mary's
preference until the fact fluttered out before
everybody's eyes, like a startled bird from its
nest. For a while the mother would think
that her daughter preferred Preston. Then

she would imagine that the girl was in love
with Colston. And sometimes she would con-
clude that Mary's heart had not been touched
at all. Miss Lou herself preferred Colston,
but she was not opposed to Preston. Colston had a solid fortune, and Preston — well,
Connecticut knows very well how many long
days and how many hard licks are necessary
to lay up a fortune. Young people may put
up True Love as their candidate and pout at
Hard Cash as much as they please, but if they
had to go through the experience that Connecticut and the neighboring States went
through sixty odd years ago (to go back no
farther), they would come to the conclusion
that Hard Cash has peculiar merits of its own.

Nevertheless, Miss Lou was too wise to say
anything about the matter. She knew that
her husband, although he possessed land and
negroes and money, had a certain fine scorn
for the privileges and distinctions that mere
wealth confers. He was emphatically a man
of the people, and he would have tolerated no
effort to implant false notions in his daughter's mind. Moreover, Miss Lou had great
confidence in Mary's sound judgment. It
was one comfort, the mother thought, that

Mary was not giddy. She was as gay as a lark, and full of the spirit of innocent fun, but (thank goodness) not giddy nor foolish.

But, after all, the chief worry of Miss Lou on the approach of this particular Christmas was not about Mary and her beaux. It was about the preparations that the colonel was making on his own responsibility. She saw several extra bags of meal coming in from Roach's Mill, and her heart sank within her at the thought of numberless fox-hounds swarming under the house and in the yard, and roaming around over the plantation. At the first convenient opportunity she broached the subject.

" Mr. Rivers " (she never called him colonel), " I do hope you have n't asked your friends to bring their hound-dogs with them. Why, they 'll take the whole place. You 've got twelve of your own. What on earth do you want with any more ? "

" Why, yes, honey," said the colonel, with a sigh. " Harvey Dennis and Matt Kilpatrick and Tom Collingsworth will fetch their dogs, and I reckon maybe Jack Casswell and Bill Hearn will fetch theirs."

Mrs. Rivers dropped her hands in her lap

in helpless dismay. " Mercies upon us! I thought you surely had dogs enough of your own."

" Why, honey," the colonel expostulated, " you 've let the niggers chunk my dogs till they are no manner account."

" Well, I do hate hound-dogs! " exclaimed Miss Lou; " sneaking around, sticking their noses in the pots and pans, and squalling like they 're killed if you lift your hand. Why, the foxes come right up in the yard and take off the geese and ducks, where your dogs could see them if they were n't too lazy to open their eyes."

" Those are just the foxes we 're going to catch, honey," remarked the colonel sooth- ingly.

" Well, I 'd rather feed the foxes a whole year than to have forty or fifty hound-dogs quartered on this place three or four days."

The colonel made no reply, and after a while his wife remarked, pleasantly, if not cheer- fully, " Well, I guess I 'll have bigger trou- bles than that before I die. If I don't, it will be a mercy."

" If you don't, honey, you 'll live and die a happy woman," responded the colonel.

Miss Lou wiped her face on her apron and sat absorbed in thought. Presently, Mary came dancing in. Her face was shining with health and high spirits.

"Just think, folks!" she exclaimed. "Four more days and I'll be eighteen! A woman grown, but with the sweet disposition of a child!"

The colonel laughed and his wife flushed a little. "Where did you hear that?" she asked her daughter.

"Why, I heard you say those words to father no longer than last night. Look, father! mother is actually blushing!"

"I believe I did say something like that," said Miss Lou. "I intended to tell your father afterward that very few children have sweet dispositions. But my mind has been worried all day with the thought of the hound-dogs we've got to feed."

"Oh, father!" exclaimed Mary, "are we to have a fox-hunt? And may I go?" The colonel nodded a prompt assent, but Miss Lou protested. "Now, Mr. Rivers, I think that is going too far. I certainly do. I have always been opposed to it. There is no earthly reason why Mary at her age should

get on a horse and go galloping about the
country with a crowd of yelling men and
howling dogs. It may be well enough for
the men, — though I think they could be better employed, — but I think the line ought to
be drawn at the women."

"Why, mother, how many times have I
been fox-hunting with father ? "

"Just as many times as you have made
me miserable," replied Miss Lou; "just that
many times and no more."

"Now, momsy ! don't scold your onliest
and oldest daughter," pleaded Mary.

"Don't wheedle around me ! " cried Miss
Lou, pretending to be very angry. "Mr.
Rivers, you need n't be winking at Mary behind your paper. I do think it is a shame
that you should allow your daughter to go
ripping and tearing about the country hunting foxes. I think it is a burning shame. I
positively do."

"Well, honey " —

"I don't care what anybody says," Miss
Lou broke in. "Here is Mary old enough
to get married, and now she must go scampering about with a lot of men on horseback.
It is ridiculous ! "

"You hear that, father? Momsy says I'm old enough to get married. I'll marry the man that brings me the fox's brush the day after Christmas. And momsy shall bake the cake, and she'll burn it just as the cake is burning now."

Miss Lou lifted her nose in the air. "I declare, if old Dilsey has gone to sleep and left that fruit-cake to burn, I'll send her to the overseer!"

Whereupon she skipped from the room, and soon after the colonel and Mary heard her laughing at something the fat old cook had said. Miss Lou's temper was all on the surface.

The colonel looked at his daughter over his spectacles and smiled. "I reckon you know, precious, that we'll have to catch the fox before your beau can give you the brush. But we'll have some good dogs here. So you'd better tell your sweetheart to stir his stumps. Maybe the wrong chap will get the brush."

"Why, you won't let me have one little joke, father," cried Mary. "Of course I won't marry the man that gives me the brush" — she paused, went to the long mir-

ror that slanted forward from the wall, and
made a pretty mouth at herself — " unless
he's the right person." Then she ran away,
laughing.

Preparations for the Christmas festival
went forward rapidly, and when the day came
a goodly company had assembled to do honor
to the hearty hospitality of Colonel Rivers.
As Miss Lou had foreseen, the yard fairly
swarmed with dogs. Harvey Dennis brought
seven, Matt Kilpatrick ten, Tom Collingsworth twelve, Jack Casswell eight, and Bill
Hearn fourteen — about fifty hounds in all.
Colston and Preston had arrived the night
before. Colston had dogs, but he left them
at home. He knew the prejudices of Mary's
mother. Preston was not a planter and had
no dogs, but he was very fond of cross-coun-
try riding, and never lost an opportunity to
engage in the sport.

The colonel was in ecstasies. The wide
fireplace in the sitting-room was piled high
with half-seasoned hickory wood, and those
who sat around it had to form a very wide
half-circle indeed, for the flaring logs and
glowing embers sent forth a warmth that
penetrated to all parts of the room, big as it
was.

And it was a goodly company that sat around the blazing fire, — men of affairs, planters with very large interests depending on their energy and foresight, lawyers who had won more than a local fame, and yet all as gay and as good-humored as a parcel of schoolboys. The conversation was seasoned with apt anecdotes inimitably told, and full of the peculiar humor that has not its counterpart anywhere in the world outside of middle Georgia.

And the dinner was magnificent. Miss Lou was really proud of it, as she had a right to be. There are very few things that a Georgia plantation will not produce when it is coaxed, and the colonel had a knack of coaxing that was the envy of his neighbors. Miss Lou could not doubt the sincerity of the praise bestowed on her dinner. All the guests were high-livers, and they declared solemnly that they had never before sat down to such a royal feast.

The servants moved about as silently as ghosts. There were four negro girls to wait on the table, and they attended to their duties with a promptness and precision that were constant tributes to the pains that Miss

Lou had taken to train them, and to the vigilance with which she watched their movements.

Over the dessert, the colonel grew communicative. "This mince-pie," he said, "was made by Mary. I don't think she put enough of the twang into it."

"It is magnificent!" exclaimed Colston.

"Superb!" Preston declared.

"It's as good as any," said Tom Collingsworth; "but this pie business is mighty deceiving. Miss Molly is eighteen, and if she can bake a pone of corn-bread as it ought to be baked, she's ready to get married."

"That is her strong point!" cried the colonel. "She beats anybody at that."

"Well, then," said Collingsworth, "you just go and get her wedding goods."

"I'm beginning to think so, too," replied the colonel. "No longer than the other day she declared she'd marry the man that brings her the fox's brush to-morrow. What do you think of that?"

"Why, father!" exclaimed Mary, blushing violently.

"Then it's just as good as settled," replied Collingsworth gravely. "I'm just as

certain to tail that fox as the sun shines. I
rubbed my rabbit-foot on Music and Rowdy
before I started, and I 'll whistle 'em up and
shake it at 'em to-night."

"But remember, Mr. Collingsworth, you
are already married," Mary suggested archly.

"I know — I know! But my old woman
has been complaining might'ly of late — complaining might'ly. When I started away, she
says, 'Tom, you ought n't to ride your big
gray; he's lots too young for you.' But
something told me that I'd need the big
gray, and, sure enough, here's right where
the big gray comes in."

"I brought my sorrel along," remarked
Colston, sententiously.

"Oh, you did?" inquired Collingsworth,
sarcastically. "Well, I'll give your sorrel
half-way across a ten-acre field and run right
spang over you with my big gray before you
can get out of the way. There ain't but one
nag I'm afraid of, and that's Jack Preston's
roan filly. You did n't bring her, did you,
Jack? Well," continued Collingsworth with
a sigh, as Jack nodded assent, "I'll give
you one tussle anyhow. But that roan is a
half-sister of Waters's Timoleon. I declare,

Jack, you ought n't to be riding that filly around in the underbrush."

"She needs exercise," Preston explained. "She's been in the stable eating her head off for a week."

Collingsworth shook his head. "Well," he said, after a while, "just keep her on the ground and I'll try to follow along after you the best I can."

That day and nearly all night there was fun in the big house and fun on the plantation. The colonel insisted on having some yam-potatoes roasted in the ashes to go along with persimmon beer. The negroes made the night melodious with their play-songs, and everything combined to make the occasion a memorable one, especially to the young people. Toward bedtime the hunters went out and inspected their dogs, and an abundant feed of warm ash-cake was served out to them. Then Tom Collingsworth hung his saddle-blanket on the fence, and under it and around it his dogs curled themselves in the oak-leaves; and the rest of the dogs followed their example, so that when morning came not a hound was missing.

During the night Mary was awakened by

the tramping of feet. Some one had come
in. Then she heard the voice of Collingsworth.

" How is it, Harvey ? "

" Splendid ! Could n't be better. It 's
warmer. Been drizzling a little."

" Thank the Lord for that ! " exclaimed
Collingsworth.

Then Mary heard the big clock in the hall
chime three. In a little while she heard
Aunt Dilsey, the cook, shuffling in. A fire
was already crackling and blazing in the sitting-room. Then the clock chimed four, and
at once there seemed to be a subdued stir
all over the house. The house-girl came
into Mary's room with a lighted candle and
quickly kindled a fire, and in a quarter of
an hour the young lady tripped lightly down-
stairs, the skirt of her riding-habit flung over
her arm.

It was not long before the company of fox-
hunters was gathered around the breakfast-
table. The aroma of Aunt Dilsey's hot coffee
filled the room, mingled with the odor of
fried chicken, and, after the colonel had
asked a blessing, they all fell to with a
heartiness of appetite that made Aunt Dil-

sey grin as she stood in the door of the
dining-room, giving some parting advice to
her young mistress.

There was a stir in the yard and in front
of the house. The dogs, seeing the horses
brought out, knew that there was fun on
foot, and they were running about and yelp-
ing with delight. And the negroes were
laughing and talking, and the horses snorting and whinnying, and, altogether, the scene
was full of life and animation. The morning
was a little damp and chilly, but what did
that matter? The drifting clouds, tinged
with the dim twilight of dawn, were more
ominous in appearance than in fact. They
were driving steadily eastward and breaking
up, and the day promised to be all that could
be desired.

At half past five the cavalcade moved off.
Mary had disposed of a possible complication
by requesting Tom Collingsworth to be her
escort until the hunt should need his attention. In addition, she had Bob, the man-of-
all-work, to look to her safety, and, although
Bob was astride of a mule, he considered
himself as well mounted as any of the rest.
So they set out, Bob leading the way to open

the plantation gates that led to the old sedge-fields, where a fox was always found.

The riders had been compelled to make a détour in order to cross Murder Creek, so that it was near half-past six o'clock when they reached the fields. Once upon a time these fields had been covered with broom-sedge, but now they had been taken by Bermuda grass, and were as clean-looking as if they were under cultivation. But they were still called the old sedge-fields.

As the east reddened, the huge shadows crept down into the valleys to find a hiding-place. They rested there a little, and then slowly disappeared, moving westward, and leaving behind them the light of day.

Tom Collingsworth had carried Mary to a hill that overlooked every part of the wide valley in which the dogs were hunting. He had been teasing her about Colston and Preston. Finally he asked : —

" Now, Miss Mary, which of the two would you like to receive the brush from ? "

" I 'll allow you to choose for me. You are a good judge."

" Well," said Collingsworth, " if a man was to back me up against the wall, and draw a knife on me, and I could n't help myself, I 'd say Preston. That 's a fact."

What Mary would have said the old hunter never knew until long afterward, for just at that moment a quavering, long-drawn note came stealing up from the valley below.

" That 's my beauty ! " exclaimed Collingsworth. " That 's Music, telling what she thinks she knows. Wait ! "

Again the long-drawn note came out of the valley, but this time it was eager, significant.

" Now she 's telling what she knows," exclaimed Collingsworth.

The dogs went scampering to the signal. Music was not indulging in any flirtation. The drag was very warm. Whalebone, Matt Kilpatrick's brag dog, picked it up with an exultant cry that made the horses prick their ears forward. Then Rowan joined in, and presently it was taken up by every ambitious dog on the ground. But there seemed to be some trouble. The dogs made no headway. They were casting about eagerly, but in confusion.

" If you 'll excuse me, Miss Mary, I 'll go down and try to•untangle that skein. That fox is n't forty yards from Music's nose."

He spurred his horse forward, but had to rein him up again. Whalebone swept out of the underbrush, a hundred yards away, followed by Music and Rowan, gave a wild, exultant challenge that thrilled and vibrated on the air, and went whirling past Mary and Collingsworth not fifty yards from where they stood. Collingsworth gave a series of yells that brought the whole field into the chase, not far behind the leaders.

The drag led through and across a series of undulations, and Miss Mary and Collingsworth, cantering leisurely along a skirting ridge, had an excellent view of hunt and huntsmen. The drag was warm enough to be inviting, but not warm enough to excite the hounds. Whalebone, Music, and Rowan were running easily twenty yards ahead of the pack, and for a good part of the time a horse-blanket would have covered them.

It was evident, Mr. Collingsworth said, that the fox had run around at the head of the valley in some confusion, and had then slipped away before the hunt came upon the ground. It was a red, too, for a gray would have played around in the undergrowth with the dogs at his heels before breaking cover.

The ridge along which Miss Mary and Collingsworth rode bore gradually to the left,
inclosing for three miles or more a low range
of Bermuda hills, and a series of sweeping
valleys, fringed here and there with pine and
black-jack thickets.

The chase led toward the point where this
ridge intersected the woodland region, so that
the young lady and Collingsworth not only
had an almost uninterrupted view of the hunt
from the moment the hounds got away, but
were taking a short cut to the point whither
the dogs seemed to be going. Both Preston
and Colston were well up with the hounds,
but Preston's roan filly was going at a much
easier gait than Colston's sorrel.

Where the ridge and the hunt entered the
woods there was what is known as a " clay
gall," a barren spot, above two acres in extent. The surface soil had been washed away
and the red clay lay bare and unproductive.
At this point the fox seemed to have taken
unto himself wings. The drag had vanished.

Who can solve the mystery of scent?
Xenophon, who knew as much (and as little)
about it as anybody knew before or has
known since, puzzled himself and his readers

with a dissertation on the subject. There is a superstition that wild animals can withhold their scent, and there is a theory held by some hunters that a fox badly frightened will leave no scent behind him at all. Those who have followed the hounds know that many a hopeful chase has suddenly come to an end under circumstances as mysterious as they were exasperating.

The old riders looked at one another significantly when the dogs ran whining about the clay gall. Matt Kilpatrick groaned and shook his head. Harvey Dennis encouraged the dogs and urged them on, and they seemed to do their best, but not a whimper came from the noisiest of the pack. Some of the huntsmen began to exhibit signs of despair. But the older ones were more philosophical.

" Wait," said Matt Kilpatrick. " Whalebone and Music and Rowan have gone off to investigate matters. Let 's hear what they have to say."

This seemed to be a pretty tame piece of advice to give a parcel of impatient people who had just got a taste of the chase, but it was reasonable ; and so they waited with such appearance of resignation as they could mus-

ter. They did not have long to wait. By
the time Collingsworth could throw a leg over
the pommel of his saddle and take out his
pocket-knife preparatory to whittling a twig,
Whalebone gave a short, sharp challenge a
quarter of a mile away. He was joined instantly by Rowan and Music, and then Bob,
the negro, gave a yell as he heard Old Blue,
the colonel's brag dog, put in his mouth.
The rest of the dogs joined in the best they
could, but a good many were thrown out, for
the fox had been taking matters easily, it
seems, until he heard the dogs coming over
the hills, and then he made a bee-line for Little River, seven miles away.

The chase went with a rush from the moment Whalebone picked up the drag in the
big woods. When the fox broke away he
turned sharply to the left, and in a few moments the dogs streamed out into the open
and struck across the Bermuda hills. Mr. Collingsworth, still escorting Mary, was compelled
to let his big gray out a few links. It was
fun for the young lady, who had a quick eye
and a firm hand. She gave the black she was
riding two sharp strokes with her whip, and,
for a couple of miles, she set the pace for the

riders. But it was a pace not good for the horses, as the older hunters knew, and Collingsworth remonstrated.

"Don't ride so hard, Miss Mary," he said. "You'll have plenty of hard riding to do when that old red comes back. I'm going to take my stand on yonder hill, and if you'll keep me company, our horses will be fresh when the big scuffle comes."

So they took their stand on the hill, and the hounds swept away toward the river, followed by the more enthusiastic riders. They were riders, however, who seemed to have a knack of taking care of their horses. When the hounds went over a hill the music of their voices rose loud and clear; when they dipped down into the valleys, it came sweet and faint. They disappeared in the woods, two miles away, and their melody swelled out on the morning air like the notes of some powerful organ softly played. Then the music became fainter and fainter, falling on the ears as gently as a whisper, and finally it died away altogether.

"Now," said Collingsworth, "we'll ride a half-mile to the left here, and I think we'll then be in the hock of the ham."

" In the hock of the ham ! " exclaimed
Mary.

" Oh, I was talking to myself," explained
the gray cavalier, laughing. " If you 'll put
a ham on the ground and make an outline of
it, you 'll get a good map of this chase, in my
opinion. The line at the big end of the ham
will be Little River. The·line on the right
will be the way the fox went, and the line on
the left will be the way he 'll come back. If
you ask me why a fox will run up stream
when he 's not hard pushed, I 'll never tell
you, but that 's the way they do."

A quarter of an hour passed — a half-hour
— three quarters. Then, far to the left, there
came upon the morning wind a whimpering
sound that gradually swelled into a chorus of
hounds.

" He 's cut out a bigger ham than I
thought he would," said Collingsworth.

The sun was now shining brightly. An
old bell-cow, browsing on the Bermuda roots
on the hillside, lifted her head suddenly as
she heard the hounds, and the kling-kolangle
of the bell made a curious accompaniment
to the music of the dogs, as they burst from
a thicket of scrub-pine and persimmon bushes

that crowned the farthest hill on the left.
There was a short pause as the leading dogs
came into view — a "little bobble," as Mr.
Collingsworth phrased it — and they deployed
about very rapidly, knowing by instinct that
they had no time to lose. Old Blue, the
colonel's dog, was still with the leaders, and
seemed to be as spry as any of them. It was
Old Blue, in fact, that recovered the drag a
little to the right of the point where the dogs
had made their appearance. The chase then
swerved somewhat to the right, and half-way
down the hill the dogs took a running jump
at a ten-rail fence. Whalebone took it in
grand style, knocking the top-rail off behind him. Rowan and Music went over
easily, but Old Blue had to scramble a little.
He made up for lost time when he did get
over, and Mary grew enthusiastic. She declared that hereafter Old Blue should be
treated with due respect.

By this time the rest of the dogs had made
their appearance. It was a pretty sight to
see them swarming, helter-skelter, over the
fence, and the sweet discord their voices
made was thrilling indeed.

A rider appeared on the hill to the left.

It was Preston, and he seemed to be riding easily and contentedly. On the hill to the right the silhouette of another rider appeared. It was Colston, and he was going as hard as he could. The fox, too, had given Colston a decided advantage, for he had swerved considerably to the left, a fact that placed Preston nearly a half-mile farther from the dogs than Colston was.

Collingsworth glanced at Mary and smiled, but she did not return the smile. She was very pale, and she swished the air with her riding-whip so suddenly and so vigorously that her horse jumped and snorted.

"Don't do that, child!" said Collingsworth, in a low tone. His eye had run ahead of the dogs, and he caught sight of the fox, doubling back up the valley, the dogs going down on one side of a low swampy growth that extended part of the way through the low ground, and the fox going back on the other side. He was going very nimbly, too, but his brush was heavy with dew, and his mouth was half open.

Mary glanced at Collingsworth, but that gentleman was looking steadily at Preston. Then a singular thing happened. Preston, riding to the hounds, raised his right hand above his head and held it there an instant. As quick as a flash, Collingsworth leaned from his saddle and shook his left hand, and then bent and unbent his arm rapidly. Preston's roan filly seemed to understand it, for she made three or four leaps forward, and then came to a standstill.

At this juncture Mr. Collingsworth gave the view halloo, — once, twice, thrice, — and then spurred his big gray toward the fox, which was now going at full speed. Whalebone responded with a howl of delight that rang clear and sharp, and in another moment he and Rowan and Music and Old Blue were going with their heads up and tails down. When Bob, the negro, saw Old Blue going with the best, he gave utterance to a shout which few white men could imitate, but which no sensible dog could misunderstand. At that instant the four dogs caught sight of the fox, and they went after him at a pace that neither he nor any of his tribe could improve on. He plunged into the swampy barrier, was forced out, and the dogs ran into him at the roan filly's feet. He leaped into the air with a squall, and fell into the red jaws of Whalebone and Old Blue.

Preston leaped from the filly so quickly that some of the others thought he had been thrown. When he rose to his feet he held the coveted brush in his hand, and without saying " By your leave," tied it to Miss Mary's saddle - bow. Mr. Collingsworth growled a little because Music was not the first to touch the fox. But otherwise he seemed to be very happy. Colston rode up, a little flushed, but he was not sulky. Mary seemed to pay no attention whatever to the little episode. Her face was somewhat rosier than usual, but this was undoubtedly due to the excitement and exercise of the chase.

When the belated hunters arrived — those who had ambled along with the colonel — the whole party turned their horses' heads toward the Rivers place, and, as they went along, Collingsworth noticed that Mary kept watching the brush to see that it was not lost.

A good deal more might be said, but I simply set out to explain why Matt Kilpatrick of Putnam used to laugh and say that his dog Whalebone caused a wedding.

THE COLONEL'S "NIGGER DOG"

ONE morning Colonel Rivers of Jasper, standing on his back porch, called to a negro man who was passing through the yard.

"Ben!"

"Yasser!"

"How's everything at the home place?"

"Tollerble, suh, — des tollerble."

"Tell Shade I want to see him this morning."

"Unk Shade done gone, suh. He sho is. He done gone!"

"Gone where?"

"He done tuck ter de woods, suh. Yasser! he done gone!"

A frown clouded the colonel's otherwise pleasant brow.

"What is the matter with the old simpleton?"

"Some kinder gwines on 'twix him an' Marse Preston, suh. I dunno de rights un it. But Unk Shade done gone, suh!"

" When did he go ? "

" Yistiddy, suh."

The colonel turned and went into the house, and the negro passed on, shaking his head and talking to himself. The colonel walked up and down the wide hall a little while, and then went into his library and flung himself into an easy-chair. As it happened, the chair sat facing his writing-desk, and over the desk hung a large portrait of his mother. It was what people call " a speaking likeness," and the colonel felt this as he looked at it. The face was full of character. Firmness shone in the eyes and played about the lips. The colonel regarded the portrait with an interest that was almost new. Old Shade in the woods, — old Shade a runaway ! What would his mother say if she were alive ? The colonel felt, too, — he could not help but feel, — that he was largely responsible for the fact that old Shade was a fugitive.

When Mary Rivers married Jack Preston, the colonel, Mary's father, insisted that the couple should live at the old home place. The desire was natural. Mary was the apple of his eye, and he wanted to see her rule in the home over which his mother had reigned. The colonel himself had been born there, and his mother had lived there for more than forty years. His father had died in 1830, but his mother lived until the day after the fiftieth anniversary of her wedding.

For near a quarter of a century this excellent lady had been the manager of her own estate, and she had succeeded, by dint of hard and pinching economy and untiring energy, in retrieving the fortune which her husband had left in a precarious condition. It was said of the colonel's father, William Rivers, that he was a man perverse in his ways and with a head full of queer notions, and it seems to be certain that he frittered away large opportunities in pursuit of small ones.

When William Rivers died he left his widow as a legacy four small boys — the colonel, the oldest, was in his teens — a past-due mortgage on the plantation, and a whole raft (as you may say) of small debts. She had one consolation that she breathed often to her little boys, — their father had lived temperately and died a Christian. Besides that consolation, she had an abundance

of hope and energy. She could have sold a
negro or two, but there were only a dozen of
them, big and little, and they were all members of one family. The older ones had grown
up with their mistress, and the younger ones
she had nursed and attended through many
an hour's sickness. She would have parted
with her right hand sooner than sell one of
them. She took her little boys from school
— the youngest was ten and the oldest fourteen — and put them to work in the fields
with the negroes for one year. At the end
of that period she began to see daylight, as
it were, and then the boys went back to
school, but their vacations for several years
afterward were spent behind the plough. She
was as uncompromising in her business as in
her religion. In one she stickled for the last
thrip that was her due ; in the other she believed in the final perseverance of the saints.

It is enough to say that she succeeded.
She transacted her own business. She did
it well at the very beginning, and thereafter
with an aptitude that was constantly growing. She paid the estate out of debt, and
added to it, and when her oldest son gradu-
ated at Princeton, she had the finest and

most profitable plantation in Jasper County.
All the old people said that if her father,
Judge Walthall, could have returned to life,
he would have been proud of the success of
his daughter, which was in that day and still
remains the most remarkable event in the
annals of Jasper County.

The main dependence of Mrs. Rivers, even
after her boys grew up, was a negro man
named Shadrach. He grew old with his mistress and imbibed many of her matter-of-fact
ways and methods. At first he was known
as Uncle Shed, but the negro pronunciation
lengthened this to Shade, and he was known
by everybody in the counties round as Uncle
Shade.

Uncle Shade knew how important his services were to his mistress and what store she
set by his energy and faithfulness, and the
knowledge made him more independent in
his attitude and temper than the average
negro. The truth is, he was not an average negro, and he knew it. He knew it by
the fact that the rest of the negroes obeyed
his most exacting orders with as much alacrity as they obeyed those of white men, and
were quite as anxious to please him. He

knew it, too, by the fact that his mistress had selected him in preference to his own father to take charge of the active management of the plantation business.

The selection was certainly a good one. Whatever effect it may have had on Uncle Shade, it was the salvation of the plans of his mistress. The negro seemed to have a keen appreciation of the necessities of the situation. He worked the hands harder than any white man could have worked them, and kept them in a good humor by doing as much as any two of them. The Saturday half-holiday was abolished for a time, and the ploughs and the hoes were kept going just as long as the negroes could see how to run a furrow.

A theory of the neighborhood was that Uncle Shade was afraid of going to the sheriff's block, and if this theory was wrong it was at least plausible. The majority of those who worked under Uncle Shade were his own flesh and blood, but his mistress had made bold to hire four extra negroes in order to carry out the plans she had in view, and these four worked as hard and as cheerfully as any of the rest.

Such was the energy with which Uncle Shade managed the rougher details of the plantation work, that at the end of the first year his mistress saw her way clear to enlarging her plans. She found that within five years she would be able to pay off all the old debts and make large profits to boot. So she sent her boys back to school, bought two of the four hired hands, and hired four more. These new ones, under Uncle Shade's management, worked as willingly as the others. In this way the estate was cleared of debt, and gradually enlarged, and Mrs. Rivers had been able, in the midst of it all, to send her boys to Princeton, where they took high rank in their studies.

The youngest drifted to California in the fifties, and disappeared; the second went into business in Charleston as a cotton factor and commission merchant. The oldest, after taking a law course, settled down at home, practiced law a little and farmed a great deal. He finally fell in love with a schoolma'am from Connecticut. His mother, who had been through the mill, as the saying is, and knew all about the dignity and lack of dignity there is in labor, rather approved the match,

although some of the neighbors, whose pre-
tensions were far beyond their possessions,
shook their heads and said that the young
man might have done better.

Nevertheless, the son did very well indeed.
He did a great deal better than some of those
who criticised his choice, for he got a wife
who knew how to put her shoulder to the
wheel when there was any necessity for it,
and how to economize when her husband's
purse was pinched. The son, having married
the woman of his choice, built him a home
within a stone's throw of his mother's, and
during her life not a day passed but he
spent a part of it in her company. He had
always been fond of his mother, and as he
grew older, his filial devotion was fortified
and strengthened by the profound impression
which her character made on him. It was a
character that had been moulded on heroic
lines. As a child, she had imbibed the spirit
of the Revolution, and everything she said
and did was flavored with the energy and independence that gave our colonial society its
special and most beautiful significance, — the
significance of candor and simplicity.

Something of his mistress's energy and independence was reflected in the character of Uncle Shade, and the result of it was that he was not very popular with those that did not know him well. The young master came back from college with a highly improved idea of his own importance. His mother, although she was secretly proud of his airs, told him with trenchant bluntness that his vanity stuck out like a pot-leg and must be lopped off. This was bad enough, but when Uncle Shade let it be understood that he was n't going to run hither and yon at the beck and call of a boy, nothing prevented a collision but the firm will that controlled everything on the plantation. After that, both the young master and the negro were more considerate of each other, but neither forgot the little episode.

When the young man married, he and Uncle Shade saw less of each other, and there was no more friction between them for four or five years. But in 1850 the negro's mistress died, and he and the rest of the negroes, together with the old home place, became the property of the son, who was now a prosperous planter, looked up to by his neighbors, and given the title of colonel by those who knew no other way of showing their respect and esteem. But in her will the colonel's mother made ample provision, as she thought, for the protection of Uncle Shade. He was to retain, under all circumstances, his house on the home place; he was never to be sold, and he was to be treated with the consideration due to a servant who had cheerfully given more than the best part of his life to the service of the family.

The terms of the will were strictly complied with. The colonel had loved his mother tenderly, and he respected her memory. He made it a point to treat Uncle Shade with consideration. He appealed to his judgment whenever opportunity offered, and frequently found it profitable to do so. But the old negro still held himself aloof. Whether from grief at the death of his mistress, or for other reasons, he lost interest in the affairs of the plantation. The other negroes said he was "lonesome," and this description of his condition, vague as it was, was perhaps the best that could be given. Except in the matter of temper, Uncle Shade was not the negro he was before his old mistress died.

This was the state of affairs when the colonel's daughter, Mary, married Jack Preston in 1861. When this event occurred, the colonel insisted that the young couple should take up their abode at the old home place. He had various sentimental reasons for this. For one thing, Mary was very much like her grandmother, in spite of her youth and beauty. Those who had known the old lady remarked the " favor " — as they called it — as soon as they saw the granddaughter. For another, the old home place was close at hand, almost next door, and the house and grounds had been kept in apple-pie order by Uncle Shade. The flower-garden was the finest to be seen in all that region, and the house itself and every room of it was as carefully kept as if the dead mistress had simply gone on a visit and was likely to return at any moment.

Naturally, the young couple found it hard to resist the entreaties of the colonel, particularly as Mary objected very seriously to living in town. So they went to the old home place, and were affably received by Uncle Shade. They found everything arranged to their hands.

Their first meal at the old home place was

dinner. The colonel had told Uncle Shade that he would have company at noon, and they found the dinner smoking on the table when they arrived. A young negro man was set to wait on the table. He made some blunder, and instantly a young negro girl came in, smiling, to take his place. Uncle Shade, who was standing in the door of the dining-room, dressed in his Sunday best, took the offender by the arm as he passed out, and in a little while those who were at table heard the swish of a buggy whip as it fell on the negro's shoulders. The unusual noise set the chickens to cackling, the turkeys to gobbling, and the dogs to barking.

"Old man," said Preston, when Uncle Shade had gravely resumed his place near the dining-room door, "take 'em farther away from the house the next time you kill em."

"I 'll do so, suh," replied Uncle Shade dryly, and with a little frown.

Matters went along smoothly enough for all concerned, but somehow Preston failed to appreciate the family standing and importance of Uncle Shade. The young man was as genial and as clever as the day is long, but he knew nothing of the sensitiveness of an old family servant. On the other hand, Uncle Shade had a dim idea of Preston's ignorance, and resented it. He regarded the young man as an interloper in the family, and made little effort to conceal his feelings.

One thing led to another until finally there was an explosion. Preston would have taken harsh measures, but Uncle Shade gathered up a bundle of " duds," and took to the woods.

Nominally he was a runaway, but he came and went pretty much as suited his pleasure, always taking care to keep out of the way of Preston.

At last the colonel, who had made the way clear for Uncle Shade to come back and make an apology, grew tired of waiting for that event ; the longer he waited, the longer the old negro stayed away.

The colonel made one or two serious efforts to see Uncle Shade, but the old darky, mis-understanding his intentions, made it a point to elude him. Finding his efforts in this di-rection unavailing, the colonel grew angry. He had something of his mother's disposition — a little of her temper if not much of her energy — and he decided to take a more serious view of Uncle Shade's capers. It was a shame and a disgrace, anyhow, that one of the Rivers negroes should be hiding in the woods without any excuse, and the colonel determined to put an end to it once for all. He would do more — he would teach Uncle Shade once for all that there was a limit to the forbearance with which he had been treated.

Therefore, after trying many times to capture Uncle Shade and always without success, the colonel announced to his wife that he had formed a plan calculated to bring the old negro to terms.

" What is it ? " his wife asked.

" Well, I 'll tell you," said the colonel, hesitating a little. " I 'm going to get me a nigger dog and run old Shade down and catch him, if it takes me a year to do it."

The wife regarded the husband with amazement.

" Why, Mr. Rivers, what are you thinking of ? " she exclaimed. " You don't mean to tell me that you are going to put yourself on a level with Bill Favers and go trolloping around the country, hunting negroes with hound-dogs ? I never heard you say that any of your family ever stooped to such as that."

"They never did," the colonel rejoined testily. "But they never had such a rantankerous nigger to deal with."

"Just as he is, just so he was made," was Mrs. Rivers's matter-of-fact comment.

"I know that mighty well," said the colonel. "But the time has come when he ought to be taken in hand. I could get Bill Favers's dogs and run him down in an hour, but I'm going to catch my own nigger with my own nigger dog."

"Why, Mr. Rivers, you have n't a dog on the place that will run a pig out of the garden, much less catch a negro. There are ten or fifteen hound-dogs around the yard, and they are actually too no-account to scratch the fleas off."

"Well," replied the colonel, wincing a little, "Matt Kilpatrick has promised to give me one of his beagles, and I'm going to take him and train him to track niggers."

"Another dog on the place!" exclaimed Mrs. Rivers. "Well, you'll have to sell some negroes. We can't afford to feed a lot of no-account negroes and no-account dogs without selling something. You can't even give the dogs away — and I would n't let you impose on anybody that way, if you could; so you 'll have to sell some of the negroes. They are lazy and no-account enough, goodness knows, but they can manage to walk around and pick up chips and get a thimbleful of milk from twenty cows, and sweep off the porch when there 's anybody to keep them awake."

Nevertheless, the colonel got his beagle, and he soon came to take more interest in it than in all his other dogs. He named it Jeff, after Matt Kilpatrick's old beagle, and Jeff turned out to be the cutest little dog ever seen in that section. The colonel trained him assiduously. Twice a day he 'd hold Jeff and make one of the little negroes run down by the spring-house and out across the cow-lot. When the little negro was well out of sight the colonel would unleash Jeff and away the miniature hunt would go across the fields, the colonel cheering it on in regulation style.

The colonel's "nigger dog" was eight months old when he was taken in hand, and by the time he was a year old he had developed amazingly. The claim was gravely made that

he had a colder nose than Bill Favers's dog
Sound, who could follow a scent thirty-six
hours old. It is not to be supposed that the
training of Jeff went no farther than tracking
the little negroes within sight of the house.
The time speedily came when he was put
on the trails of negroes who had hours the
start, — negroes who crept along on fences
and waded wide streams in their efforts to
baffle the dog.

But Jeff was not easily baffled. He developed such intelligence and such powers of
discriminating scent as would have put to
shame the lubberly and inefficient dogs known
as bloodhounds. Bloodhounds have figured
very largely in fiction and in the newspapers
as the incarnation of ferocity and intelligence.
As a matter of fact, Jeff, the little beagle,
could have whipped a shuck-pen full of them
without ever showing his teeth, and he could
run half a mile while a bloodhound was
holding his senseless head in the air to give
tongue.

Naturally the colonel was very proud of
Jeff. He had the dog always at his heels,
whether going to town or about the plantation, and he waited for the opportunity to

come when he might run Uncle Shade to his
hiding-place in the swamps of Murder Creek
and capture him. The opportunity was not
long in coming, though it seemed long to the
colonel's impatience.

There was this much to be said about Uncle
Shade. He had grown somewhat wary, and
he had warned all the negroes on both plantations that if they made any reports of his
movements, the day of wrath would soon
come for them. And they believed him fully,
so that, for some months, he might have been
whirled away on a cloud or swallowed by the
earth for all the colonel could hear or discover.

But one day, while he was dozing in his
library, he heard a dialogue between the
housemaid and the cook. The housemaid
was sweeping in the rear hall, and the cook
was fixing things in the dining-room. They
judged by the stillness of the house that there
was no one to overhear them.

" Mighty quare 'bout Unk Shade," said the
house-girl.

" Huh ! dat ole nigger-man de devil, mon ! "
replied the cook, rattling the dishes.

" I boun' ef 'twuz any er we-all gwine on

dat away runnin' off an' comin' back when we
git good an' ready, an' eatin' right dar in de
house in broad daylight, an' marster gwine
right by de do' — I boun' you we 'd be kotch
an' fotch back," remarked the girl, in an in-
jured tone.

"La! I ain't studyin' 'bout ole Shade
kingin' it 'roun' here," exclaimed the cook.
"He been gwine on dat away so long dat
't ain't nothin' new." Here she paused and
laughed heartily.

"What you laughin' at?" inquired the
girl, pausing in her work.

"At de way dat ole nigger man been gwine
on," responded the cook. "I hear tell dat
marster got dat ar little houn'-dog trainin'
now fer ter track ole Shade down. Dar de
dog an' dar old Shade, but dey ain't been no
trackin' done yit. Dat dog bleedzter be no
'count, kaze all he got ter do is to go down
dar by the house whar ole Shade live at
'twix' daybreak an' sun-up, an' dar he 'll
fin' de track er dat ole nigger man hot an'
fresh."

"I don't keer ef dey does ketch 'im," said
the house-girl, by way of comment. "De wuss
frailin' I ever got he gi' me. He skeer'd

me den, an' I been skeer'd un 'im fum dat
day."

"De white folks kin git 'im any time dey
want 'im," said the cook. "But you hear
me! — dey don't want 'im."

"Honey, I b'lieve you," exclaimed the girl.

At this juncture the colonel raised his head
and uttered an exclamation of anger. Instantly there was the most profound silence
in the dining-room and in the hall. The
house-girl slipped up the stairway as noise-
lessly as a ghost, and the cook disappeared
as if by magic.

The colonel called both negroes, but they
seemed to be out of hearing. Finally the cook
answered. Her voice came from the spring
lot, and it was the voice of conscious innocence. It had its effect, too, for the colonel's
heavy frown cleared away, and he indulged
in a hearty laugh. When the cook came up,
he told her to have breakfast the next morning by sunrise.

The woman knew what this meant, and she
made up her mind accordingly. In spite of
the fact that she pretended to despise Uncle
Shade, she had a secret respect for his independence of character, and she resolved to

repair, as far as she knew how, the damage her unbridled tongue had wrought.

Thus it was that when Uncle Shade made his appearance that night he found the cook nodding by the chimney corner, while his wife was mending some old clothes. A covered skillet sat near the fire, and a little mound of ashes in one corner showed where the ash-cake was baking or the sweet potatoes roasting. Uncle Shade said nothing. He came in silently, placed his tin bucket in the hearth, and seated himself on a wooden stool. There was no greeting on the part of his wife. She laid aside her mending, and fixed his supper on a rude table close at hand.

" I speck you mus' be tired," she said when everything was ready — " tired and hongry too."

Uncle Shade made no response. He sat gazing steadily into the pine-knot flame in the fireplace that gave the only light in the room.

" De Lord knows I 'd quit hidin' out in de woods ef I wuz you," said his wife. " I would n't be gwine 'roun' like some wil' varmint — dat I would n't ! — I 'd let um come git me an' do what dey gwine ter do. Dey can't kill you."

"Dat's so," exclaimed the cook, by way of making herself agreeable.

Uncle Shade raised his eyebrows and looked at the woman until she moved about in her chair uneasily.

"How come you ain't up yonder whar you b'long?" he asked. He was not angry; the tone of his voice was not even unkind; but the cook was so embarrassed that she could hardly find her tongue.

"I'm here kaze marster tol' me ter get brekkus by sun-up, an' I know by de way he done dat he gwine ter come and put dat ar nigger dog on yo' track."

"What good dat gwine ter do?" Uncle Shade asked.

"Now, ez ter dat," replied the cook, "I can't tell you. It may do harm, an' it may not, but what good it gwine ter do, I'm never is ter tell you."

"What de dog gwine ter do?" inquired Uncle Shade.

The cook looked at the other woman and laughed, and then rose from her seat, adjusting her head handkerchief as she did so.

"You mos' too much fer me," she remarked as she went toward the door. "Mos' a long ways too much. Ef you kin git off de groun' an' walk in de elements, de dog ain't gwine do nothin'. Maybe you kin do dat; I dunno. But ef you can't dat ar dog 'll track you down sho ez you er settin' dar." Then she went out.

Uncle Shade ate his supper and then sat before the fire smoking his pipe. After a while he got a piece of candle out of an old cigarbox, lit it, and proceeded to ransack a wooden chest which seemed to be filled with all sorts of odds and ends, — gimlets, hinges, horn buttons, tangled twine, quilt pieces, and broken crockery. At the bottom he found what he was looking for, — a letter that had been rolled in cylindrical shape. Around it had been wrapped a long strip of cloth. He unrolled the package, took the letter out and looked at it, rolled it up again, and then placed it carefully in his hat.

"Well, den," said his wife, "what you gwine ter do?"

"I'll tell you," he said. He leaned over and placed one hand on her knee. "Ef he don't ketch me, I ain't comin' back. Ef he ketch me, I'll show 'im dat," — indicating the letter, — "an' ef dat ain't do no good,

I 'm gwine ter jump off Injun Bluff in de river."

" Sho nuff ? " his wife asked, in a low voice.

" Sho nuff ! " he answered, in a voice as low.

The woman sighed as she rose from her chair to clear away the little table. In a little while she began to sing a hymn, and by that time Uncle Shade, lying across the foot of the bed, was fast asleep.

The cook, out of abundant caution, gave her master his breakfast before sunrise. The colonel called Jeff into the dining-room and gave him some substantial scraps of warm victuals — an unheard-of proceeding in that house.

After breakfast the colonel mounted his horse, which was standing saddled at the gate, and rode over to the old home place. He rode straight to Uncle Shade's house, called a negro to hold his horse, and went in, followed by Jeff.

" Where did Shade sleep last night ? " he asked of Shade's wife.

" Well, suh, what little sleepin' he done, he done right dar, suh — right dar in de baid, suh."

The colonel pulled off one of the blankets, made Jeff smell of it, and then went out and mounted his horse. Once in the saddle, he spoke an encouraging word to the dog. The task set for Jeff was much more difficult than the colonel thought it was. The dog circled around the house, once, twice, thrice, his nose to the ground. Then he ran back to the door, and tried to unravel the riddle again. He went off a little way, flung back, and entered the house, nosed the bed carefully, and then came out, giving tongue for the first time.

Near by was a low wooden bench. Jeff leaped upon it and gave tongue again. A piece of bacon-rind lay on the bench. The dog nosed around it very carefully. The colonel clenched his teeth together. "If he eats that meat-skin," he thought, "I'll go get my gun and kill him." But Jeff did no such thing. He had solved a problem that had puzzled his intelligent nose, and he sprang away from the bench with a ringing challenge.

Some of the negroes who had been watching the dog looked at each other and shook their heads. As a matter of fact, Uncle Shade

had sat on that bench and greased the soles
of his shoes with the bacon-rind. He had a
theory of his own that the dog would be
unable to follow him after his shoes were
greased.

It is certain that Jeff had considerable difficulty in getting away from the negro quarters, for Uncle Shade, true to his habits, had
gone to several of the cabins and issued his
orders, laying off a week's work for the
plough-hands, and telling them what to do
in the event that rains suspended their operations. Patiently Jeff threaded the maze of
the old negro's comings and goings, and at
last he found the final clue at the stile that
led from the negro quarters into the avenue.

The colonel rode around by the big gate,
and when he passed through Jeff was going
down the big avenue at a pretty lively clip,
but he was not running as freely as his custom was. Where a bush or a weed touched
the footpath, he would examine it with his
nose, but he kept the colonel's horse in a
canter. When he left the avenue for the
public road he ran in a more assured manner,
and the colonel was compelled to force the
canter into a gallop.

This was nothing like a fox-hunt, of course. The excitement of companionship and rivalry, and the thrill of the restless and eager-moving pack were lacking, but the enthusiasm of the colonel was mingled with pride as he rode after the dog that was guiding him so swiftly and unerringly. The enthusiasm was as persistent as the pride. But Jeff had no room for such emotions. The path of duty, straight or crooked, lay before him, and he followed it up as nimbly as he could.

The colonel was puzzled by the route they were taking. He had heard a good deal of runaway negroes, and had seen some after they were caught, but he had always imagined that they went into the deep woods or into the dim swamps for shelter and safety. But here was old Shade going poling down the public road where every passer-by could see him. Or was the dog at fault? Was it some visiting negro who had called in to see the negroes at the home place, and had then gone home by the road?

While the colonel was nursing these suspicions, Jeff paused and ran back toward him. At a low place in the fence, the dog hesitated

and then flung himself over, striking into a
footpath. This began to look like business.
The path led to a ravine, and the ravine must
naturally lead to a swamp. But the path
really led to a spring, and before the colonel
could throw a few rails from the fence and
remount his horse, Jeff had reached the
spring and was clicking up the hill beyond
in the path that led back to the road.

It appeared that Uncle Shade had rested
at the spring a while, for the dog went forward more rapidly. The spring was six
miles from the colonel's house, and he began
to have grave doubts as to the sagacity of
Jeff. What could have possessed old Shade
to run away by this public route? But if
the colonel had doubts, Jeff had none. He
pressed forward vigorously, splashing through
the streams that crossed the road and going
as rapidly up hill as he went down.

The colonel's horse was a good one, but
the colonel himself was a heavy weight, and
the pace began to tell on the animal. Nevertheless, the colonel kept him steadily at his
work. Four or five miles farther they went,
and then Jeff, after casting about for a while,
struck off through an old sedge field.

Here, at last, there was no room for doubt, for Jeff no longer had to put his nose to the ground. The tall sedge held the scent, and the dog plunged through it almost as rapidly as if he had been chasing a rabbit. The colonel, in his excitement, cheered the dog on lustily, and the chase from that moment went at top speed.

Uncle Shade, moving along on a bluff overlooking Little River, nearly a mile away, heard it and paused to listen. He thought he knew the voices of man and dog, but he was not sure, so he lifted a hand to his ear and frowned as he listened. There could be no doubt about it. He was caught. He looked all around the horizon and up at the glittering sky. There was no way of escape. So he took his bundle from the end of his cane, dropped it at the foot of a huge hickory-tree, and sat down.

Presently Jeff came in sight, running like a quarter-horse. Uncle Shade thought if he could manage to kill the dog, there would still be a chance for him. His master was not in sight, and it would be an easy matter to slip down the bluff and so escape. But, no; the dog was not to be trapped. His

training and instinct kept him out of the old
negro's reach. Jeff made a wide circle around
Uncle Shade and finally stopped and bayed
him, standing far out of harm's way.

The old negro took off his hat, folded it
once and placed it between his head and
the tree as a sort of cushion. And then the
colonel came galloping up, his horse in a
lather of sweat. He drew rein and con-
fronted Uncle Shade. For a moment he
knew not what to say. It seemed as though
his anger choked him; and yet it was not so.
He was nonplussed. Here before him was
the object of his pursuit, the irritating cause
of his heated and hurried journey. There
was in the spectacle that which drove the
anger out of his heart, and the color out
of his face. Here he saw the very essence
and incarnation of helplessness, — an old
man grown gray and well-nigh decrepit in
the service of the family, who had witnessed
the very beginning and birth, as it were,
of the family fortune.

What was to be done with him? Here in
the forest that was almost a wilderness, the
spirit of justice threatened to step forth from
some convenient covert and take possession

of the case. But the master had inherited
obstinacy, and pride had added to the store.
Anger returned to her throne.

"What do you mean by defying me in this
way?" the colonel asked hotly. "What do
you mean by running away, and hiding in
the bushes? Do you suppose I am going to
put.up with it?"

The colonel worked himself up to a terri-
ble pitch, but the old negro looked at his
master with a level and disconcerting eye.

"Well, suh," replied Uncle Shade, fumbling with a pebble in his hand, "ef my
mistiss wuz 'bove groun' dis day I 'd be
right whar she wuz at, — right dar doin' my
work, des like I usen ter. Dat what I mean,
suh."

"Do you mean to tell me, you impudent
rascal, that because your mistress is dead you
have the privilege of running off and hiding
in the woods every time anybody snaps a
finger at you? Why, if your mistress was
alive to-day she 'd have your hide taken off."

"She never is done it yet, suh, an' I been
live wid 'er in about fifty year."

"Well, I 'm going to do it," cried the colonel excitedly. He rode under a swinging

limb and tied his horse. A leather strap
fixed to a wooden handle hung from the horn
of his saddle. "Take off that coat," he exclaimed curtly.

Uncle Shade rose and began to search in
his pockets. "Well, suh," he said, "'fo' I
does dat I got sump'n here I want you to
look at."

"I want to see nothing," cried the colonel.
"I've put up with your rascality until I'm
tired. Off with that coat!"

"But I got a letter fer you, suh, an' dey
tol' me to put it in yo' han' de fus time you
flew'd up an' got mad wid me."

It is a short jump from the extreme of
one emotion to the extreme of another. The
simplicity and earnestness of the old negro
suddenly appealed to the colonel's sense of
the ridiculous, and once more his anger took
wings. Uncle Shade searched in his pockets
until he suddenly remembered that he had
placed it in the lining of his hat. As he
drew it forth with a hand that shook a little
from excitement, it seemed to be a bundle of
rags. "It's his conjure-bag," the colonel
said to himself, and at the thought of it he
could hardly keep his face straight.

Carefully unrolling the long strip of cloth, which the colonel immediately recognized as part of a dress his mother used to wear, Uncle Shade presently came to a yellow letter. This he handed to the colonel, who examined it curiously. Though the paper was yellow with age and creased, the ink had not faded.

"What is this?" the colonel asked mechanically, although he had no difficulty in recognizing the writing as that of his mother, — the stiff, uncompromising, perpendicular strokes of the pen could not be mistaken. "What is this?" he repeated.

"Letter fer you, suh," said Uncle Shade.

"Where did you get it?" the colonel inquired.

"I tuck it right out 'n mistiss' han', suh," Uncle Shade replied.

The colonel put on his spectacles and spread the letter out carefully. This is what he read: —

My dear Son: I write this letter to commend the negro Shade to your special care and protection. He will need your protection most when it comes into your hand. I have told him that in the hour when you read these lines he may surely depend on you. He has been a faithful servant to me — and to you. No human being could be more devoted to my interests and yours than he has been. Whatever may have been his duty, he has gone far beyond it. But for him, the estate and even the homestead would have gone to the sheriff's block long ago. The fact that the mortgages have been paid is due to his devotion and his judgment. I am grateful to him, and I want my gratitude to protect him as long as he shall live. I have tried to make this plain in my will, but there may come a time when he will especially need your protection, as he has frequently needed mine. When that time comes I want you to do as I would do. I want you to stand by him as he has stood by us. To this hour he has never failed to do more than his duty where your interests and mine were concerned. It will never be necessary for him to give you this letter while I am alive; it will come to you as a message from the grave. God bless you and keep you is the wish of your

MOTHER.

The colonel's hands trembled a little as he folded the letter, and he cleared his throat in a somewhat boisterous way. Uncle Shade held out his hand for the letter.

"No, no!" the colonel cried. "It is for me. I need it a great deal worse than you do."

Thereupon he put the document in his pocket. Then he walked off a little way and leaned against a tree. A piece of crystal quartz at his feet attracted his attention. A mussel shell was lying near. He stooped and picked them both up and turned them over in his hand.

"What place is this?" he asked.

"Injun Bluff, suh."

"Didn't we come out here fishing once, when I was a little boy?"

"Yasser," replied Uncle Shade, with some animation. "You wa'n't so mighty little, nudder. You wuz a right smart chunk of a chap, suh. We tuck 'n' come'd out here, an' fished, an' I got you a hankcher full er deze here quare rocks, an' you played like dey wuz diamon's, an' you up'd an' said that you liked me better 'n you liked anybody 'ceppin' yo' own blood kin. But times done change, suh. I'm de same nigger, but yuther folks ain't de same."

The colonel cleared his throat again and pulled off his spectacles, on which a mist had gathered.

" Whose land is this?" he asked presently.

" Stith Ingram's, suh."

"How far is his house?"

" Des cross dat fiel', suh."

" Well, take my hankcher and get me some more of the rocks. We'll take 'em home."

Uncle Shade gathered the specimens of quartz with alacrity. Then the two, Uncle Shade leading the horse, went across the field to Stith Ingram's, and, as they went, Jeff, the colonel's " nigger dog," fawned first on one and then on the other with the utmost impartiality, although he was too weary to cut up many capers.

Mr. Ingram himself, fat and saucy, was sitting on his piazza when the small procession came in sight. He stared at it until he saw who composed it, and then he began to laugh.

" Well, I declare!" he exclaimed. " Well, the great Tecumseh! Why, colonel! Why, what in the world! I'm powerful glad to see you! Is that you, Shade? Well, take your master's horse right round to the lot and brush him up a little. Colonel, come in! It's been a mighty long time since you've darkened this door. Where've you been?"

"I've just been out training my nigger dog," the colonel replied. "Old Shade started out before day, and just kept moving. He was in one of his tantrums, I reckon. But I'm glad of it. It gives me a chance to take dinner with you."

"Glad!" exclaimed Mr. Ingram. "Well, you ain't half as glad as I am. That old Shade's a caution. Maybe he was trying to get away, sure enough."

"Oh, no," replied the colonel. "Shade knows well enough he couldn't get away from Jeff."

That afternoon, Mr. Ingram carried the colonel and Jeff home in his buggy, and Uncle Shade rode the colonel's horse.

A RUN OF LUCK

Iᴛ was natural that the war and its results should bring about great changes in the
South; but I never fully realized what a
wonderful change had been wrought until,
a dozen years after the struggle, business,
combined with pleasure, led me to visit the
old Moreland Place, in middle Georgia. The
whole neighborhood for miles around had
been familiar to my youth, and was still dear to
my memory. Driving along the well-remem-
bered road, I conjured up the brilliant and
picturesque spectacle that the Moreland Place
presented when I saw it last : a stately house
on a wooded hill, the huge, white pillars that
supported the porch rising high enough to
catch the reflection of a rosy sunset, the porch
itself and the beautiful lawn in front filled
with a happy crowd of lovely women and gallant men, young and old, the wide avenues
lined with carriages, and the whole place lit
up (as it were) and alive with the gay commo-

tion of a festival occasion.   And such indeed
it was — the occasion of the home-coming of
Linton Moreland, the master, with a bride he
had won in far-off Mississippi.

The contrast that now presented itself
would have been pathetic if it had not been
amazing.   The change that had taken place
seemed impossible enough to stagger belief.
It had been easier to imagine that some con-
vulsion had swept the Moreland Place from
the face of the earth than to believe that in
twenty years neglect and decay could work
such preposterous ravages.   The great house
was all but dismantled.   One corner of the
roof had fallen in.   The wide windows were
mere holes in the wall.   The gable of the
porch was twisted and rent — so much so that
two of the high pillars had toppled over,
while another, following the sinking floor, had
parted company with the burden it was intended to support and sustain.   The cornices,
with their queer ornamentation, had disappeared, and more than one of the chimney-
tops had crumbled, leaving a ragged pile of
bricks peeping above the edge of the roof.
The lawn and avenues leading to it were
rankly overgrown with weeds.   The grove of

magnificent trees that had been one of the
features of the Place had not been spared.
Some were lying prone upon the ground and
others had been cut into cord-wood, while
those that had been left standing had been
trimmed and topped and shorn of their
beauty.

Even the topography of the Place had
changed. The bed of the old highway leading to the gate that opened on the main
avenue had now become a gully, and a new
highway had been seized upon — a highway
so little used that it held out small promise to
the stranger who desired to reach the house.
The surroundings were so strange that I was
undecided whether to follow the new road,
and my horse, responsive to the indecision of
my hand, stopped still. At this an old negro
man, whom I had noticed sitting on the trunk
of a fallen tree not far from the house, rose
and came forward as fast as his age would
permit him. I knew him at once as Uncle
Primus, who had been the head servant in the
Place in Linton Moreland's day — carriage-
driver, horse-trainer, foreman, and general
factotum. I spoke to him as he came forward, hat in hand and smiling.

He bowed in quite the old fashion. "Howdy, suh! I 'low'd you wuz tryin' fer ter fin' yo' way ter de house, suh. Dat what make I come. De time wuz, suh, when my ole Marster wuz 'live, en long atter dat, dat nobody on top er de groun' hatter ax de way ter dat house up yander. But dey's been a mighty churnin' up sence dem days, suh, en in de churnin' de whey done got de notion dat it's more wholesomer dan de butter — en I speck it is, suh, ter dem what like whey."

He paused and looked at me with a shrewd twinkle in his eye, which quickly faded away when, in responding to his remark, I called his name again. He regarded me closely, but not impolitely, and then began to scratch his head in a puzzled way. I was on the point of telling him who I was when he raised his hand, a broad grin of pleasure spreading over his face.

"Wait, suh! des wait! I ain't gwine ter be outdone dataway. Ain't you de same little boy what show'd me whar de buzzud nes' wuz on de two-mile place, en' which he use ter go 'possum-huntin' long wid me?" Assuring Uncle Primus that his identification was complete in all particulars, he brought his two

hands together with a resounding clap, exclaiming, " Ah-yi! Primus gittin' ol', suh,
but he ain't gwine ter be outdone when it
come ter knowin' dem what he use ter know,
an' mo' speshually when he know'd 'em endurin' er de farmin' days. You er kind er
fleshened up, suh, en you look like you er mo'
settled dan what you wuz in dem days. Kaze
I dunner how come you 'scaped breakin' yo'
neck when you wuz stayin' at de Terrell plantation."

I was as much pleased at Uncle Primus's
recognition after these long and fateful years
as he seemed to be, and we had much to say
to each other as he piloted me along the new
road to the new gate. The house and the
home place were now owned by a Mr. Yarbrough, who had at one time followed the calling of an overseer. Having bought the house,
it was a marvel why he allowed it to go to
rack, but he did. Instead of repairing the
fine old house and living in it, he built a
modest dwelling of his own. There is a psy-
chological explanation of this, into which it
is not necessary now to go. At the time I
could find small excuse for the man who could
use the Moreland house as a storage place for

corn, wheat, potatoes, and fodder, and that, too, when there were no locks on the doors, and only boards nailed across the lower windows.

But Mr. Yarbrough gave me a good dinner, as well as a good part of the information I had come in search of, and it would have become me ill to inquire too closely into his motives for abandoning the Moreland dwelling to the elements. After dinner, I walked about the place with Uncle Primus, visiting first the rock-spring, that I remembered well, and the old family burying-ground in the orchard. Here all the marbles were old and weather-beaten, and I had much trouble in making out some of the names and dates. I knew that Linton Moreland had returned home after the war, with some military reputation, which he tried in vain to turn to account in business matters. Farming was such a precarious affair directly after the war that he gave it up in disgust, and moved to Savannah, where he took charge of the general agency of an insurance company. Lacking all business training, and wanting the instinct of economy in all things, great or small, it was no surprise to his friends when he gave up

the insurance agency in disgust, and went off
to Mississippi.

I had often heard of old family servants
attaching themselves to their masters' families,
and I wondered why Uncle Primus had not
accompanied Linton. The old negro either
divined my thoughts, or I expressed my wonder in words not now remembered, for he began to shake his head solemnly, by way of
protest.

" Well, suh," he said, after a while, " I come
mighty nigh gwine off wid my young marster.
I 'speck I 'd 'a' gone ef he 'd 'a' had any chillun, but he ain't had a blessed one. En it
look like ter me, suh, dat ef de Lord gwine
ter stan' by a man, He gwine ter gi' 'im chillun. But dat ain't all, suh. I done been
out dar ter Massysip wid my young marster,
en dat one time wuz too much fer me. Fust
dar wuz de rippit on de steamboat, en den dar
wuz de burnin' er de boat, en den come de
swamps, en de canebrakes ; en I tell you right
now, suh, I dunner which wuz de wuss — de
rippit on de boat, er de fier, er de swamps,
er de canebrakes. Dat ain't no country like
our'n, suh. Dey 's nuff water in de State er
Massysip fer ter float Noah's ark. Hit 's in

de ve'y lan' what dey plant der cotton in, suh. De groun' is mushy. En black! You may n't b'lieve me, suh, but dey wuz times when I wuz out dar, dat I 'd 'a' paid a sev'mpunce fer ter git a whiff er dish yer red dus' up my nose. When you come to farmin', suh, gi' me de red lan' er de gray. Hit may not make ez much cotton in one season, but it las's longer, en hit 's lots mo' wholesome."

To pass the time away, I asked Uncle Primus about the " rippit" on the boat, as he called it. He shook his head and groaned. Finally he brightened up, and said : —

" You ain't know much about my young marster, suh ; you wuz too little ; but he had de fam'ly failin', ef you kin call it dat. He wuz up fer whatsomever wuz gwine on, let it be a fight, er let it be a frolic. 'T wuz all de same ter him, suh; yit, ef he had de choosin', 't would 'a' bin a fight mighty nigh all de time. I dunner but what he wuz wuss at dat dan ole marster wuz, en de Lord knows he wuz bad 'nuff.

" Well, suh, nothin 'd do my young marster but he mus' travel, but stidder travelin' up dar in Boston, en Phillimindelphy, whar folks live at, he tuck de notion dat he mus' go out

dar in de neighborhoods er Massysip. En I
had ter go 'long wid 'im. I kinder hung
back, kaze I done hearn tell 'bout de gwines-
on dey had out dar ; but de mo' I hung back,
de mo' my young marster want me ter go.
I wuz lots younger den dan what I is now, en
lots mo' soopler, en I 'low ter myself dat ef
anybody kin stan' fer ter go out dar spectin'
ter come back wid breff in um, dat somebody
wuz Primus. 'T wuz like de ol' sayin,' suh —
start out wid a weak heart ef you want ter
come home wid a whole hide. En so we start
off. My young marster wuz mighty gayly.
He cracked jokes, en went on mighty nigh
de whole time ; en I 'spicioned den dat dey
wuz gwine ter be some devilment cut up 'fo'
we got back. En sho nuff dey wuz.

" Well, suh, stidder gwine right straight
to'rds Massysip, we tuck de stage en went ter
Nashville, en den ter Kaintucky, en den fum
dar up ter St. Louis. Hit look like dat wharsomever dey wuz a hoss-race, er a chicken
fight, er a game er farrer gwine on, right dar
we wuz, en dar we staid twel de light wuz out,
ez you may say. En when dey 'd move, we 'd
move. Ef it had n't 'a' been fer me, suh,
my young marster would 'a' teetotally ruint

hisse'f wid gamblin' en gwine on. I seed dat
sump'n had ter be done, en dat mighty quick,
so I tuck 'im off one side en ax 'im ef he 'd
bet on de hoss what I 'd pick out fer 'im de
next day. Dat wuz des fun fer my young
marster, suh. He tuck me right up, en des
vowed he 'd put his las' dollar on 'im.

" 'T wa'n't no mo' trouble ter me, suh, ter
pick out de winnin' hoss dan 'twuz ter wash
my face. Dat night I made my young marster gi' me a tickler full er dram, en den I
went 'mong de stables whar dey kep' de race-
hosses, en 't w'an't no time 'fo' I know'd eve'y
hoss dat wuz gwine ter win de nex' day, en
de day arter, en de day arter dat — kaze de
nigger boys, what rode de hosses, know'd,
en dey tol' me what dey would n't dast ter
tell no white man dat ever wuz born'd.

" Well, suh, we sorter helt back on de fust
two races, but de nex' un wuz de big un, en
my young marster plankt down all he had
on de hoss I picked, en we walked 'way fum
dar wid mighty nigh 'nuff money ter fill a
bedtick. De biggest pile my young marster
got, he won'd fum a great big man, wid white
whiskers en blue eyes. He look mo' like a
preacher dan any hoss-race man I ever is see.

De man wid de white whiskers en blue eyes counted out de bills slow, en all de time he wuz doin' it he look hard at me en my young marster. Arter we got back in de tavern, my young marster say, 'Primus!' I say, 'Suh!' He 'low, 'Is you see how dat ol' man look at us whence he wuz countin' out dat money?' I 'low, 'Well, suh, I notice 'im glance at us mo' dan once.' He say, 'You know what dat means?' I say, 'No, suh, less'n hit's kaze he hate ter drap so much good money.' He 'low, 'Dat man got de idee in 'im big ez a mule dat I 'm a swindler. Damn 'im! I 'll put a hole thoo 'im de fust chance I git.' I 'low, 'Better wait twel we git some mo' er his money.' But my young marster tuck it mighty hard. He walk de flo' en walk de flo'. But ez fer me — well, suh, I des set down at de foot er de bed, en de fus news I know'd I wuz done gone ter de land er Nod.

" Well, suh, we went on cross de country twel we come ter St. Louis. We ain't do much dar, 'cept ter spen' money, en bimeby my young marster tuck a notion dat he 'd go ter New 'leans. I 'low, 'Dar now!' but dat ain't do no good. My young marster done make up his min'. So I got ev'rything ready, en terreckly atter dinner we went down en got on de boat. Hit look like ter me, suh, dat she wuz bigger dan a meetin'-house. Mon, she loomed up so high, dat I got sorter skittish, en den on top er dat wuz two great big smoke-stacks, scolloped on de aidge, en painted red roun' de rim. En de smoke dat come a-bilin' out'n um wuz dat black en thick dat it look like you might er cut it wid a kyarvin' knife.

" I followed 'long atter my young marster, I did, en when we got up on top dar whar de balance er de folks wuz, de fust man I laid eyes on wuz dat ar man wid de white whiskers en de blue eyes what my young marster won de big pile er money fum. He look mo' like a preacher man dan ever, kaze he wuz drest up mo' slicker dan what he had been. I ain't blame 'im fer dat when I seed what he had wid 'im. I done laid eyes on lots er purty white ladies, but I ain't seed none no purtier dan de one what dat ar preacher-lookin' man had wid 'im. She walk, suh, like she wuz on springs, en when she laugh it look like she lit up de boat, en her ha'r shine like when de sun strike down thoo de

trees whar de water ripple at. When de man
'ud look at her, hit seem like his eyes got
mo' bluer, but dey wa'n't no mo' bluer dan
what her 'n wuz en not more 'n half ez big.
I know'd by de way she hung on de man's
arm en projicked wid 'im, dat dey wuz some
kin er nudder, en I say ter myse'f, 'Name
er de Lord, white man, why n't you drap dis
gamblin' business en settle down some'ers en
take keer er dat gal?' Bless yo' soul, suh,
whiles I wuz sayin' dat de gal wuz pullin' at
de man's whiskers; en bimeby, she up en —
smack ! — she kissed 'im, en den I know'd
he wuz her daddy.

"My young marster wuz watchin' all deze
motions mo' samer dan what I wuz. He
watch de gal so close dat bimeby de man
kotch 'im at it, en when my young marster
seed he wuz kotched he up en blush wuss 'n
de gal did. But de preacher-lookin' man
ain't say nothin'. He look at my young
marster an grin des nuff fer ter show his
tushes. 'T wa'n't no laugh; 't wuz one er
deze yer grins like you see on er dog des
'fo' he start ter snap you. Den he hustled
de gal off, en I dunner whar dey went.

"Arter supper some er de men what my

young marster been talkin' wid said sump'n
'bout gittin' up a little game. Dey talked
en smoked, en bimeby my young marster en
two mo' 'greed ter try dey han' at poker.
Dey went off to'rds a little room what dey
had at one een' er de boat, en I went 'long
wid um. My fust notion wuz ter go off
some'ers en go ter bed, but when I got ter
whar dey wuz gwine, dar wuz de preacher-
lookin' man settin' in dar by his lone se'f
shufflin' a deck er kyards. He look up, he
did, when my young marster en de yuthers
went in, en den he showed his tushes en
bowed. But he kep' on settin' dar shufflin'
de kyards, en it look like ter me dat he done
been shuffle kyards befo'. I been see lots er
men shuffle kyards in my day, but dat ar
preacher-lookin' man, he beat my time by de
way he handle dat deck. 'T wuz slicker dan
sin.

"Right den en dar, suh, I say ter myse'f
dat dish yer preacher-lookin' man wuz one er
dem ar river-gamblers, what you hear folks
talk 'bout, en dat he wa'n't doin' nothin' in
de roun' worl' but layin' fer my young marster. Dey sorter pass de time er day, dey
did, en my young marster 'low dat he hope

he ain't doin' no intrusion, en de preacher-
lookin' man say ef dey's anybody doin' any
intrusion, it's him, kaze he ain't doin' nothin'
but settin' dar projickin' with de kyards
waitin' fer bed-time. Den my young marster ax 'im ef he won't jine in de game, en
he 'low he don't keer ef he do, but he say it
twon't do no good fer ter jine in de game
ef my young marster know ez much 'bout
kyards ez he do 'bout race-hosses. Wid
dat, my young marster 'low dat he never
won'd a dollar on any hoss what he pick
out hisse'f. Dis make de preacher-lookin'
man open his eyes wide, en dey look mo'
bluer dan befo'; en he 'low : —

"'Who does de pickin' fer you?'

"My young marster nod his head to'rds
me. 'Dar's my picker.'

"De man say, 'Who larnt you so much
'bout race-hosses?'

"I make answer, 'Well, suh, hit's mighty
much de same wid hosses ez 't is wid folks.
Look at um right close en watch der motions,
en you'll know what dey got in um, but you
won't know how you know it.'

"De man say, 'Kin you pick out kyards
same ez you does hosses?'

" I 'low, ' Well, suh, I has played sev'm-up
on Sundays, en I ken pick out de kyards
when I see um.'

" Dis make de man grin mo' samer dan
befo', but my young marster looks mighty
sollum.   He drum on de table wid his fingers
like he studyin' 'bout sump'n, en bimeby he
say : —

" ' Primus, I wus des 'bout ter sen' you off
ter bed, but I reckon you better set dar be-
hine me en gi' me good luck.'

" De man look at me, en den he look at my
young marster.   I 'low : —

" ' I 'll set behime you en nod, Marse Lint,
ef dat 'll gi' you good luck.'

" Well, suh, dey started in wid de game.
Dey had corn fer chips, en er empty seegyar
box wuz de bank.   I watched um long ez I
could, en den I drapt off ter sleep.   I dunner
how long I sot dar en nodded, but bimeby I
hear a shufflin', en dat woke me.   De two
men what come in wid my young marster had
done got tired er playin', en dey draw'd out
en went off ter bed.   My young marster wuz
fer drawin' out too, but de preacher-lookin'
man would n't hear ter dat.   He say, ' Gi'
me er chance ter win my money back,' en I

know'd by dat dat my young marster ain't been losin' much.

"Dey played on, en I kinder kep' one eye on de game. My young marster played des like he tryin' ter lose. But 't wa'n't no use. Luck wuz runnin' his way, en she des run'd all over him. She got 'im down en wallered 'im, en den she sot on top un 'im. Dey ain't no use talkin', suh : hit wuz des scanlous. Dey wa'n't no sleep fer me while dat wuz gwine on. I des sot dar wid bofe eyes open, en my mouf too, I speck. De kyards runded so quare, suh, dat dey fair made my flesh crawl, kaze I know'd how it bleedze ter look like swindlin' ter de man what wuz so busy losin' all his money. Ef I had n't er know'd my young marster, nobody could n't er tol' me dat he wa'n't playin' a skin game, kaze I would n't b'lieved um. En dat 's de way 't wuz wid dat ar preacher-lookin' man. He played en played, but bimeby he put his kyards down on de table, en draw'd a long breff, en look at my young marster. Den he 'low : —

"'I seed lots er folks in my day en time, but you en your dam nigger is de slickest pair dat I ever is lay eyes on.'

"My young marster sorter half-way shet his eyes en lean on de table en look at de man. He ax : —

" 'What yo' name?'

"Man say, ' Barksdale er Loueeziana.'

"My young marster had his han' on a tum'ler er water, en he 'low, ' Well, Barksdale er Loueeziana, ol' ez you is, I 'll hatter l'arn you some manners.'

"Wid dat, he dash de water in de man's face wid one han' en draw'd his gun wid de yuther. De man wipe de water out er his eyes wid one han' en draw'd *his* gun wid de yuther. Leas'ways, I speck he draw'd it, kaze de pistol what my young marster had wuz so techous, ez you may say, dat I duckt my head when I seed 'im put his han' on it.

"But 'fo' anybody could do any damage, suh, I heerd a squall dat make my blood run col'. Hit come fum a 'oman, too, kaze dey ain't nothin' ner nobody what kin make dat kinder fuss 'cep' it 's a 'oman er a mad hoss. I raise my head at dat, en dar stood my young marster en de man wid der han's on der guns en de table 'twix' um. De squall ain't mo' dan die away, 'fo' somebody holler ' *Fier !* ' en time dat word come, I could see

de red shadder flashin' on de water, en den
hit come 'cross my min' dat dey wuz one nigger man a mighty fur ways from home, en hit
make me feel so sorry fer de nigger man dat
I could n't skacely keep fum bustin' out en
cryin' boo-hoo right den en dar. De man
look at my young marster en say : —

" ' 'Scuze me des one minnit. My daughter ' —

" ' Certn'y, suh ! ' sez my young marster,
en den he bowed des ez perlite ez ef he 'd a
had a fiddle stidder a pistol. De man, he
bowed back, en went out, en my young marster follered arter. By dat time de folks in
de boat (en dey wuz a pile un um, mon !)
come a-rushin' out'n der rooms, en 'fo' you
kin wink yo' eyeball dey wuz a-crowdin' en
a-pushin' en a-pullin' en a-haulin', en a-cryin'
en a-fightin', en a-cussin' en a-prayin'.

" Well, suh, I put it down in my min' den,
en I ain't never rub it out, dat ef you take
proudness out'n de white folks dey er des ez
skeery ez de niggers. En dem white folks
on dat boat dat night had all de proudness
out'n um, en dey went on wuss 'n a passel er
four-footed creeturs. Hit 's de Lord's trufe,
suh, — all 'cep'n my young marster en de

preacher-lookin' man. Dem two wuz des ez
cool ez cowcumbers, en I say ter myse'f, I did,
'I 'll des up en wait twel dey gits skeer'd, en
den I 'll show um how skeer'd a nigger kin
git when he ain't got nothin' on his min'.'

" Dat ar Mr. Barksdale, he wuz fur shovin'
right 'long froo de crowd, but my young
marster say dey better stay on de top deck
whar dey kin see what gwine on. 'Bout dat
time I cotch sight er de young 'oman in de
jam right close at us, en I p'int her out ter
my young marster. Time he kin say, ' Dar
yo' daughter right nex' ter de railin',' de
crowd sorter swayed back, de rope railin' give
'way, en inter de water de gal went, wid a lot
mo' un um. My young marster han' me his
coat en pistol en over he went; I han' um
ter Mr. Barksdale, whiles he sayin', ' Oh,
Lord ! oh, Lordy ! ' en over I went, — kaze
in dem days I ain't had no better sense dan
ter go whar my young marster went. I hit
somebody when I struck de water, en I like
ter jolted my gizzard out, en when I riz hit
look like de boat had done got a mile away,
but she wuz headin' fer de bank, suh, en she
flung a broadside er light on de water, en I
ain't hit mo'n a dozen licks 'fo' I seed my

young marster hol'in' de gal, an' swimmin'
'long easy.

" Well, suh, what should I do but des up
en fetch one er dem ar ol'-time fox-huntin'
hollers, en I boun' you mought er heerd it
two mile. My young marster make answer,
en den I know'd de res' wuz easy. Kaze me
an' him wuz at home in de water. I holler
out, I did, ' Gi' me room, Marse Lint ! ' en I
pulled up 'long side er him same ez a pacin'
hoss. My young marster say sump'n, I disremember what, en den he laugh, en when
de young 'oman hear dis, she open her eyes,
en make some kind er movement. My young
marster 'low, ' Don't grab me, please, ma'am,'
en she say she ain't skeer'd a bit. 'Bout dat
time we come up wid a nigger man in a
canoe. Stidder tryin' ter save us, ef we
needed any savin', he done his level best ter
git away. But he ain't hit two licks wid de
paddle 'fo' I had de boat, en I say, ' You
dunner who you foolin' wid, nigger ! '

" Well, suh, he dez riz up in de boat en
light out same ez a bull-frog in a mill-pon'.
My young marster say he wuz a runaway
nigger, en I speck he wuz, kaze what business
he got jumpin' in de water des kaze we want

ter git in his boat? Dat zackly what he
done; he lipt out same ez er bull-frog. Now,
some folks dunner how ter git in a boat fum
de water when dey ain't nobody in it, but
here's what does. De sides is lots too tick-
lish. I dez grab de een' en sorter spring up
en down twel I got de swing un it, en den I
straddle it des like playin' lip-frog. Dat
done, dey wa'n't no trouble 't all. I lif' de
young 'oman in, en den my young marster he
clomb in, en dar we wuz a little chilly in de
win', but warm 'nuff fer ter thank de Lord
we had life in us. I tuck de paddle, I did,
en look at my young marster. He nod his
head to'rd de burnin' boat. De young 'oman
wuz cryin' en moanin', en gwine on turrible
'bout her daddy, but I des jerk dat canoe
along. Her daddy wuz dead, she des know'd
it; sump'n done tol' her so; en nobody ner
nothin' can't make her b'lieve he 'live, no
matter ef day done seed 'im 'live en well.
You know how de wimmin folk runs on, suh.
But while she gwine on dat a-way, I wuz des
makin' dat canoe zoon, pullin' fust on one
side en den on t'er.

"By dis time, suh, de burnin' boat done
been run on de bank, en, mon, she lit up de

worl'. De fier wuz shootin' mos'ly fum de
middle, en mos' all de folks wuz at de een'
nex' ter de bank, but on de hine een' en way
on de top deck dey wuz a man standin'. He
wuz wringin' his han's en lookin' out on de
water, en he wa'n't no mo' tryin' ter save hisse'f dan de smoke-stacks wuz. De light
shined right on 'im, en I know'd de minnit
I seed 'im dat 't wus dat ar Mr. Barksdale.
So I turn my head en say ter de young
'oman, ' Mistiss, yon' yo' pa now.' She ain't
look up 't all. She 'low, ' I don't b'lieve it!
I never is ter b'lieve it!' I say, ' Marse Lint,
who dat ar gemman on de top deck all by his
own 'lone se'f?' My young marster 'low,
' Hit 's Mr. Barksdale.' De young 'oman
moan en cry out, ' Oh, it can't be!'

"But I des drove dat ar canoe 'long, en
bimeby we wuz right at de hine een', en my
young marster sot in ter holler at dat ar Mr.
Barksdale. But look like he can't make 'm
hear, de folks on de een' wuz makin' sech a
racket, en de fier wuz ro'in so. I say, ' Wait,
Marse Lint,' en den I back de canoe out in
de light, en fetched one er dem ol'-time corn-
shuckin' whoops. Dis make de man look
down. I holler, ' Here yo' daughter waitin'
for you! Climb down — climb down!'

" Well, suh, he sorter rub his han' 'cross his eyes, en den de young 'oman fetched a squall en called 'im by name. Wid dat, he stoop down en pick up my young marster's coat en den he clomb down des ez cool ez a cowcumber. 'T wa n't long atter dat 'fo' we made a landin'. You may n't b'lieve it, suh, but folks in gettin' off dat burnin' boat, what wid der crowdin' en der pushin', would drown deyse'f in water dat wa n't up ter der chin ef dey 'd a stood up. It's de Lord's trufe. Not one here en dar, suh, but a whole drove un um.

" De folks in de neighborhood seed de light en know'd purty much what de matter wuz, en 't wa'n't long 'fo' here dey come wid der buggies, en der carryalls, en der waggins, en by sunup me an' my young marster, en de young 'oman en her daddy, wuz all doin' mighty well at a house not mo'n two mile fum de river. Leas'ways, I know I wuz doin' mighty well, suh, kaze I wuz drinkin' hot coffee en eatin' hot biscuits in de kitchen, en I speck de yuthers wuz doin' de same in de house. En what better kin you ax dan dat?

" Atter dinner, whiles I wuz settin' out on de hoss-block sunnin' myse'f — kaze de sun

feel mighty good, suh, when you done got
yo' fill er vittles — 1 wuz settin' dar, I wuz,
kinder huv'rin' 'twix' sleep en slumber, when
I hear my young marster talkin'. I open
my eyes, en dar wuz him en Mr. Barksdale
comin' down fum de house. Dey stop not so
mighty fur fum whar I wuz, en talk mighty
sollum. Bimeby Mr. Barksdale beckon to me.
He 'low —

"'Come yer, boy. You wuz de onliest
one what hear what I say ter yo' young
marster las' night, en I want you ter hear
what I say now, en dat's dis : I'm ready ter
git on my knees, en 'polergize on account er
de insults what passed.'

"I say : 'Yasser, I know'd sump'n n'er
had ter be done 'bout dat, kaze my white
folks ain't got no stomach fer dat kind er
talk, let it come fum who it shill en whence
it mought.'

"He look at me right hard, en den he
laugh, en 'low: 'Shake han's wid me. Nigger ez you is, you er better dan one half de
white folks dat I'm 'quainted wid.'

"Well, suh, you wuz 'roun' here when my
young marster come back wid my young
mistiss? Dat wuz de upshot un it. We

went home wid Marse Barksdale, en when we
come 'way fum dar, Marse Lint brung wid
'im de gal what he pick up in de river.

"Dey ain't but one thing 'bout my young
marster dat I can't onkivver en onravel.
What in de name er goodness de reason dat
he can't stay right here whar he born'd at,
stidder gwine out dar in Massysip er Loueez-
iany, er wharsomever hit is? Dat what I
want ter know."

When I last saw him, Uncle Primus was
sitting on a log, evidently still trying to solve
that problem.

THE LATE MR. WATKINS OF GEORGIA

HIS RELATION TO ORIENTAL FOLK-LORE

OWING to the fact that I have compiled and published from time to time such stories of the Southern plantations as chanced to fall in my way, an opinion has gone abroad that if I am not a genuine professor of the science of folk-lore I at least know all about the comparative branch of the subject. There is no mystery as to how this impression got abroad. I beat my forehead in the dust at the reader's feet and make a full confession. It is all owing to the wonderfully learned introduction to the volume of plantation stories called "Nights with Uncle Remus." There is nothing egotistical in my characterization of that introduction. I speak as a spectator, — an outsider, as it were. I am not a bit proud of it, but I marvel at it. Where did I get hold of all the information that seems to be packed in those unobtrusive pages, and how did I have the patience to string it out

and make it fit so the joints would n't show?
It is the habit of man, the world over, to
stand in awe, secret or avowed, of that which
he does not understand. When I say, therefore, that the introduction is wonderfully
learned, I mean that I do not understand it.

To that introduction I owe my reputation
abroad (very much abroad) as a student or a
professor of folk-lore. To that introduction
also the reader owes the curious narrative (or
narratives) which I have concluded to put on
record here, in order (if I may be so fortunate) to put an end to a bitter dispute that
has raged and is still raging in the various
folk-lore societies in Europe and Asia, from
Jahore to London, — a dispute that is not
the less bitter or demoralizing because it is
carried on in seven different languages and
thirteen different dialects.

The way of it was this. On the 16th of
February, 1892, — the date is in my note-
book, though it is not of the slightest importance, — I received a communication from
Sir Waddy Wyndham, one of her Majesty's
officials at Jahore. Sir Waddy evidently had
plenty of time at his command, for his letter
contained fourteen sheets of note-paper, con-

taining by actual count two hundred and
eleven words to the page. The envelope to
the letter had a weather-beaten appearance.
It was literally covered with post-marks, save
the address and one little spot in a corner,
where some one, evidently a postal-clerk in
Georgia, had written, "All for Joe!" Sir
Waddy's cramped handwriting was trying,
but I managed to make out that he had read
with great pleasure the learned introduction
to the plantation stories, and was proud to
know that he and his coadjutors in India and
other parts of the world had so worthy a co-
worker in the fertile fields of South America.
Without further introduction he would take
the liberty of sending me a story which he
regarded as the key to the folk-lore of India.
"If you can find even a trace of this story
on the South American plantations," he
wrote, "you will solve a riddle that has
been puzzling us for years, and give the science of folk-lore a new claim to the consideration of the thoughtful." The story that
Sir Waddy sent is interesting enough to nar-
rate here. I have taken the liberty to tell it
in my own way, — which is decidedly not the
way of a professional folk-lorist.

THE SYMPATHETIC VINE

At a certain place, which is marked by a river, a furrow, a hedge, and a range of hills, there dwelt a prince who made his people very unhappy. A Brahmin, going into the forest to do penance, had told the prince that there was a great supply of gold in his dominions.

"How shall I get it?" the prince inquired.

"Dig for it," said the Brahmin.

"Where shall I dig?" asked the prince.

"In the space of land," replied the Brahmin, "that is marked off by a river, a furrow, a hedge, and a range of hills."

The Brahmin, after receiving the kindest treatment, took his leave and went forward into the forest. The prince immediately summoned his subjects and told them that, as there was to be a great scarcity of food the next year, the best thing they could do would be to become farmers.

"You have little land," said the prince, "but I have plenty. Go yonder where the land is marked off by a river, a furrow, a hedge, and a range of hills. Dig there, and make the ground arable. The mists will rise from the river and help you, and the dew will fall from the hills and make the soil sweet."

So they went, some gladly, but others with a bad grace.

" How shall we begin ? " asked one old man.

" Dig," said the prince.

" When we have dug, what then ? " asked a young man.

" Continue to dig," replied the prince.

Now, the prince, being afraid that the people would find the gold and hide it, took his stand by a tree on the range of hills and watched them, and at night when they could no longer work he caused the laborers to pass near him, in single file, so that he might question them. To each he said, " What have you found ? " and the reply was, " Nothing but the trouble of digging."

This happened day after day, and the workers got no rest except the little they found at night. The young men asked when it could end, and the old men shook their heads. Life is a little span, but greed runs from generation to generation. So the people dug and dug from day to day, and the prince sat by the tree and watched them.

At last, one day, an old man, while digging wearily, turned up a lump of gold. It was dingy and dirty, but he knew it was gold because it was hard and very heavy. After this, it seemed that the field was full of gold, and when night had come, each took a lump, intending to give it to the prince who was watching by the tree. So they came to him, and an old man said, "Your high mightiness, we have found something."

But the prince answered not a word. He sat there still and cold. A quick-growing vine had wrapped around his body, crushing his bones and strangling him. The Brahmin, coming out of the forest, saw the people gathered together. He went to them and said, "What you have found is yours; what your master has found is his."

So they went to their homes, leaving the prince dead and covered with ants.

I need not quote Sir Waddy Wyndham's letter, nor recite the history of this legend as he had traced it through the several Indian dialects. It struck me as being very tame at best, lacking both the humor and the picturesque verity (if I may say so) of plantation stories with which I am familiar.

For a time Sir Waddy's letter and the story, and all his remarks about Bidpai and other fabulists passed out of my mind. But one day, a few months ago, while adjusting the fixtures of the pump near the kitchen door, I overheard a conversation between my cook, Mrs. Edie Strickland, and Mrs. Caroline Biggers, a colored lady who cooks for a neighbor, and this conversation reminded me of Sir Waddy Wyndham's Indian story. I concluded at once that I had found it here, somewhat disfigured, it is true, but still able to speak for itself. Without loss of time, I reduced the story I had heard in the kitchen to writing, and sent a brief outline of it to Sir Waddy. Perhaps this was a mistake, and yet my intentions were of the best. I regret now that I violated a rule made several years ago, not to reply to letters from strangers. No doubt Sir Waddy regrets it too, but it is only fair to say that no word of complaint has ever come from him. Nevertheless, some one has sent me an envelope containing slips from an Indian newspaper, though neither the name of the paper nor the date accompanies them, and I gather from these that a most furious controversy has been going on

among the professors of folk-lore in that far-
away country. One communication charges
that Sir Waddy Wyndham has been deceived,
first by his own imagination, and second by
" a South American impostor." There is no
doubt that the writer of the communication
is a very learned man, and he touches on the
folk-tales of India in a way that shows his
familiarity with the foot-notes and appen-
dices of a great number of volumes. The
next in order is a card from Sir Waddy himself, who explains that the attack on him and
his " South American correspondent " is the
result of a professional grudge, Sir Waddy
having refused to admit that either the Indian story or the alleged South American
" fragment " is intended to typify the eclipse
of the sun.

I have reason to believe that this unhappy
controversy has spread or is spreading to
other countries, and, in order to prevent any
misconception or misunderstanding, — seeing
that the outline of the American story on
which Sir Waddy bases his defense is imper-
fect, — I deem it best to give here a correct
version of the story as told by Mrs. Caroline
Biggers to Mrs. Edie Strickland, and repeated

to me by Mrs. Biggers a few weeks ago. This can be done in the language of Mrs. Biggers, who is a pleasant and fairly well educated young woman.

"I thought Miss Edie done mighty funny when she told me you wanted to see me," said Mrs. Biggers, striving to hide her embarrassment. She laughed and went on. "I declare, if you had n't come out there just when you did, I would have been gone — gone. Yes, sir, I would. If I could tell tales like my grandmother did, I could keep you up at night. But nobody can tell tales unless they 're sitting in front of a big wood fire, where the sparks will fly out and spangle right before your eyes. My grandmother always said that what was a good tale at night was mighty weak talk in the daytime. And I reckon it 's so, because she was a mighty old woman. I can tell you what I told Miss Edie, but I know mighty well it won't sound right." Whereupon Mrs. Biggers settled herself, and told

THE STORY OF MR. WATKINS

"Maybe you did n't know much about the Watkinses. Well, they lived in Jasper

County, and a mighty big family it was. Some of 'em was good people, but one — old Mr. Watkins — was mean as gar-broth. He was mean and rich. You take notice, and 'most all the time you'll see the meanest folks have more money than anybody else. I don't know why it is, unless it's because they are just too mean to spend it. Well, this Mr. Watkins was so mean that he had all the chincapin-trees, and all the chestnut-trees, and all the muscadine vines, and all the plum-bushes on his place cut down to keep the children from getting them. Now, you know that wa'n't right, was it? I tell you, now, when anybody gets that mean, something will certainly happen to 'em.

" It seemed like everybody knew how mean this Mr. Watkins was, and they tried to shun him. When people went by his house going to church, or coming back from frolics, they'd stop talking and laughing. Some of 'em would say, 'Hush! Mr. Watkins may be out on his front porch;' and then they'd go by just like somebody was dead in the house. And my grandmother used to say that sometimes they'd hear noises like somebody was in great pain.

" But Mr. Watkins did n't pay any attention to how people done, so long as they
did n't come bothering him. He was all
crippled up like he had the palsy or something, and he had to be moved about from
room to room. He could walk a little by
holding on to two of his negroes and shuffling along, but in general they toted him
about on a chair. Once a week he went to
town. They toted him out to his buggy and
wrapped a blanket around his legs, and then
a little negro, about the size of Miss Edie's
Zach, got in the buggy and drove him to
town. There he 'd get his jimmy-john filled,
and then he 'd go back home and sit in his
front porch and talk to himself all day when
he was n't dozing.

" I can't tell it like my grandmother did.
She used to get started, and she 'd stand up
on the floor and shuffle around and roll her
eyeballs and skeer us children mighty near to
death.

" Now, you 'd think that nobody would be
afraid of Mr. Watkins, weak and crippled
like that ; but he had everybody on his place
under his thumb. Temper ! he was rank
poison. And cuss ! my grandmother used to

say he'd lean back in his seat and cuss till he'd make the cold chills run up and down your back. He could sit right still and run the chickens out of the garden and drive the dogs off the place. Now, you know a man must be mighty mean when he can stay right still and do all that.

"This was during the week-days. On Sunday — well!" Here Mrs. Biggers raised both hands vigorously, and then permitted them to fall helplessly in her lap. "That was the day he let his meanness come out, sure enough. I know you ain't ready to believe what I'm going to tell you. The children believed it because my grandmother told it at night when she was combing her hair. She said her grandmother was well acquainted with Mr. Watkins, because she lived on a joining plantation. Some things she heard tell of, and some she saw with her own eyes. I told you that Mr. Watkins was rich. Well, I don't know whether he had much money, but he had a heap of negroes. And he made 'em work. Yes, sir, work! Up in the morning by the crack of day — work, work — until dark, and, if the moon shone, until away in the night. And that wa'n't all.

No, sir! He made 'em work Sundays! I'm telling you the truth. Sundays! I know that it don't look like the truth, but my grandmother heard her grandmother tell about it, and this much she saw with her own eyes.

" Yes, sir! That old man, crippled and trembly as he was, made his negroes work on Sunday same as any other day. He'd make 'em tote him out to the field and put him up on a stump close by the big road, and there he'd stay all day. If he saw anybody coming along the road, he'd wave his stick, and the negroes would lay down in the field till the people went by. Then he'd wave his stick, and the negroes would get up and go to work again.

" I don't know how long this went on — I can't tell it like my grandmother did, because she went through the motions; but Mr. Watkins made his negroes work Sunday after Sunday. They worked until he waved his walking-cane or called them, and then they'd come and tell him how much they had done. Then they'd take him off the stump and put him in his chair and tote him to the house.

" Well, one Sunday, while the negroes were

at work, a man passed along the road, and Mr. Watkins did n't wave his cane. But the negroes stopped work anyhow and looked at him. The man was tall and dark-looking. He had on black clothes, and he rode a big black horse. When he came close to Mr. Watkins there was a flash of fire. Some said the man's horse hit his shoe against a flint rock and made the blaze, and some said not. My grandmother did n't know how that was, because her grandmother was n't there to see. But there was the tall dark man riding a big black horse, and there was the flash of fire, and there on the stump was Mr. Watkins.

" Well, sir, when the time come for the negroes to quit work, Mr. Watkins did n't wave his cane, and so they kept on until it got too dark to work. Then they went to where Mr. Watkins was perched up on the stump, and asked him if it was time to quit. He would n't say anything, so they hung around and did n't know what to do. They thought they could smell brimstone; but they wa'n't certain. Anyhow, when they tried to lift Mr. Watkins off the stump they could n't budge him. No, sir! They could n't budge him. Some of the negroes run to the house and told Mr. Watkins's family, and they got torches and went to see about it.

" Well, sir, Mr. Watkins had done growed to the stump. I know you won't believe me, because I 'm half laughing when I tell you about it, but my grandmother, she could tell it with a straight face. She was old and settled. Yes, sir! Mr. Watkins was growed to the stump, and they could n't pull him loose. First they pulled and then they tried to prize him up. But there he was. It seemed like the stump had fastened to him somehow. They sent for the doctor, but you know yourself the doctor could n't do nothing for a man in that kind of a fix. He might drench him with horse medicine, and even that would n't do any good. Mr. Watkins was there on the stump, and no doctor could n't take him loose. The doctor came, but what good could the doctor do ? He just looked at Mr. Watkins and felt of him, and looked at the stump and felt of it, and then he shook his head and rubbed his chin. You know how it is when a doctor shakes his head and rubs his chin. That was the way it was with Mr. Watkins.

" People come and looked at him, but they could n't do any good, and, after so long a time, the negroes dug the stump up and put it in a wagon with Mr. Watkins and carried 'em both home. There they was, Mr. Watkins and the stump. Then when the time come to bury Mr. Watkins, they had to bury the stump with him. I won't blame you if you don't believe all this, but my grandmother vowed that her grandmother saw Mr. Watkins on the stump, and if you could hear her tell it you 'd feel like every word of it was so, and you 'd never forget it as long as you lived."

This is the story the rough outline of which has caused such a commotion among the folk-lore students and scholars in India, in Bombay and Jahore. There are symptoms that the controversy is to be transferred, in part at least, to these shores, and I feel it to be due to all concerned that a true version of the story of the late Mr. Watkins of Georgia, together with all the facts in the case, should be laid before the public. No one can regret more than I do that any act or word of mine, however well intended, should have provoked, even indirectly, a controversy that has resulted in the resignation of Sir Waddy Wyndham as secretary of the Folk-Lore Society of Jahore, a position he has adorned during the last five years.

The question arises, What bearing has the Indian folk-lore story on the final episode in the career of the late Mr. Watkins of Georgia?

A BELLE OF ST. VALERIEN

I

You will flit through on the steam cars, or
rush along the great winding river, and say,
" It is a very fine life here in New France."
You will look to the right, you will look to
the left, and, as far as the eye can see, the
roofs and steeples of the little churches will
be sparkling in the sun, and you will say,
" How beautiful !   How full of peace and repose ! " and if you go away from the river
and the railway you will say, " What simplicity !   What contentment ! "   When you
come to St. Valerien, you will say, " The life
here is the most beautiful of all."   Yes ; that
is because you want to get away from the
noise and confusion.   It is very beautiful at
St. Valerien.   The gentle curé, smiling always, moves slowly along the board walk to
the little church.   The bright-eyed boys who
attend the school of the Frères Maristes, close
by, are not boisterous at their play.   The

neighbors do not talk loudly when they gossip together, and the cattle lie down in the
fields long before noon. Everything has the
air of repose; contentment seems to brood
everywhere.

Very well. But suppose you were compelled to remain in St. Valerien, and partake
of its peace and contentment from year's end
to year's end? A few weeks in the summer,
when the children are picking wild raspberries
in the fields near by, and singing their songs,
— that is not much. But a whole lifetime!
Well, yes, that is another matter. Look at
Monsieur Phaneuf. Seventy-seven years here
at St. Valerien, and every hour of them spent
within sight of the shining church steeple.
You think he is contented? Well, then, keep
away from him, if you do not want to hear
your funeral preached. Look at Madame
Delima Benoit. Born here at St. Valerien;
married three husbands here, and buried two.
You think she ought to be happy and contented? Well, then, don't pass her doors
without putting your fingers in your ears.
You see Aimé Joutras, the tall shoemaker;
Aimé, but yes, it is a friendly name. You
see him there on the corner — tap, tap, tap,

— stitch, stitch, stitch, — all day long, and humming a tune; you see him cut out the *sabot*, you see him fashion the *soulier-de-bœuf*, and you think, " Here is a man who ought to glow with happiness." But good! Wait till you hear him railing at his little ones, and growling at the *belle-mère* who is at once his slave and his benefactress. Wait till you see him jostle rudely against the old *pepère* who sits drooling and dribbling in the corner, and then tell me whether he is happy and contented. Look, yonder is Euphemie Toupin, running lightly across the fields, the roses blooming in her face, her eyes sparkling with youth and hope, and her beautiful hair flying loose in the wind. Presently you will hear her calling the cows, — " Come thou! Come thou on!" and the echo will fall softly and sweetly on her own ears, — " Come thou! Come thou on!" And then the memory of another voice calling thus in a neighboring field will rise in her heart, and she will clasp her hands together and give way to her misery.

No, no, messieurs, the peace and contentment at St. Valerien, as elsewhere, are found in the deep skies, in the purple mists that settle over the far-lying fields, and in the little garden of the dead. There is life here, and where there is life there you will find trouble and passion, doubt and despair, and, whirling in and around these, the stinging swarm of worries and vexations that belong to human experience. Is it not so, Caderet? Is it not so, Desmoulins? Where men and women meet and look at each other, and smile and take hold of hands, there is much to be forgotten and forgiven.

There was Euphrasie Charette. Is it true, then, that you have never heard of her? I wonder at that, for it was a fine piece of gossip she set going about here. The men shrugged their shoulders and lifted their eyebrows, and the women put their heads together over the palings and in the chimney corners. Pouah! to hear the chatter was sickening, and it was kept up until, one Sunday, Père Archambault stood up in his pulpit and looked at the people a long time. Then he hung his head and sighed, saying, "My friends, to-day I shall preach you two sermons. My first sermon is this: What is bolder than innocence?" Then he paused again, turned over the leaves of the Book, read from the gospel, and preached his second sermon, on charity.

Well, the gossip soon died out, and no wonder; for, with all her beauty and wild impulsiveness, where could be found a purer or a tenderer-hearted girl than Euphrasie Charette? It will be very many years before another such as she will be running and romping and singing through the village, laughing with the young and sympathizing with the old. This was when the great world beyond St. Valerien was a dream as vague to her as the story of *le loup-garou*. Then, when she was a little older and more beautiful than ever, she was sent to the convent at St. Hyacinthe, and there she heard larger rumors of the great world. She had not much to learn in music, — her whole nature was tuned to melody; but while she was learning her English and her other lessons, she was also learning something of the world she had barely caught a glimpse of. Not much, no, but something, — just a little. Two of her school friends were from the States. French, yes; their families belonged near Montreal, but had gone to the States, where work is easy and wages are good. Euphrasie, inquis-

itive as a weasel, found out everything her
school friends knew; how their mothers
worked in the big cotton-mills, and how their
older sisters clerked in the stores. She saw
some photographs of these sisters, and oh,
how lovely they looked, with their lace and
finery, and their hair *frisé !* And she saw
some of the letters the girls wrote, telling of
the gay times the young people had in the
mill town.

All this in the ears of a child of St. Valerien. She was not young, — seventeen is
neither old nor young, — but she was at the
turning-point. Take it to yourself ! Would
you prefer the life in St. Valerien to that in
the mill town in the States, where everything
is gay ? Think of it ! All the summer long,
calling the cows and milking them, cooking,
scrubbing, working, raking hay ; all the winter long, mending, scrubbing, washing, spinning, weaving, and attending to the sheep
and cattle. It is very nice, you think. Yes,
for a little while, but wait until you have tried
it for a whole lifetime, and then tell me what
you think.

Well, Ma'm'selle Charette was old enough to
look at these things, and she made up her

mind. She liked St. Valerien, and she was
fond of the people here ; and she was so fond
of Joi Billette, her little cavalier, that the
children had long ago run their names together in some nonsense rhymes. Euphrasie
Charette, little Joi Billette, — you see how
they go ? She made up her mind that she
would see something of those gay times in
the mill town in the States, and so when she
came home from the convent there was no
longer any peace among the Charettes. Euphrasie could not go to the mill town in the
States ; that was settled. Madame Charette
said so, and madame had a quick temper
and a sharp tongue. "And you!" she would
say to Euphrasie, — "how would you look,
a young girl like you, running away to the
States ? Have you any shame ?" But Pierre
Charette, the father, sat in the corner and
smiled to himself. He had been in the
States, and he knew it was no great journey.
"Would you then go away and leave Joi and
St. Valerien ?" madame would say.

"What, then," Euphrasie would reply, "is
Joi a stick that he can no longer walk ? And
what storm is to blow St. Valerien away ?"

Then letters came to Euphrasie from her

school friends; and finally her sister, the wife
of Victor Donais, made up her mind to go to
the States. As for Victor, he said that where
the tongs went the shovel must go, and that
was all. Madame Charette made a fine quarrel,
— the sheep in the fields could hear her; but
Pierre Charette sat in the corner smoking his
black pipe and smiling to himself; and when
madame could quarrel no more, he rubbed his
knees, and said that Euphrasie would find
much benefit in traveling in the States.

" Oho! a fine lady! traveling in the
States! But yes, a fine lady! She will have
money, — oh, a great pocketful! Oh, certainly!" Madame Charette made a grand
gesture.

" Well, then," remarked Joi Billette, who
was sitting near Euphrasie, his head leaning
on his hands, " she can have some money
from me."

" Yes? Then you would do well to keep
it for yourself."

" It is hers," Joi said. " I can make
more."

There was nothing to do but for Madame
Charette to give her consent; and though
her tongue was sharp her heart was tender,

for she wept more than any one when Euphrasie was going, and in the long nights
afterwards she lay awake to weep. But there
was so much to do nobody could sit and
grieve. Joi Billette worked harder than ever,
and he found time to help the madame. He
cut wood and carried water, and she told him
he was handier about the house than Euphrasie, who had too many ideas from books.

It was not such a long year, after all. In
the spring and summer there was the farm
work to do, the milk to be carried to the
cheese factory, and the bark to be gathered
for the tannery. Everybody was busy, and
Joi Billette was busiest of all. For a little
while Euphrasie wrote to him every week,
and then she wrote no more. Joi said nothing. He could hear of her through Madame Charette, and that was enough. Perhaps she was too busy, — perhaps everything,
except that she had forgotten him. So the
year went on, and at last Euphrasie wrote
that she was coming home for the *fête* of
Jour de l'An. It is the custom here for the
absent ones to return home on the first day
of the year, to ask their father's blessing;
and there is often a friendly contest among

the members of the family as to which shall get the blessing first.

Euphrasie came on the Day of the New Year, and she was dressed very fine, — oh, ever so much finer than any girl you see here in St. Valerien. When her father had given her his blessing, he sat and watched her curiously a long time without smiling. Then he said in English, speaking slowly : —

" I ting you toss you' 'ead too much."

" Me toss my 'ead too much ! " replied Euphrasie. " Well, you should see dem girl of Fall River. If you can see dem girl toss 'er 'ead, I ting you won't say I toss my 'ead too much."

" I ting you 'ave too much feader on de 'at," suggested the father, not without some display of diffidence. His daughter had developed into a beautiful young woman, and her finery was not unbecoming.

" Well, now ! " Euphrasie retorted triumphantly, "if you only can see how much feader dem oder girl 'ave, I ting you will say dere is not one feader on my 'at."

" What is it, then ? " cried the madame sharply. She could not understand English.

" C'est rien, ma bonne femme," the old man sighed.

" I ting I give you good 'ug for dat." Euphrasie put her arms around her father's neck.

He shook his head slowly as he filled his pipe, and said no more.

Joi Billette sat in the corner, watching everything and listening. He was restless and uneasy. He was quick to see the great change that had come over Euphrasie. She was no longer his little girl of St. Valerien. The change meant more to him than it did to the others. More than once it seemed to him that some other girl had donned Euphrasie's face and voice for a New Year's masquerade. He had heard of such things in the fireside folk tales. Would Euphrasie look at him scornfully or speak to him mockingly, as this vision of beauty did? No, it could not be so. He looked at his hard and horny hands, at his coarse and dirty shoes, at his rough clothes, and then at the trim, neat figure of Euphrasie, her white hands and dainty feet. He rose, playing with his hat nervously, and would have slipped away, but Pierre Charette laid a detaining hand on his arm.

" Wouldst thou go, then? Thy place is here. Let the women talk."

At that moment Euphrasie was busy telling Suzette Benoit about a Monsieur Sam Pettingill, who had come all the way from Fall River to Montreal, and who was coming to St. Valerien. Pierre Charette was carrying his pipe to his mouth, but he paused, with his hand suspended in the air.

"'Ow you call 'is name?" he asked in English.

"M'sieu Sam Pattangeel," said Euphrasie, reddening a little.

"You know 'im, you?"

"Oh, yes; 'e was clerk in de mill store."

"'E clerk dere no more; no?"

"Of course, yes. 'E is taking his recess. 'E belong at de store." Euphrasie continued to redden. English was not often heard in that house, and the women were vainly straining their ears to catch the meaning.

"Aha-a-a!" exclaimed the old man. There was the faintest trace of contempt in his tone.

"'E say 'e come to see de country, if 'e like it or not," explained Euphrasie.

"If 'e like it, den 'e carry it back to 'is 'ouse?" Pierre Charette suggested.

"'Ow 'e can do dat?" asked Euphrasie.

"I 'ave seen dem clerk, me," said the old

man. " Dey de mos' pow'ful of all. If dis one like de country so 'e mus' take it back, what we goin' do? If 'e don't like it so 'e mus' take 'is scissor to cut it off, what we goin' do?"

Euphrasie could not misunderstand the sarcasm that seasoned the old man's tongue. It touched her temper.

"If 'e come visitin' de country, 'ow I can 'elp 'im? If you can 'elp 'im, den go 'elp 'im." Her tone was sharper than her words.

"Ah-h-h!" cried Pierre Charette, "dat is 'ow you fine ladies talk to old man!"

"No, no," said the girl impulsively, "I mean not dat. No, no." She went to her father and would have embraced him, but he pushed her away and resumed his pipe, while Euphrasie threw herself on a chair and began to cry.

But it was a small storm, more wind than rain, as the farmers say, and it soon passed over, but not until the madame had made some vigorous remarks, aimed at those who forget themselves sufficiently to quarrel in the English tongue. It was a queer father who would abuse his daughter the instant she set foot in the house, and it was a queer

daughter who would be disrespectful to the
father she had not seen for a year, — and all
in English, too. Well, madame knew men,
large and small, and she knew girls, old and
young, but never did she know such a man
as this, never did she see such a girl. As for
the English, — bah! C'est la blague!

II

Around the corner from Pierre Charette's
and not very far up the street is the little
auberge, kept by Toussaint Chicoine. There
Joi Billette went when he could slip out of
the family storm, and there he found some of
his village comrades sitting around the huge
stove in the public room, listening to the
famous stories told by Chicoine. Of course
you will think Chicoine is nobody, because
he can do nothing but keep this tavern, with
his mother and his sisters and his old father.
But good! You wait! Before long you will
see that man in the Parliament at Quebec.
When he is not telling stories he is talking
politics. Some people are quick to forget.
Chicoine is fifty, and remembers. A Liberal?
Yes, and better, — a Red; *le Rouge* written
in his glowing eyes and in his quick gestures.

No sooner had Joi Billette settled himself to listen to Chicoine's tremendous yarns than the sound of sleighbells was heard coming over the snow.

"One dollar it is Barie's horse," said Chicoine, — "Barie of Upton."

"How then can you know?" asked Joi Billette.

"Hard-head! It is by the sound of the bells. Listen!"

"It is even so," said Pierre Charette, who had followed Joi.

At that moment the sleigh paused at the door, and Barie himself called out: —

"Hey, Chicoine! Hey! Are you deaf, then?"

"Good-day, Barie," said Chicoine, opening the door. "Good-day, m'sieu. Within you will find it warmer."

"It is to be hoped," replied Barie dryly. "I have brought you a customer, Chicoine," he continued. "Lift your feet; make some stir."

The customer Barie had brought was Mr. Sam Pettingill, of Fall River. He was nice looking, yes, but you would not say he was fine. He had yellow hair and gray eyes, and one of his front teeth was gone. He was smoking a cigarette, and he had a look on his face as if he knew a great deal more than older people. He kept trying to twist his little mustache, which was too thin to be twisted.

" Great Scott ! " he exclaimed, as he got out of the sleigh ; " is this the Hotel Imperial ? "

" 'Ow you please," replied Chicoine gravely. " 'Otel, auberge, 'ouse, — it all de same when you git col' an' 'ungry. You spik French ? No ? "

" Rats ! " cried young Mr. Pettingill. " How can I speak French in this weather ? It freezes everything except American cusswords. You ask his Nibs, here, if it don't." Barie shrugged his shoulders and threw the sleigh robe over his horse. " You may n't have much of a hotel," said Pettingill, " but maybe you 've got a fire. It 's colder 'n Flujens."

With his hat on the side of his head, and his red cravat creeping from under his overcoat, Pettingill swaggered into the little tavern and stood close to the big stove. Joi Billette looked at the new-comer, and then at

Pierre Charette. Pierre Charette looked at
the new-comer, and then at Joi Billette.
Each, by an almost imperceptible shrug of
the shoulders, telegraphed his comment. You
know how the shoulders and the eyebrows can
talk here in St. Valerien: a word, a glance, a
little movement of the shoulders, and much
more than a long story is told.

"Say !" said Pettingill, removing his overcoat, "I don't see no hotel register around
here, but I guess that's all skewvee. My
name's Pettingill, and it would be the same
if it was wrote down in a book."

"Hall ri', m'sieu," returned Toussaint Chicoine, bowing. "You 'ear dat, Joutras?
You 'ear dat, Billette ? You 'ear dat, everybody? M'sieu Pattungeel."

"Kee-rect," said Pettingill approvingly.
"You flatten it a little too much in the middle, and pull it out too much at the end, but
that's my maiden name." He shook himself,
and strode around the room, looking at the
cheap prints pasted on the wall. The little
company looked at each other somewhat
sheepishly, all save Charette and Chicoine.
Charette stood gloomily by the stove, while
Chicoine, with his arms akimbo and his chin

drawn in until it was hid by the muscles of his neck, watched Pettingill closely.

At one end of the room, above a worn and battered sofa, hung a faded tintype. It was the picture of a very old man. He was leaning forward on a stout cane, and a weak and trembling smile had been caught and fastened on his face.

" What old duck is this?" asked Pettingill, after studying the picture. Receiving no answer, he turned and looked at Chicoine.

" 'Ow you call it, m'sieu?" Surely there was no menace in the sweetly spoken accent. Yet something that he heard or felt caused Pettingill to change his question.

" What old gent is this?" he asked.

" Dat my fader," replied Chicoine.

" Is he still kicking?"

" 'Ow, m'sieu?"

" Is he dead?"

" No, no, m'sieu. 'E right in dis 'ouse."

" Well, I wanter know!" Pettingill exclaimed, with genuine admiration. "I thought old uncle Cy Pettingill, down to Pittsfield, was the oldest inhabitant, but the colonel here can give him odds and beat him thirteen laps in a mile."

"'Ow you say, m'sieu?" asked Chicoine.

"I was lettin' out a family secret. Uncle Cy Pettingill is so old he can't see nothin' but a silver dollar, but the colonel here lays a long ways over him. I'd like to see them two old coons git together and jabber about the landin' of Christopher Columbus."

"Yes, yes, m'sieu, pair'aps dat would be nice." Chicoine spoke so seriously that Pettingill had to lean against the wall to laugh.

"Just have my grip sent up to my room," he said, after a while. "I'll hang out here a day or two, and see how the climate suits my complexion. And while you're about it, you might jest as well show me where I am to roost."

"You want fin' you' room? Well, I show you."

He led Monsieur Pettingill up a narrow stairway into a snug little attic.

"It ain't bigger 'n a squirrel cage," said the American.

"It 'ave comfort." Chicoine stretched his hand toward the stovepipe, which ran through a sheet-iron drum; then he went down.

Charette, Billette, Joutras, and the rest sat just as he had left them. They had neither moved nor spoken. Chicoine stood and glared at them, his arms akimbo, his chin drawn into his neck, and his under lip stuck out ominously. Suddenly he raised his right arm, and brought down his clenched fist in the palm of the other hand with a tremendous whack.

"Pig! beast! that he should strut in this place! But that I had pity on him I would have crushed him with my hand." Toussaint Chicoine's eyes gleamed.

"Softly, softly!" Pierre Charette raised his hand.

"*Ah-h-h!* Softly, yes, softly. Good! But I have seen my old father take off his hat and bend his knee to just such a man as that. Yes, me! I have seen that. I am old enough. When the lord of the land came where his slaves could see him — off hat! bend knee! Well, yes, I have seen that." The veins in Chicoine's neck stood out angrily.

"But those days, they are no more." Charette spoke gently.

"No?" Chicoine made a hideous grimace. "Well, they are here!" With that he struck his broad breast a tremendous blow. "For what does he come?"

Joi Billette rose and shook himself viciously, and turned his back to the stove. "This ugly beast is detestable!"

"But wait, then!" It was Joutras who spoke. "What the thunder! Are we all taking leave of ourselves? Let this pig alone. Is he stealing corn from our pen? Well, then, show it to me."

Pierre Charette chuckled to himself, and Joi Billette shrugged his shoulders.

It was not long before Monsieur Pettingill came down from his room. He found only Chicoine and Joi Billette. As if to refresh his memory or to confirm some afterthought, he went again to the portrait of old Anthime Chicoine. He looked at it a little while, and then shook his head.

"That lays over uncle Cy Pettingill," he repeated, with admiration. "He 's mighty nigh too old to make a shadder." He paused a moment, and then, with just the faintest trace of embarrassment, remarked: "Say! can any of you chaps tell me where Miss Euphrasie Charette lives? As long as I 'm in town, with nothin' much to prey on my mind, I might as well drop in an' tell her I 'm still her humble-come-tumble. See?"

"I dunno if I can show you," said Chicoine; "pair'aps M'sieu Billette will show
you de 'ouse. He been dere some time befo'
now. Is not that so, M'sieu Billette?" he
went on, switching off into French. "I have
told m'sieu that you would have much pleasure to show him the house of Charette. Is
it not so, then? Ah, little boy! make not
your face to wrinkle so. At forty you will
laugh at the physic of this kind."

Billette shrugged his shoulders, but he did
not smile.

"'E spik only French," said Chicoine to
Pettingill, by way of explanation, "but dat
make no diffrance. 'E can show you de
'ouse."

"All skewvee," said Pettingill. "If he
can walk in English, that's enough for me."

Joi Billette, coiled in the chair, had seemed
to be an insignificant creature, but when he
rose, glancing furtively at Chicoine, it was seen
that he was taller than Pettingill, — taller
and stronger, and much handsomer. The
innocence of youth shone in his face. Without a word, he went out at the door, followed
by Pettingill. Billette's slouching gait carried
him forward swiftly, and in a few moments

he paused, waved his hand toward Charette's house, from which the blue smoke cheerfully curled, and stood watching Pettingill as he made his way to the door. He saw the door open, and heard Euphrasie's exclamation : —

"Ah, 't is you. I di' n' ting you come so soon."

When the door was closed, Billette went forward to the house, and passed through the yard and into the kitchen. There he found Pierre Charette enjoying his pipe. As Joi entered, Charette nodded his head toward the inner room and shrugged his shoulders.

"Yes," said Joi, "it is the stranger. Euphrasie was glad to see him, then ?"

"How can I know ?" responded Charette. "Of the women we know nothing. They pet the pig and scald it. Go see for yourself if she is glad. The man cannot comprehend."

"No, no," said Joi, the blood mounting to his face.

"You have fear, then ? Yes ?"

For reply Joi laughed loudly, and the sound was so harsh and unnatural that those in the next room paused to listen, and madame put her head in the door to make inquiry.

"Prutt! prutt!" exclaimed Pierre Charette, mimicking the inquisitive turkey hen.
"Allez-vous-en! Back to the pig."

Then there was silence in the kitchen.
The old man and the young man sat smoking. Each had his own thoughts. One was
thinking how much money his grain and hay
would fetch; the other was thinking bitterly
of the day, a year ago, when he and Euphrasie, with their village companions, sang their
holiday songs together. Ah! they were happy
then, but now —

Madame Charette was surely at her best
this day. She rattled away at Pettingill in
French, and Euphrasie interpreted the words
the best she knew how; but she could not
keep up, madame was so jolly and hearty.
Pettingill had never been in such a storm of
French and broken English, and he wished
himself well out of it. All he could do was
to sit and grin helplessly, and mop his face
aimlessly with his gorgeous silk handkerchief.
Euphrasie, too, was jolly, or pretended to be,
and she carried on her interpretations with a
great deal of laughter.

"Ma mère say if you like dis country?"
she remarked.

"Just tell her," said Pettingill, "that if she will give me the daughter she may keep the country."

"'Ush up, you!" said Euphrasie, blushing; "you too bad." To her mother, "He is very fond of the country, oh, — much."

This caught the ear of Pierre Charette, and it recalled him from his mental grain speculation. He turned in his chair and looked at Billette with half-closed eyes. At this moment there was a shuffling of feet and a moving of chairs in the next room. Some of the girls and boys of the village had come in to see Euphrasie. Presently, madame, glowing with hospitality, came into the kitchen for more chairs.

"It is the whole village," she explained. "And Joi hiding like a thief! Shame upon him! Take these chairs, then, and cease to be a stick. Leave dozing to the gray cat."

Joi Billette took the chairs, but with no good grace. He was not himself. He placed them around the room mechanically, and stood in the midst of his friends, awkward and ill at ease. Some wanted to laugh at him, while others tried to tease him, but his air of preoccupation restrained them; they

were already somewhat subdued by the presence of a stranger. In this diffident company Pettingill sat serene, smiling and con-
fident. He was even patronizing. When
an embarrassing silence was about to fall on
all, he was superior to circumstances.

"Rats!" he exclaimed. "Don't set here
moping. Can't we have some play-songs?"

"Oh," said Euphrasie, trying to understand, "some play-song, — yes."

"Something like 'Here's a young man set
down to sleep'" —

"Oh, to sleep! I know," said Euphrasie.

"'He needs a young girl to keep him
awake.'"

"Oh, yes, — to kip 'im 'wake!" Then
she rattled away in French to the rest. The
result was that all the young men chose part-
ners, except Joi, — there was no partner for
him to choose, — and proceeded to promenade slowly around the small room, singing
as they went. The song was about a maiden
and her bashful lover, and the clear voice of
Euphrasie carried the tune. The cavalier
sees his sweetheart laughing; then runs the
song : —

> "Qu'avez-vous, belle ?   Qu'avez-vous, belle ?
>   Qu'avez-vous à tant rire ?"

Whereupon the girl replies : —

> "Je ris de moi, je ris de toi,
>   De nos fortes entreprises :
>   C'est d'avoir passé le bois
>   Sans un petit mot me dire ! "

The maiden is going away from the lover, who is too bashful to speak the little word. She is supposed to be waving her hand in the distance.   Then the lover is aroused.

> "Revenez, belle !   Revenez, belle !
>   Je vous donnerai cent livres !"

But the girl does n't want his fortune.   She has had a glimpse of a larger world.

> " Ni pour un cent, ni pour deux cent,
>   Ni pour cinq cent mille livres :
>   Il fallait mangé la perdrix
>   Tandis qu'elle était prise ! "

And the pretty little partridge will never come back.   The girl, still going, cries : —

> " La perdrix a pris sa volée,
>   Elle se mit en ville ;
>   Je vois mes amants promener
>   Dans le parc de la ville ! "

All through the singing Joi Billette kept his eyes on Euphrasie, and he thought she was singing at him. The motions of her pretty head, the glances of her bright eyes, — in every way she seemed to be saying that she would not return, but would promenade with other lovers. Joi understood it so, too, for by the time the song was ended he had disappeared, and the small company saw him no more that day. But they heard of him, — oh, yes!

He went into the kitchen, and sat with his face in his hands. No one could say whether his attitude was one of laziness or despair, so little do we know of what is going on before our very eyes. For a while he sat still as death; then he rose and went about the room, searching for something. On the wall hung a piece of looking-glass. He looked into it as he passed, and saw that his face was very white. He shook his head; he did not know the man that looked back at him from the glass. He went about the room, hunting in the corners, on the shelves, and under the pans. At last a long knife lay under his hand. He picked it up, looked at it curiously, and hid it under his jacket. Then he seated himself again, his face hid in his hands, and waited. Euphrasie came for a drink of water; he knew the rustle of her dress, the sound of her footsteps, but he did not stir. She looked at him and tossed her head. She

said to herself, " Now he is angry ; to-morrow
he will feel better." He sat and waited, his
face in his hands. Some one went away, —
that was Hélène Joutras ; he knew her voice.
One by one they all went away, except the
serene and smiling stranger. Then, too, after
a while, he was ready to go. Euphrasie went
to the door with him. Her broken English
seemed very queer to Joi Billette, and very
beautiful, too. The door was closed, and
then Joi heard the stranger's feet crunching
in the snow. He rose from his chair, feeling
strangely oppressed. He was so weak he was
compelled to steady himself. It was not
fear ; it was pity. He heard Pettingill going
along whistling a gay tune, and he pitied
him. But what was pity ? There are other
things more important than pity. He went
out at the back door, and the cold air stung
his face and made him feel stronger.

Once out of the gate, he pressed forward
rapidly. Just ahead of him Pettingill was
sauntering along, still whistling. The stranger was in no hurry, then ? So much the
better. Joi Billette was so intent on carrying out the purpose he had formed that he
did not hear heavy footsteps behind him, nor

did he hear a strong voice call his name. He
had eyes and ears for no one but Pettingill.
As he went forward, he drew the knife from
beneath his jacket and held it firmly in his
hand, quickening his pace. Pettingill's careless swagger whetted his anger. The wretch!
Would he come here, then, and lord it over
the village ?

Pettingill, hearing footsteps behind him,
paused and looked around. He saw Joi Billette coming swiftly towards him, followed as
swiftly by a tall, black-robed figure. Like a
flash his mind recurred to the stories he had
read of Roman Catholics, and now, here
before his eyes, as he imagined, was an emis-
sary of the Pope about to administer discipline.

" Run, buster ! he 's gainin' on you ! " he
called out gayly. He had no opportunity to
say more. At that moment Joi Billette seized
him by the arm and swung him around violently.

" Beast ! devil ! " the Canadian hissed
through his clenched teeth. " Take that ! "
He made an effort to plunge the knife into
the American, but a powerful hand was laid
on his arm. He turned, looked into the eyes

of the *frère directeur* of the Maristes, and then sank trembling on the snow. The Mariste stood over him, tall and severe.

"What, then, have I taught thee to assassinate?" There was grief in his voice and supreme pity.

"Say!" exclaimed Pettingill, who had been too much astonished to speak, "what kinder game is he up to? Ain't he off his kerzip?"

"Go!" The Mariste waved his hand imperiously.

"Come off!" Pettingill spoke roughly. "Wait till I give you a pointer. Don't you let that chap rush after me. Because if you do"— he drew a shining pistol from his overcoat pocket — "I'll give him a tetch of the United States that 'll last him."

"Go!" the Mariste repeated.

"So long," said Pettingill, whereupon he turned on his heel and went away.

The Mariste lifted Joi Billette to his feet, brushed the snow from his clothes, took him by the hand, and led him back the way he had come. Past Charette's, past all the houses, they went, the Mariste still holding Joi by the hand. At the end of the street,

"GO!" THE MARISTE REPEATED

the white crosses of the little cemetery
gleamed almost as white as the snow piled
up on the graves. Into the garden of the
dead they went, and there the Mariste led
Joi to one of the little white crosses. In the
centre of the cross had been fixed a small
frame, and in this frame was the likeness of
a young woman, a souvenir of the dead. It
was a common tintype, but there was an air
of nobility about it. It had the beauty of
youth and the tenderness of maturity. It
was the picture of Joi Billette's mother. He
fell on his knees before it, and sobbed convulsively. The Mariste stood, with hat off
and folded arms, his black hair blown about
by the wind. Aimé Joutras, watching from
a distance, saw the two emerge from the
cemetery and go into the church, not far
away. Then he saw them no more.

When Pettingill returned to the little auberge, he found Barie still there, tasting and
testing Chicoine's *la p'tite bière*, and it was
not long before he was seated in the grizzled
habitant's sleigh, on his way to Upton. One
day passed, then two days, then three. Pettingill could be accounted for, — he had gone

away; but where was Joi Billette? The times were not so gay at Charette's as before. Euphrasie ceased to toss her head and forgot to put on her fine airs. She was continually looking up the street for Joi, but no Joi came. She went to see André Billette, Joi's father, but André looked at her coldly and shook his head. He had no information to give. Joi was of age: he could take care of himself.

"You know where he is?" said Euphrasie.

"I know where I am, ma'm'selle," said André. "I bother nobody."

There was no comfort for the girl in such talk as that. Then there was the story that Joutras told of seeing Joi with the *frère directeur* of the Mariste school. To the school Euphrasie went. One of the pupils opened the door, and in a little while the *frère directeur* came. He was very grave, but there was a twinkle of fun in his eyes when he saw Euphrasie. The girl was excited and defiant. Her face was very white, and her hands trembled. She made no salutation.

"Where is Joi Billette?" she asked bluntly.

The Mariste regarded her curiously.

"Why do you come to me for Joi Billette?" he asked gently. "If he is here, why disturb him? He asks to see no one. He is content."

"I ask you, where is Joi Billette?" the girl repeated. Her attitude was almost threatening.

"Why come to me?" the Mariste insisted. "What am I?"

"For you," exclaimed Euphrasie, "I do not care that!" She raised her hand and snapped her fingers. "Where is Joi Billette?"

Her voice rang through the hallway, and at that moment Joi appeared behind the Mariste, his face pale and his eyes full of wonder. When Euphrasie saw him she turned away from the door and began to weep. Joi looked at the Mariste for an explanation, but, without waiting for it, he ran to Euphrasie, as she was going away, and threw his arms around her.

The Mariste nodded his head approvingly, and closed the door.

THE COMEDY OF WAR

I

ON THE UNION SIDE

PRIVATE O'HALLORAN, detailed for special duty in advance of the picket line, sat reclining against a huge red oak. Within reach lay a rifle of beautiful workmanship. In one hand he held a blackened brier-root pipe, gazing on it with an air of mock regret. It had been his companion on many a weary march and on many a lonely day, when, as now, he was doing duty as a sharpshooter. But it was not much of a companion now. It held the flavor, but not the fragrance, of other days. It was empty, and so was O'Halloran's tobacco-pouch. It was nothing to grumble about, but the big, laughing Irishman liked his pipe, especially when it was full of tobacco. The words of an old song came to him, and he hummed them to himself : —

" There was an ould man, an' he had a wooden leg,
　An' he had no terbacky, nor terbacky could he beg ;
　There was another ould man, as keen as a fox,
　An' he always had terbacky in his ould terbacky box.

" Sez one ould man, ' Will yez give me a chew ? '
　Sez the other ould man, ' I 'll be dommed ef I do.
　Kape away from them gin-mills, an' save up yure rocks,
　An' ye 'll always have terbacky in yer ould terbacky box.' "

What with the singing and the far-away
thoughts that accompanied the song, Private
O'Halloran failed to hear footsteps approaching until they sounded quite near.

"Halt !" he cried, seizing his rifle and
springing to his feet. The newcomer wore
the insignia of a Federal captain, seeing
which, O'Halloran lowered his weapon and
saluted. " Sure, sor, you 're not to mind me
capers. I thought the inimy had me com-
plately surrounded — I did, upon me sowl."

"And I," said the captain, laughing,
"thought the Johnnies had caught me. It
is a pleasant surprise. You are O'Halloran
of the Sharpshooters ; I have heard of you
— a gay singer and a great fighter."

"Sure it 's not for me to say that same. I
sings a little bechwane times for to kape up
me sperits, and takes me chances, right and
lift. You 're takin' a good many yourself,

sor, so far away from the picket line. If I make no mistake, sor, it is Captain Fambrough I'm talkin' to."

"That is my name," the captain said.

"I was touchin' elbows wit' you at Gettysburgh, sor."

The captain looked at O'Halloran again. "Why, certainly!" he exclaimed. "You are the big fellow that lifted one of the Johnnies over the stone wall."

"By the slack of the trousers. I am that same, sor. He was nothin' but a bit of a lad, sor, but he fought right up to the end of me nose. The men was jabbin' at 'im wit' their bay'nets, so I sez to him, says I, 'Come in out of the inclemency of the weather,' says I, and thin I lifted him over. He made at me, sor, when I put 'im down, an' it took two men for to lead 'im kindly to the rear. It was a warm hour, sor."

As O'Halloran talked, he kept his eyes far afield.

"Sure, sor," he went on, "you stand too much in the open. They had one muddle-head on that post yesterday; they'll not put another there to-day, sor." As he said this, the big Irishman seized the captain by the arm and gave him a sudden jerk. It was an unceremonious proceeding, but a very timely one, for the next moment the sapling against which the captain had been lightly leaning was shattered by a ball from the Confederate side.

" 'T is an old friend of mine, sor," said O'Halloran ; " I know 'im by his handwritin'. They had a muddlehead there yesterday, sor. I set in full sight of 'im, an' he blazed at me twice ; the last time I had me fist above me head, an' he grazed me knuckles. ' Bedad,' says I, ' you 're no good in your place ; ' an' when he showed his mug, I plugged 'im where the nose says howdy to the eyebrows. 'T was no hurt to 'im, sor ; if he seen the flash, 't was as much."

To the left, in a little clearing, was a comfortable farmhouse. Stacks of fodder and straw and pens of corn in the shuck were ranged around. There was every appearance of prosperity, but no sign of life, save two bluebirds, the pioneers of spring, that were fighting around the martin gourds, preparing to take possession.

" There 's where I was born." The captain pointed to the farmhouse. " It is five years since I have seen the place."

" You don't tell me, sor! I see in the ' Hur'ld ' that they call it the Civil War, but it's nothin' but oncivil, sor, for to fight agin' your ould home."

" You are right," assented the captain. " There's nothing civil about war. I suppose the old house has long been deserted."

" Sure, look at the forage, thin. 'T is piled up as nately as you plaze. Wait till the b'ys git at it! Look at the smoke of the chimbly. Barrin' the jay-birds, 't is the peacefullest sight I 've seen."

" My people are gone," said the captain. " My father was a Union man. I would n't be surprised to hear of him somewhere at the North. The day that I was eighteen he gave me a larruping for disobedience, and I ran away."

" Don't spake of it, sor." O'Halloran held up his hands. " Many 's the time I 've had me feelin's hurted wit' a bar'l stave."

" That was in 1860," said the captain. " I was too proud to go back home, but when the war began I remembered what a strong Union man my father was, and I joined the Union army."

" 'T is a great scheme for a play," said the big Irishman solemnly.

" My mother was dead," the captain went
on, "my oldest sister was married, and my
youngest sister was at school in Philadelphia,
and my brother, two years older than myself,
made life miserable for me in trying to boss
me."

" Oh ! " exclaimed O'Halloran, " don't I
know that same ? 'T is meself that 's been
along there."

Captain Fambrough looked at the old place,
carefully noting the outward changes, which
were comparatively few. He noted, too, with
the eye of a soldier, that when the impending conflict took place between the forces
then facing each other, there would be a
sharp struggle for the knoll on which the
house stood ; and he thought it was a curious feat for his mind to perform, to regard
the old home where he had been both happy
and miserable as a strategic point of battle.
Private O'Halloran had no such memories to
please or to vex him. To the extent of his
opportunities he was a man of business. He
took a piece of white cloth from his pocket
and hung it on the broken sapling.

" I 'll see, sor, if yon chap is in the grocery
business."

As he turned away, there was a puff of smoke on the farther hill, a crackling report, and the hanging cloth jumped as though it were alive.

"Faith, it's him, sor!" exclaimed O'Halloran, "an' he's in a mighty hurry." Whereupon the big Irishman brushed a pile of leaves from an oil-cloth strapped together in the semblance of a knapsack.

"What have you there?" asked Captain Fambrough.

"Sure, 't is me grocery store, sor. Coffee, tay, an' sugar. Faith, I'll make the divvle's mouth water like a baby cuttin' his stomach tathe. Would ye mind comin' along, sor, for to kape me from swindlin' the Johnny out of all his belongin's?"

II

ON THE CONFEDERATE SIDE

THREE men sat in a gully that had once been a hillside ditch. Their uniforms were various, the result of accident and capture. One of them wore a very fine blue overcoat which was in queer contrast to his ragged pantaloons. This was Lieutenant Clopton, who had charge of the picket line. Another had on the uniform of an artilleryman, and his left arm was in a sling. He had come out of the hospital to do duty as a guide. This was Private John Fambrough. The third had on no uniform at all, but was dressed in plain citizen's clothes, much the worse for wear. This was Jack Kilpatrick, scout and sharpshooter, — Happy Jack, as he was called.

How long since the gully had been a ditch it would be impossible to say, but it must have been a good many years, for the pines had grown into stout trees, and here and there a black-jack loomed up vigorously.

"Don't git too permiscus around here," said Happy Jack, as the others were moving about. "This ain't no fancy spot." He eased himself upward on his elbow, and made a swift but careful survey of the woodland vista that led to the Federal lines. Then he shook down the breech of his rifle, and slipped a long cartridge into its place. "You see that big poplar over yonder? Well, under that tree there's a man, leastways he ought to be there, because he's always hangin' around in front of me."

" Why don't you nail him ? " asked Fambrough.

" Bosh ! Why don't he nail me ? It's because he can't do it. Well, that's the reason I don't nail him. You know what happened yesterday, don't you? You saw that elegant lookin' chap that came out to take my place, did n't you ? Did you see him when he went back ? "

Lieutenant Clopton replied with a little grimace, but Fambrough said never a word. He only looked at Kilpatrick with inquiring eyes.

" Why, he was the nicest lookin' man in the army — hair combed, clothes brushed, and rings on his fingers. He was all the way from New 'leans, with a silver-mounted rifle and a globe sight."

" A which ? " asked Fambrough.

" A globe sight. Set down on yourself a little further, sonny," said Happy Jack ; " your head 's too high. I says to him, says I, ' Friend, you are goin' where you 'll have to strip that doll's step-ladder off'n your gun, an' come down to business,' says I. I says, says I, ' You may have to face a red-headed flannel-mouthed Irishman, and you don't want

to look at him through all that machinery,'
says I."

"What did he say?" Fambrough asked.

"He said, 'I'll git him.' Now, how did
he git him? Why, he come down here,
lammed aloose a time or two, and then hung
his head over the edge of the gully there,
with a ball right spang betwixt his eyes. I
went behind the picket line to get a wink of
sleep, but I had n't more 'n curled up in the
broom-sage before I heard that chap a-bangin'
away. Then come the reply like this" —
Happy Jack snapped his fingers; "and then
I went to sleep waitin' for the rej'inder."

Kilpatrick paused, and looked steadily in
the direction of the poplar.

"Well, dog my cats! Yonder 's a chap
standin' right out in front of me. It ain't
the Mickey, neither. I'll see what he 's up
to." He raised his rifle with a light swinging
movement, chirruped to it as though it were
a horse or a little child, and in another moment the deadly business of war would have
been resumed, but Fambrough laid his hand
on the sharpshooter's arm.

"Wait," he said. "That may be my old
man wandering around out there. Don't be

too quick on trigger. I ain't got but one old man."

"Shucks!" exclaimed Kilpatrick pettishly; "you reckon I don't know your old man? He's big in the body, an' wobbly in his legs. You 've spiled a mighty purty shot. I believe in my soul that chap was a colonel, an' he might 'a' been a general. Now that's funny."

"What's funny?" asked Fambrough.

"Why, that chap. He 'll never know you saved him, an' if he know'd it he would n't thank you. I 'd 'a' put a hole right through his gizzard. Now he 's behind the poplar."

"It 's luck," Lieutenant Clopton suggested.

"Maybe," said Kilpatrick. "Yonder he is ag'in. Luck won't save him this time." He raised his rifle, glanced down the barrel, and pulled the trigger. Simultaneously with the report an expression of disgust passed over his face, and with an oath he struck the ground with his fist.

"Don't tell me you missed him," said Clopton.

"Miss what?" exclaimed Kilpatrick scornfully. "If he ain't drunk, somebody pulled him out of the way."

"I told you it was luck," commented Clopton.

"Shucks! don't tell me. Luck 's like lightnin'. She never hits twice in the same place."

Kilpatrick sank back in the gully and gave himself up to ruminating. He leaned on his elbows and pulled up little tufts of grass and weeds growing here and there. Lieutenant Clopton, looking across towards the poplar, suddenly reached for the sharpshooter's rifle, but Kilpatrick placed his hand on it jealously.

"Give me the gun. Yonder 's a Yank in full view."

Kilpatrick, still holding his rifle, raised himself and looked.

"Why, he 's hanging out a flag of truce," said Clopton. "What does the fellow mean?"

"It 's a message," said Kilpatrick, "an' here 's the answer." With that he raised his rifle, dropped it gently in the palm of his left hand, and fired.

"You saw the hankcher jump, did n't you?" he exclaimed. "Well, that lets us out. That 's my Mickey. He wants tobacco, and I want coffee an' tea. Come, watch me swap him out of his eye teeth."

Then Kilpatrick went to a clump of broom-sedge and drew forth a wallet containing several pounds of prepared smoking tobacco and a bundle of plug tobacco, and in a few moments the trio were picking their way through the underwood towards the open.

III

ON NEUTRAL GROUND

MATTERS were getting critical for Squire Fambrough. He had vowed and declared that he would never be a refugee, but he had a responsibility on his hands that he had not counted on. That responsibility was his daughter Julia, twenty-two years old, and as obstinate as her father. The Squire had sent off his son's wife and her children, together with as many negroes as had refused to go into the Union lines. He had expected his daughter to go at the same time, but when the time arrived, the fair Julia showed that she had a mind of her own. She made no scene, she did not go into hysterics; but when everything was ready, she asked her father if he was going. He said he would follow along after a while. She called to a negro, and made him take her trunks and band-boxes from the wagon and carry them into the house, while Squire Fambrough stood scratching his head.

"Why don't you make her come?" his daughter-in-law asked, somewhat sharply.

"Well, Susannah," the Squire remarked, "I ain't been a jestice of the peace and a married man, off and on for forty year, without findin' out when to fool with the wimen sek an' when not to fool wi' 'em."

"I'd make her come," said the daughter-in-law.

"I give you lief, Susannah, freely an' fully. Lay your baby some'rs wher' it won't git run over, an' take off your surplus harness, an' go an' fetch her out of the house an' put her in the buggy."

But the daughter-in-law treated the courteous invitation with proper scorn, and the small caravan moved off, leaving the fair Julia and her father in possession of the premises. According to human understanding, the refugees got off just in the nick of time. A day or two afterwards, the Union army, figuratively speaking, marched up,

looked over Squire Fambrough's front palings, and then fell back to reflect over the
situation.   Shortly afterwards the Confederate army marched up, looked over the Squire's
back palings, and also fell back to reflect.
Evidently the situation was one to justify
reflection, for presently both armies fell back
still farther.   These movements were so courteous and discreet — were such a colossal
display of etiquette — that war seemed to be
out of the question.   Of course there were
the conservative pickets, the thoughtful ve-
dettes, and the careful sharpshooters, ready
to occasion a little bloodshed, accidentally or
intentionally.   But by far the most boister-
ously ferocious appendages of the two armies
were the two brass bands.   They were continually challenging each other, beginning
early in the morning and ending late in the
afternoon; one firing off " Dixie," and the
other " Yankee Doodle."   It was " Yankee
Doodle, howdy do ? " and " Doodle-doodle,
Dixie, too," like two chanticleers challenging
each other afar off.

This was the situation as it appeared to
Squire Fambrough and his daughter.   On
this particular morning the sun was shining

brightly, and the birds were fluttering joyously in the budding trees. Miss Julia had brought her book out into the grove of venerable oaks which was the chief beauty of the place, and had seated herself on a rustic bench that was built around one of the trees. Just as she had become interested, she heard a rifle-shot. She moved uneasily, but fell to reading again, and was apparently absorbed in the book, when she heard another shot. Then she threw the book down and rose to her feet, making a very pretty centrepiece in the woodland setting.

" Oh ! what is the matter with everything ? " she exclaimed. " There 's the shooting again ! How can I read books and sit quietly here while the soldiers are preparing to fight ? Oh, me ! I don't know what to do ! If there should be a battle here, I don't know what would become of us."

Julia, in her despair, was fair to look upon. Her gown of striped homespun stuff, simply made, set off to admiration her strong but supple figure. Excitement added a new lustre to her eye and gave a heightened color to the rose that bloomed on her cheeks. She stood a moment as if listening, and then a faint smile showed on her lips. She heard her father calling : —

"Jule! Jule! O Jule!"

"Here I am, father!" she cried. "What is it?"

"Well, the Lord he'p my soul! I 've been huntin' for you high an' low. Did you hear that shootin'? I 'lowed may be you 'd been took prisoner an' carried bodaciously off. Did n't I hear you talkin' to somebody?"

Squire Fambrough pulled off his hat and scratched his head. His face, set in a fringe of gray beard, was kindly and full of humor, but it contained not a few of the hard lines of experience.

"No, father," said Julia, in reply to the squire's question. "I was only talking to myself."

"Jest makin' a speech, eh? Well, I don't blame you, honey. I 'm a great mind to jump out here in the clearin' an' yell out my sentiments so that both sides can hear 'em."

"Why, what is the matter, father?"

"I 'm mad, honey! I 'm jest nachally stirred up, — dog my cats ef I ain't! Along at fust I did hope there would n't be no fightin' in this neighborhood, but now I jest want to see them two blamed armies light into one another, tooth and toe-nail."

" Why, father ! " Julia made a pretty gesture of dismay. " How can you talk so ? "

" Half of my niggers is gone," said Squire Fambrough ; " one side has got my hosses, and t' other side has stole my cattle. The Yankees has grabbed my grist mill, an' the Confeds has laid holt of my corncrib. One army is squattin' in my tater patch, and t' other one is roostin' in my cow pastur'. Do you reckon I was born to set down here an' put up wi' that kind of business ? "

" But, father, what can you do ? How can you help yourself ? For heaven's sake, let 's go away from here ! "

" Great Moses, Jule ! Have you gone an' lost what little bit of common sense you was born with ? Do you reckon I 'm a-goin' to be a-refugeein' an' a-skeedaddlin' across the country like a skeer'd rabbit at my time of life ? I hain't afeared of nary two armies they can find room for on these hills ! Hain't I got one son on one side an' another son on t' other side ? Much good they are doin', too. If they 'd 'a' felt like me they 'd 'a' fit both sides. Do you reckon I'm a-gwine to be drove off'n the place where I was born, an' where your granpappy was born, an' where your mother lies buried ? No, honey ! "

" But, father, you know we can't stay here. Suppose there should be a battle ? "

" Come, honey ! come ! " There was a touch of petulance in the old man's tone. " Don't get me flustrated. I told you to go when John's wife an' the children went. By this time you'd 'a' been out of hearin' of the war."

" But, father, how could I go and leave you here all by yourself ? " The girl laid her hand on the squire's shoulder caressingly.

" No," exclaimed the squire angrily ; " stay you would, stay you did, an' here you are ! "

" Yes, and now I want to go away, and I want you to go with me. All the horses are not taken, and the spring wagon and the barouche are here."

" Don't come a-pesterin' me, honey ! I'm pestered enough as it is. Lord, if I had the big men here what started the war, I'd take 'em an' butt their cussed heads together tell you would n't know 'em from a lot of spiled squashes."

" Now, don't get angry and say bad words, father."

" I can't help it, Jule; I jest can't help it. When the fuss was a-brewin' I sot down an' wrote to Jeems Buchanan, and told him, jest as plain as the words could be put on paper, that war was boun' to come if he did n't look sharp; an' then when old Buck dropped out, I sot down an' wrote to Abe Lincoln an' told him that coercion would n't work worth a cent, but conciliation " —

" Wait, father ! " Julia held up her pretty hand. " I hear some one calling. Listen ! "

Not far away they heard the voice of a negro. " Marse Dave Henry ! O Marse Dave Henry ! "

" Hello ! Who the nation are you hollerin' at ? " said Squire Fambrough as a youngish-looking negro man came in view. " An' where did you come from, an' where are you goin' ? "

" Howdy, mistiss, — howdy, marster ! " The negro took off his hat as he came up.

" What 's your name ? " asked the squire.

"I'm name Tuck, suh. None er you all ain't seed nothin' er Marse" —

"Who do you belong to?"

"I b'longs ter de Cloptons down dar in Georgy, suh. None er you-all ain't seed nothin'" —

"What are you doin' here?" demanded Squire Fambrough, somewhat angrily. "Don't you know you are liable to get killed any minute? Ain't you makin' your way to the Yankee army?"

"No, suh." The negro spoke with unction. "I'm des a-huntin' my young marster, suh. He name Dave Henry Clopton. Dat what we call him, — Marse Dave Henry. None er you-all ain't seed 'im, is you?"

"Jule," said the squire, rubbing his nose thoughtfully, "ain't that the name of the chap that used to hang around here before the Yankees got too close?"

"Do you mean Lieutenant Clopton, father?" asked Julia, showing some confusion.

"Yessum." Tuck grinned and rubbed his hands together. "Marse Dave Henry is sholy a lieutender in de company, an' mistiss she say he'd a done been a giner'l ef dey wa'n't so much enviousness in de army."

"I saw him this morning, — I mean" — Julia blushed and hesitated. "I mean, I heard him talking out here in the grove."

"Who was he talking to, Jule?" The squire put the question calmly and deliberately.

There was a little pause. Julia, still blushing, adjusted an imaginary hairpin. The negro looked sheepishly from one to the other. The squire repeated his question.

"Who was he talking to, Jule?"

"Nobody but me," said the young lady, growing redder. Her embarrassment was not lessened by an involuntary "eh — eh," from the negro. Squire Fambrough raised his eyes heavenwards and allowed both his heavy hands to drop helplessly by his side.

"What was he talkin' about?" The old man spoke with apparent humility.

"N-o-t-h-i-n-g," said Julia demurely, looking at her pink finger-nails. "He just asked me if I thought it would rain, and I told him I didn't know; and then he said the spring was coming on very rapidly, and I said, 'Yes, I thought it was.' And then he had found a bunch of violets and asked me if I would accept them, and I said, 'Thank you.'"

"Land of the livin' Moses!" exclaimed Squire Fambrough, lifting his hands above his head and allowing them to fall heavily again. "And they call this war!"

"Yessum!" The negro's tone was triumphant. "Dat sholy wuz Marse Dave Henry. War er no war, dat wuz him. Dat des de way he goes 'mongst de ladies. He gi' 'um candy yit, let 'lone flowers. Shoo! You can't tell me nothin' 't all 'bout Marse Dave Henry."

"What are you wanderin' 'round here in the woods for?" asked the squire. His tone was somewhat severe. "Did anybody tell you he was here?"

"No, suh!" replied Tuck. "Dey tol' me back dar at de camps dat I 'd fin' 'im out on de picket line, an' when I got dar dey tol' me he wuz out dis a-way, whar dey wuz some sharpshootin' gwine on, but I ain't foun' 'im yit."

"Ain't you been with him all the time?" The squire was disposed to treat the negro as a witness for the defense.

"Lor, no, suh! I des now come right straight fum Georgy. Mistiss, — she Marse Dave Henry's ma, — she hear talk dat de solyers ain't got no cloze fer ter w'ar an' no vittles fer ter eat, skacely, an' she tuck 'n made me come an' fetch 'im a box full er duds an' er box full er vittles. She put cake in dar, yit, 'kaze I smelt it whiles I wuz handlin' de box. De boxes, dey er dar at de camp, an' here me, but wharbouts is Marse Dave Henry? Not ter be a-hidin' fum somebody, he de hardest white man ter fin' what I ever laid eyes on. I speck I better be knockin' 'long. Good-by, marster; good-by, young mistiss. Ef I don' fin' Marse Dave Henry nowheres, I'll know whar ter come an' watch fer 'im."

The squire watched the negro disappear in the woods, and then turned to his daughter. To his surprise, her eyes were full of tears; but before he could make any comment, or ask any question, he heard the noise of tramping feet in the woods, and presently saw two Union soldiers approaching. Almost immediately Julia called his attention to three soldiers coming from the Confederate side.

"I believe in my soul we're surrounded by both armies," remarked the squire dryly. "But don't git skeer'd, honey. I'm goin' to see what they're trespassin' on my premises for."

IV

COMMERCE AND SENTIMENT

"Upon me sowl," said O'Halloran, as he and Captain Fambrough went forward, the big Irishman leading the way, "I'm afeard I'm tollin' you into a trap."

"How?" asked the captain.

"Why, there's three of the Johnnies comin', sor, an' the ould man an' the gurrul make five."

"Halt!" said the captain, using the word by force of habit. The two paused, and the captain took in the situation at a glance. Then he turned to the big Irishman with a queer look on his face.

"What is it, sor?"

"I'm in for it now. That is my father yonder, and the young lady is my sister."

"The Divvle an' Tom Walker!" exclaimed O'Halloran. "'T is quite a family rayunion, sor."

"I don't know whether to make myself known or not. What could have possessed them to stay here? I'll see whether they know me." As they went forward, the captain plucked O'Halloran by the sleeve. "I'll be shot if the Johnny with his arm in the sling is n't my brother."

"I was expectin' it, sor," said the big Irishman, giving matters a humorous turn. "Soon the cousins will be poppin' out from under the bushes."

By this time the two were near enough to the approaching Confederates to carry on a conversation by lifting their voices a little.

"Hello, Johnny," said O'Halloran.

"Hello, Yank," replied Kilpatrick.

"What's the countersign, Johnny?"

"Tobacco. What is it on your side, Yank?"

"Tay an' coffee, Johnny."

"You are mighty right," Kilpatrick exclaimed. "Stack your arms agin a tree."

"The same to you," said O'Halloran.

The Irishman, using his foot as a broom, cleared the dead leaves and twigs from a little space of ground, where he deposited his bundle, and Kilpatrick did the same. John Fambrough, the wounded Confederate, went forward to greet his father and sister, and Lieutenant Clopton went with him. The squire was not in a good humor.

"I tell you what, John," he said to his son, "I don't like to be harborin' nary side. It's agin' my principles. I don't like this colloguin' an' palaverin' betwixt folks that ought to be by good rights a-knockin' one another on the head. If they want to collogue an' palaver, why don't they go som'ers else?"

The squire's son tried to explain, but the old gentleman hooted at the explanation. "Come on, Jule, let's go and see what they're up to."

As they approached, the Irishman glanced at Captain Fambrough, and saw that he had turned away, cap in hand, to hide his emotion.

"You're just in time," the Irishman said to Squire Fambrough in a bantering tone, "to watch the continding armies. This mite of a Johnny will swindle the Government, if I don't kape me eye on him."

"Is this what you call war?" the Squire inquired sarcastically. "Who axed you to come trespassin' on my land?"

"Oh, we'll put the leaves back where we found them," said Kilpatrick, "if we have to git a furlough."

"Right you are!" said the Irishman.

"It is just a little trading frolic among the boys!" Captain Fambrough turned to the old man with a courteous bow. "They will do no harm. I'll answer for that."

"Well, I'll tell you how I feel about it!" Squire Fambrough exclaimed with some warmth. "I'm in here betwixt the hostiles. They ain't nobody here but me an' my daughter. We don't pester nobody, an' we don't want nobody to pester us. One of my sons is in the Union army, I hear tell, an' the other is in the Confederate army when he ain't in the hospital. These boys, you see, found their old daddy a-straddle of the fence, an' one clomb down one leg on the Union side, an' t' other one clomb down t' other leg on the Confederate side."

"That is what I call an interesting situation," said the captain, drawing a long breath. "Perhaps I have seen your Union son."

"Maybe so, maybe so," assented the squire.

"Perhaps you have seen him yourself since the war began?"

Before the squire could make any reply, Julia rushed at the captain and threw her arms around his neck, crying, "O brother George, I know you!"

The squire seemed to be dazed by this discovery. He went towards the captain slowly.
The tears streamed down his face and the
hand he held out trembled.

" George," he exclaimed, " God A'mighty
knows I 'm glad to see you ! "

O'Halloran and Kilpatrick had paused in
the midst of their traffic to watch this scene,
but when they saw the gray-haired old man
crying and hugging his son, and the young
girl clinging to the two, they were confused.
O'Halloran turned and kicked his bundles.

" Take all the tay and coffee, you bloody
booger ! Just give me a pipeful of the
weed."

Kilpatrick shook his fist at the big Irishman.

" Take the darned tobacco, you redmouthed
Mickey ! What do I want with your tea
and coffee ? " Then both started to go a
little way into the woods, Lieutenant Clopton
following. The captain called them back,
but they would n't accept the invitation.

" We are just turnin' our backs, sor, while
you hold a family orgie," said O'Halloran.
" Me an' this measly Johnny will just go an'
complate the transaction of swappin'."

At this moment Tuck reappeared on the scene. Seeing his young master, he stopped still and looked at him, and then broke out into loud complaints.

"Marse Dave Henry, whar de nam er goodness you been? You better come read dish yer letter what yo' ma writ you. I'm gwine tell mistiss she come mighty nigh losin' a likely nigger, an' she 'll rake you over de coals, mon."

"Why, howdy, Tuck," exclaimed Lieutenant Clopton. "Ain't you glad to see me?"

"Yasser, I speck I is." The negro spoke in a querulous and somewhat doubtful tone, as he produced a letter from the lining of his hat. "But I'd 'a' been a heap gladder ef I had n't mighty nigh traipsed all de gladness out 'n me."

Young Clopton took the letter and read it with a smile on his lips and a dimness in his eyes. The negro, left to himself, had his attention attracted by the coffee and tobacco lying exposed on the ground. He looked at the display, scratching his head.

"Boss, is dat sho nuff coffee?"

"It is that same," said O'Halloran.

"De ginnywine ole-time coffee?" insisted the negro.

" 'T is nothin' else, simlin-head."

" Marse Dave Henry," the negro yelled, " run here an' look at dish yer ginnywine coffee! Dey 's nuff coffee dar fer ter make mistiss happy de balance er her days. Some done spill out ! " he exclaimed. " Boss, kin I have dem what 's on de groun' ? "

" Take 'em," said O'Halloran, " an' much good may they do you."

" One, two, th'ee, fo', fi', sick, sev'm." The negro counted the grains as he picked them up. " O Marse Dave Henry, run here an' look ! I got sev'm grains er ginnywine coffee. I 'm gwine take um ter mistiss."

The Irishman regarded the negro with curiosity. Then taking the dead branch of a tree he drew a line several yards in length between himself and Kilpatrick.

" D 'ye see that line there ? " he said to the negro.

" Dat ar mark? Oh, yasser, I sees de mark."

" Very well. On that side of the line you are in slavery — on this side the line you are free."

" Who ? Me ? "

" Who else but you ? "

" I been hear talk er freedom, but I ain't

seed 'er yit, an' I dunner how she feel." The
negro scratched his head and grinned expec-
tantly.

" 'T is as I tell you," said the Irishman.

" I b'lieve I 'll step 'cross an' see how she
feel." The negro stepped over the line, and
walked up and down as if to test the matter
physically. " 'T ain't needer no hotter ner
no colder on dis side dan what 't is on dat,"
he remarked. Then he cried out to his young
master : " Look at me, Marse Dave Henry;
I 'm free now."

" All right." The young man waved his
hand without taking his eyes from the letter
he was reading.

" He take it mos' too easy fer ter suit me,"
said the negro. Then he called out to his
young master again : " O Marse Dave Henry!
Don't you tell mistiss dat I been free, kaze
she 'll take a bresh-broom an' run me off'n de
place when I go back home."

V

THE CURTAIN FALLS

Squire Fambrough insisted that his son
should go to the house and look it over for

the sake of old times, and young Clopton went along to keep Miss Julia company. O'Halloran, Kilpatrick, and the negro stayed where they were — the white men smoking their pipes, and the negro chewing the first " mannyfac " tobacco he had seen in many a day.

The others were not gone long. As they came back, a courier was seen riding through the woods at break-neck speed, going from the Union lines to those of the Confederates, and carrying a white flag. Kilpatrick hailed him, and he drew rein long enough to cry out, as he waved his flag : —

" Lee has surrendered ! "

" I was looking out for it," said Kilpatrick, " but dang me if I had n't ruther somebody had a-shot me right spang in the gizzard."

Lieutenant Clopton took out his pocket-knife and began to whittle a stick. John Fambrough turned away, and his sister leaned her hands on his shoulder and began to weep. Squire Fambrough rubbed his chin thoughtfully and sighed.

" It had to be, father," the captain said. " It 's a piece of news that brings peace to the land."

" Oh, yes, but it leaves us flat. No money, and nothing to make a crop with."

" I have government bonds that will be worth a hundred thousand dollars. The interest will keep us comfortably."

" For my part," said Clopton, " I have nothing but this free nigger."

" You b'lieve de half er dat," spoke up the free nigger. " Mistiss been savin' her cotton craps, an' ef she got one bale she got two hundred."

The captain figured a moment. " They will bring more than a hundred thousand dollars."

" I have me two arrums," said O'Halloran.

" I 've got a mighty fine pack of fox-hounds," remarked Kilpatrick with real pride.

There was a pause in the conversation. In the distance could be heard the shouting of the Union soldiers and the band with its " Yankee Doodle, how d'y-do ? " Suddenly Clopton turned to Captain Fambrough : —

" I want to ask you how many troops have you got over there — fighting men ? "

The captain laughed. Then he put his hand to his mouth and said in a stage whisper : —

"Five companies."

"Well, dang my hide!" exclaimed Kilpatrick.

"What is your fighting force?" Captain
Fambrough asked.

"Four companies," said Clopton.

"Think o' that, sir!" cried the Irishman;
"an' me out there defendin' meself ag'in a
whole army."

"More than that," said Clopton, "our
colonel is a Connecticut man."

"Shake!" the captain exclaimed. "My
colonel is a Virginian."

"Lord 'a' mercy! Lord 'a' mercy!" It
was Squire Fambrough who spoke. "I'm
a-goin' off some'rs an' ontangle the tangle
we've got into."

Soon the small company separated. The
squire went a short distance towards the
Union army with his new-found son. Kilpatrick and the negro went trudging back to
the Confederate camp, while Clopton lingered
awhile, saying something of great importance
to the fair Julia and himself.

What they said was commonplace, even tri-
fling; what they meant carried their minds
and their hearts high above all ordinary mat-

ters; lifted them, indeed, into the region of poetry and romance — lifted and held them there for one brief, blissful half hour. Their questions and their answers, heavy with doubt, or light with shy hope, were such as swarm in Love's convoy whether he precedes or follows comedy or tragedy. They flourish in the thunders of war as serenely as in the sunshine of peace.

A BOLD DESERTER

I

THE war wasn't much of a bother to Hillsborough, for the town was remote from the field of operations. Occasionally news would come that made the women cry out and the old men weep, but the intervals were long between these episodes, and to all appearances affairs moved forward as serenely as ever.

This was during the first year or two of the struggle. Then came the Impressment Law, which created bad feelings and caused a good deal of grumbling. Following this came the Conscript Act, which made matters much worse, especially when strange men were sent to enforce it. This disturbed the serenity of Hillsborough very seriously.

Nevertheless, Hillsborough could have put up with the Conscript Act but for one event that stirred the little community from centre to circumference. The conscript officers had not been in the town a week before they pounced upon little Billy Cochran, the sole support of his widowed mother, who was known throughout that region as Aunt Sally. Little Billy himself was a puzzle to the more thoughtful people. He was so simple and innocent-minded, so ready to do for others what he would n't do for himself, that some said he was a half-wit, while others contended that he would have sense enough if his heart was n't so big.

But everybody liked little Billy — for his mother's sake, if not for his own, for Aunt Sally was, indeed, a good Samaritan. She seemed to know by instinct where trouble and sickness and suffering were to be found, and there, too, she was to be found. High or low, rich or poor, she passed none by. And, though she was as simple and as in-nocent-minded as little Billy, these qualities seemed to fit her better than they did her awkward and bashful boy.

Aunt Sally and little Billy were both as industrious as the day was long, yet they made but a precarious living on their little patch of ground, — a bale or two of cotton, that did n't bring a good price, and a little bit of garden truck, which, with a few chickens and eggs, they brought to town occasionally in a rickety one-horse wagon. Aunt Sally would take no pay for nursing the sick, no matter how much of her time was taken up, but she supplemented the meagre income they got from the one-horse farm by making quilts, and counterpanes, and bedspreads, and by taking in weaving, being very expert at the loom.

As may be supposed, Aunt Sally and little Billy did n't wear fine clothes nor put on any airs. Living in middle Georgia (the most democratic region, socially, in the world), they had no need for either the one or the other. They made a bare living, and were tolerably satisfied with that.

One day, shortly after the conscript officer had established his headquarters in Hillsborough, Aunt Sally and little Billy drove into town with a few dozen eggs and three or four chickens to sell. The conscript officer, sitting on the veranda of the tavern, noticed that little Billy was a well-grown lad, and kept his eye on him, as the rickety, one-horse wagon came through the public square.

There were two or three loungers sitting

on the veranda, including Major Goolsby. One of them tapped the major on the shoulder and pointed to little Billy with his forefinger and to the conscript officer with his thumb. The major nodded gravely once or twice, and presently hitched his chair closer to the conscript officer.

" You ain't a-bagging much game in these parts, I reckon," said the major, addressing the officer, with half-closed eyes.

" Business is not very good," replied the other, with a chuckle, " but we manage to pick up a few stragglers now and then. Yonder's a chap now " — pointing to little Billy — " that looks like he would be an ornament to the rear-guard in an engagement." The officer was a big, rough-looking man, and seemed to find his present duties very agreeable.

" Do you mean little Billy Cochran ? " inquired the major.

" I don't know his name," said the officer. " I mean that chap riding in the chariot with the fat woman."

" That boy," remarked the major with an emphasis that caused the conscript officer to regard him with surprise, " is the sole support of his mother.　He's all she's got to make her crop."

"May be so," the officer said, "but the law makes no provision for cases of that kind."

"You said, 'May be so,'" suggested the major.　"Do you mean to doubt my word?" His voice was soft as the notes of a flute.

"Why, certainly not!" exclaimed the officer, flushing a little.

The major made no further remark, but sat bolt upright in his chair.　The rickety wagon drove to the tavern door, and little Billy got out, a basket of eggs in one hand and the chickens in the other.　He went into the tavern, and while he was gone, Aunt Sally passed the time of day with the major and the rest of her acquaintances on the veranda.

Evidently little Billy had no difficulty in disposing of his eggs and chickens, for he soon came out smiling.　The officer arose as little Billy appeared in the door, and so did Major Goolsby.　The loungers nudged one another in a gleeful way.　As little Billy came out, the conscript officer drew a formidable-looking memorandum-book from his pocket and tapped the young man on the shoulder. Little Billy looked around in surprise, the blood mounted to his face, and he laughed sheepishly.

" What is your name? " the officer asked, poising his pencil.

" William Henry Harrison Cochran," replied little Billy.

" How old are you? "

" Twenty, April gone."

" Report at my office, under the Temperance Hall, next Wednesday morning, the day after to-morrow. The army needs your services."

" Do you want me to go to the war? " asked little Billy, a quaver in his voice.

" Yes," the officer replied. " You fall under the conscript law."

" What 'll mammy do? "

" Really, I don't know. The Confederacy needs you worse than your mammy does just now."

Little Billy hung his head and walked to the rickety wagon.

" Mind," said the officer, " Wednesday morning at ten o'clock. I don't want to send after you."

"Why, what in the round world is the matter, honey?" Aunt Sally inquired, seeing the downcast look of her son.

Little Billy simply shook his head. He could not have uttered a word then had his life depended on it.

"Git up, Beck!" exclaimed Aunt Sally, slapping her old mule with the rope reins.

Major Goolsby watched the mother and son for a few moments as they drove back across the public square. His lip quivered as he remembered how, years before, Aunt Sally had nursed his dead wife. He turned to the conscript officer and straightened himself up.

"Mister" — his voice was soft, sweet, and insinuating — "Mister, how many of your kind are loafing around in the South, picking up the mainstay of widows?"

"As many as are necessary, sir," replied the officer.

"'As many as are necessary, sir,'" said the major, turning to his acquaintances and mimicking the tones of the officer. "Boys, that's what they call statistics — the exact figures. Well, sir, if there's one for every town in the Confederacy, there's more than a regiment of 'em. Don't you reckon I 'm about right in my figures?"

"I could n't say," replied the officer, in an indifferent way. He saw that Major Goolsby was angry, but he did n't know what the major's anger meant. "I could n't say. If all of them have enlisted as many men as I have, the army will be a great deal larger in the course of the next three months."

"Don't you think you could do a great deal more damage to the Yankees, if you had the will, than that boy you 've just served notice on?" asked the major, with a little more asperity than he had yet shown. "Why don't you get a basket and catch tomtits, and send 'em on to the front? The woods are full of 'em."

"Now, if you 'll tell me how all this concerns you," said the officer, bristling up, "I 'll be much obliged to you."

The major took one step forward and, with a movement quick as lightning, slapped the officer in the face with his open hand. "That 's for little Billy!" he exclaimed.

The officer sprang back and placed his hand under his coat as if to draw a pistol. The major whipped out a big morocco pocket-book, fumbled about in it a moment, and then threw five twenty-dollar gold pieces at the feet of the officer.

" I 'll send that to your family," he said, " if you 'll pull your pistol out where I can see it."

But the officer by this time had taken a sober second thought, and he turned away from the major and went to his office across the public square. The older citizens of Hillsborough applauded his coolness and discretion, and one of them told him confidentially that if he had drawn his pistol when Major Goolsby begged him to he would have been a dead man before he could have pulled the hammer back.

II

Of course, everybody sympathized with Aunt Sally, and their sympathy added to her grief, for she was a tender-hearted woman. Moreover, when she found herself the object of so much condolence, she naturally concluded that her trouble was a great deal worse than she had any idea of, and she sat in her humble home and wept, and, like Rachel, refused to be comforted.

But the situation was not nearly so bad as Aunt Sally thought it was, or as Major Goolsby expected it would be. The major himself· sent her a little negro girl to keep her company, and the neighbors for miles around contended with one another in their efforts to make her comfortable. Not a day passed, except Sundays, that Miss Mary, the major's daughter, did n't drive out to Aunt Sally's little place and spend an hour or two with her. Miss Mary was eighteen, as pretty as a peach, and as full of fun as an egg is of meat. She was a brunette with blue eyes, and although they were laughing eyes, they could look very sad and tender when occasion called for it.

She made herself very useful to Aunt Sally. She read to her the letters that little Billy sent back from the camp of instruction at Loudersville, and answered them at Aunt Sally's dictation. In this way she came to feel that she knew little Billy better than any one else except his mother. She was surprised to find that, although little Billy had had few advantages in the way of schooling, he could write a beautiful letter. She took the fact home to her innocent bosom and

wondered how it could be that this country
lad had the knack of putting himself into his
letters along with so many other things that
were interesting. She was touched, too, by
the love for his mother that shone through
every line he wrote. Over and over again,
he called her his dear mammy and tried to
comfort her; and sometimes he spoke of Miss
Mary, and he was so deft in expressing his
gratitude to her that the young lady blushed
and trembled lest some one else was writing
little Billy's letters, as she was writing his
mother's.

And then, somehow, she never knew how,
his face came back to her memory and planted
itself in her mind and remained there. Little
Billy was no longer the green, awkward, and
ungainly country boy, peddling the scanty
fruits of his poverty about the village, but a
hero, who had no thought for anybody or
anything except his dear old mammy.

As the cold weather came on, little Billy
wrote that he would feel a great deal more
comfortable in the mind if he knew where
he could get a thick suit of clothes and a
heavy pair of shoes. But he begged his dear
mammy not to worry about that, for he had

no doubt the clothes and shoes would be forthcoming when he needed them most. Miss Mary skipped this part of the letter when she was reading it aloud to Aunt Sally, but it was n't long before the clothes were made, with the aid and under the direction of little Billy's mother; and the shoes were bought, costing Major Goolsby a pretty round sum in Confederate currency. Moreover, Miss Mary baked a fruit cake with her own hands, and this was to be put in the box with the clothes and shoes.

The next thing was to find out if anybody from Hillsborough or from the country side was going to the camp of instruction, where little Billy's headquarters were. But right in the midst of expectation and preparation Aunt Sally fell ill. She had never reconciled herself to her separation from little Billy. Until the conscript law tore him away from her side she had never been parted from him a day since the Lord sent him to her arms.

The strain was too much for the motherly heart to bear. Aunt Sally gradually pined away, though she tried hard to be cheerful, and, at last, just before little Billy's Christmas box was to be sent, she took to her bed and lay there as helpless as a child. The doctor came and prescribed, but little Billy was the only medicine that would do Aunt Sally any good. So she kept to her bed, growing weaker and weaker, in spite of everything that the doctor and the neighbors could do.

And at last, when an opportunity came to forward the box, Miss Mary wrote a note and pinned it where it could be seen the first thing. She began it with " Dear Little Billy," but this seemed too familiar, and she began it with " Mr. Cochran." She told him that his dear mammy was very ill, and if he wanted to see her he would do well to come home at once. It was a very pretty letter, brief, simple, and sympathetic.

This duty done, Miss Mary turned her attention to nursing Aunt Sally, and, except at night, was never absent from her bedside more than an hour at a time.

III

When little Billy arrived at the camp of instruction, the first person on whom his eye fell was Private Chadwick. Simultaneously the eye of Private Chadwick fell on little Billy. Mr. Chadwick was something of a humorist in his way, and a rough one, as the raw conscripts found out to their cost. A heartless jest rose to his lips, but something in little Billy's face — an expression of loneliness, perhaps — stayed it. In another moment Private Chadwick's hand fell on little Billy's shoulder, and it was a friendly hand.

" Where from ? " he asked.

" Close about Hillsborough," little Billy answered.

" I reckon you know the Tripps and the Littles ? "

" Mighty well," said little Billy.

" What name ? "

" Cochran."

" How old ? "

" Twenty, last April gone."

" You don't look like you 're fitten to do much soldierin'," suggested Private Chadwick.

" Oh, I 'm tough," said little Billy, laughing, though he had a big lump in his throat.

" Come with me, buddy," remarked the old soldier, smiling. " If I 'm ever to keep a tavern, I reckon I might as well begin with you as a boarder."

And so, for the time at least, little Billy

was installed in Private Chadwick's tent, much to the surprise of those who knew the peculiarities of the man. The camp was in charge of Captain Mosely, who was recovering from a wound, and he had selected his old comrade, Private Chadwick, as his drill-master, — a curious selection it seemed to be to those who did n't know the man, but the truth was that Private Chadwick knew as much about tactics as any West Pointer, and had the knack, too, of imparting what he knew, even if he had to use his belt-strap to emphasize his remarks.

The upshot of the matter was that little Billy went to Private Chadwick's tent and remained there. He and the private became inseparable companions when neither was on duty, and in these hours of leisure little Billy learned as much about tactics as he did from the actual practice of drilling. He seemed to take to the business naturally, and far outstripped even the men who had been drilling twice a day for three months. Naturally, therefore, Private Chadwick was very proud of his pupil, and frequently called Captain Mosely's attention to little Billy's proficiency.

Over and often during the pleasant days of

November, Private Chadwick could be seen
sitting in front of their tent engaged in earnest conversation, little Billy leaning his face
on his hands, and Private Chadwick making
fantastic figures in the sand with the point of
his bayonet. On such occasions little Billy
would be talking about his dear old mammy,
and about Miss Mary, and, although Private
Chadwick was something of a joker, in his
way, he never could see anything to laugh at
in little Billy's devotion to his mother, or in
his innocent regard for Miss Mary Goolsby.
Somehow it carried the private back to his
own boyhood days, and he listened to the lad
with a sympathy that was as quick and as
delicate as a woman's.

About the middle of December, little
Billy's box came. He carried it to Private
Chadwick's tent in great glee, and opened it
at once.

He had said to himself as he went along
that he was sure there was something nice in
the box, and he hoped to find Mr. Chadwick
either in the tent or close by ; but the drill-
master was engaged just then in making a
refractory conscript mark time in the guard
tent by jabbing a bayonet at his toes.

So, for the moment, little Billy had his precious box all to himself. He opened it and found the letter that Miss Mary had pinned to the clothes. It ran thus : —

MR. COCHRAN, — Aunt Sally is very ill now and has been ill for some time. We are afraid that you are the only person in the world that can cure her. She is calling your name and talking about you all the time. It would do her so much good to see you that I hope you can make it convenient to come home very soon, if only for a day. We should all be so glad to see you.

Your true friend,
MARY GOOLSBY.

Holding this letter in his hand, little Billy sank down on a camp-stool and sat there. He forgot all about the box. He sat as still as a statue, and he was sitting thus when Private Chadwick came into the tent a half-hour later. Little Billy neither turned his head nor moved when the drill-master came in, snorting with rage and consigning all awkward recruits to places too warm to be mentioned in polite conversation. But he pulled

himself up when he saw little Billy sitting on
the camp-stool staring at vacancy.

"Hello!" he cried. "What kind of a
picnic is this? If my nose ain't gone and
forgot her manners, I smell cake." He
paused and looked at little Billy. Seeing
that the lad was troubled about something,
he lowered his voice. "What's the matter,
old man? If it's trouble, it'll do you more
good to talk about it than to think about it."

For answer, little Billy held out the letter.
Private Chadwick took it and began to read
it. Then he held it close to his eyes.

"Now, this is right down funny," he said,
"and it's just like a gal. She's gone and
scratched out the best part." Little Billy
neither moved nor spoke, but turned inquiring eyes on his patron and friend. "She
began it 'Dear Little Billy,'" Private Chadwick continued, "and then she went and
scratched it out."

It was a very fortunate stroke indeed. The
color slowly came back into little Billy's face
and stayed there. After Private Chadwick
had read the letter, little Billy took it and
gave it a careful inspection. His face was so
full of color at what he saw that a stranger
would have said he was blushing.

" What 's to be done about it ? " Private Chadwick asked.

" I must go home and see mammy," replied little Billy.

Private Chadwick shook his head, and continued to shake it, as if by that means he would blot out the idea.

" Can't I get a furlough ? " little Billy asked, with tears in his voice.

If any other conscript had asked him this question, Private Chadwick would have used violent language, but the innocence and ignorance of little Billy were dear to him.

" Now, who ever heard of the like of that ? " he said in a kindly tone. " There ain't but one way for a conscript to leave this camp, and that is to desert."

" I 'll do it ! " exclaimed little Billy.

" You know what that means, I reckon," said Private Chadwick dryly.

" It means that I 'll see my dear mammy once more," replied little Billy. " And after that, I don't care what happens."

Private Chadwick looked at little Billy long and hard, smiling under his mustache, and then went out. He walked to the centre of the encampment, where the flag-pole stood.

This inoffensive affair he struck hard with his fist, exclaiming under his breath, " Lord, Lord! What makes some people have such big gizzards ? "

The next day little Billy was missing.

IV

Captain Mosely had the camp searched, but without result, and in a little while everybody knew that the lad was a deserter. During the morning Private Chadwick had a long talk with Captain Mosely, and the result of it was that no immediate arrangements were made to send a guard after little Billy.

Meanwhile, Aunt Sally was growing weaker and weaker. Sometimes, in her troubled dreams, she imagined that little Billy had come, and at such moments she would cry out a glad welcome, and laugh as heartily as ever. But, for the most part, she knew that he was still absent, and that all her dreams were futile and fleeting.

Nevertheless, one bright morning in the latter part of December, little Billy walked into his mother's humble home, weary and footsore. Aunt Sally heard his footstep on the door-sill, and, weak as she was, sat up in

bed and held out her arms to him. Her
dreams had come true, but they had come
true too late. When little Billy removed the
support of his arms, in order to look at his
dear mammy's face, she was dead. The joy
of meeting her son again was too much for
the faithful and tender heart.

All that could be done by kind hearts and
willing hands was done by Miss Mary and the
neighbors. Little Billy shed no tears. The
shock had benumbed all his faculties. He
went about in a dazed condition. But when,
the day after the funeral, he went to tell Miss
Mary good-by, the ineffable pity that shone
in her face touched the source of his grief,
and he fell to weeping as he had never wept
before. He would have kissed her hand, but
she drew it away, and, as he straightened
himself, tiptoed and kissed him on the forehead. With that she, too, fell to weeping,
and thus they parted. But for many a long
day little Billy felt the pressure of soft and
rosy lips on his forehead.

He sold the old mule that had served his
dear mammy so faithfully, and this gave him
sufficient money to pay his way back to camp
on the railroad, with some dollars to spare.

As good fortune would have it, the first man he saw when the train stopped at the station nearest the camp was Private Chadwick. Little Billy spoke to his friend with as much cheerfulness as he could command.

"I'm mighty glad to see you, old man," said Chadwick. "I knowed in reason that you was certain to come back, — and, sure enough, here you are. You've had trouble, too. Well, trouble has got a long arm and a hard hand, and I ain't never saw the livin' human bein' that could git away from it when it begins to feel around for 'em."

"Yes," replied little Billy simply; "I'll never have any more trouble like that I've had."

"It's mighty hard at first, always," remarked Private Chadwick, with a sigh, "but it's mighty seasonin'. The man that ain't the better for it in the long run ain't much of a man. That's the way I put it down."

"Am I a deserter, sure enough?" asked little Billy, suddenly remembering his position.

"Well, it's a mixed case," answered the private. "You've gone and broke the rules and articles of war, — I reckon that's what

they call 'em. You took Dutch leave. The
Cap said if you did n't come back in ten days
he 'd send a file of men after you, and then
your cake would 'a' been all dough. But
now you 've come back of your own free will,
and the case is mixed. You are bound to be
arrested. All that 's been fixed, and that 's
the reason I 've been comin' to the train every
day sence you 've been gone. I wanted to
arrest you myself."

" Then I 'm a prisoner," suggested little
Billy.

" That 's about the size and shape of it,"
replied Private Chadwick.

His tone was so emphatic that little Billy
looked at him. But there was a kindly light
in the private's eyes and a pleasant smile
lurking under his mustache : so that the
young fellow thought he might safely go
back to his grief again.

When they arrived at camp, Private Chadwick, with a great show of fierce formality,
led little Billy to the guard tent, and there
placed him in charge of a newly-made cor-
poral, who knew so little of his duties that he
went inside the tent, placed his gun on the
ground, and had a long familiar chat with
the prisoner.

After the camp had gone to bed, Private Chadwick relieved the guard, and carried little Billy to his own tent, where Captain Mosely was waiting.

This rough old soldier gave little Billy a lecture that was the more severe because it was delivered in a kindly tone. At the end he informed little Billy that the next day a squad of picked men from the conscript camp was to go to the front in charge of Private Chadwick, the enemy having shown a purpose to make a winter campaign.

"Would you like to go?" the captain asked.

Little Billy seized the captain's arm. "Don't fool me," he cried. "If I am fit to go, let me go. That's what I am longing for."

The captain felt about in the dark for little Billy's hand, and grasped it. "You shall go," he said, and walked from the dark tent into the starlight outside.

The nights are long to those who sleep with sorrow, but, after all, the days come quickly, as little Billy soon found out. The next morning he found himself whirling away to Virginia, where some cruel business was on foot. The days went fast enough then, and the railway train, with its load of soldiers, puffed and snorted as if it wanted to go faster, too; but it went fast enough, — just fast enough to be switched off to the right of Richmond and plunge its load of conscripts and raw recruits unprepared into a furious battle that had just reached the high tide of destruction. Private Chadwick was swept along with the rest, and he tried hard to keep his eye on little Billy, but found it impossible, since they were soon mixed with men who were wounded and with men who were running away. Some of the latter turned again when they saw the reinforcements rushing forward pellmell.

Little Billy was far in front of the others. He heard the crackle of musketry and the thunder of the cannon, and ran toward the smoke and confusion. A shell dropped in front of him and spun around, spitting fire, but he ran on, and never even heard the explosion that shattered the trees around, and played havoc with the reinforcements that were following. He jumped over men that were lying on the ground, whether dead or wounded, he never knew. Some one, apparently in command, yelled at him with a savage curse, but he paid no attention to it. Directly in front of him he saw a battery of three guns. Two were in action, but one had no one to manage it. On each side of this battery, and a little to the rear, the line of battle stretched away.

Seeing little Billy running forward, followed by the recruits from the train, the line of battle began to cheer, and at the same time to advance. He had practiced with an old six-pounder at the conscript camp, and he now ran, as if by instinct, to the gun that had been silenced. The Confederates charged, but had to fall back again, and then they began to retire, slowly at first, and then with some haste. Little Billy paid no attention to this movement at all. He continued to serve his gun and fire it as rapidly as he could. Shot and shell from the Federal batteries plowed up the ground around him, but never touched him. Presently a tall man with a long brown beard rode out of the smoke and ordered little Billy to retreat, pointing, as he did so, to the bristling line of Federals charging up the hill.

"Take hold of my stirrup," said the tall

man. He spurred his horse into a rapid trot, and little Billy trotted by his side, mightily helped by holding on to the stirrup. In this way they were soon out of it, and in a little while had caught up with the main body, which had planted itself a couple of miles farther back, while the brigade in which little Billy had fought was holding the enemy at bay.

Little Billy's face was black with powder, but his eyes shone like stars. He knew now that never again would danger or the fear of death cause him to flinch.

"What regiment do you belong to?" asked the tall man as they went along.

"None," replied little Billy simply. Then he told how he was just from a conscript camp in Georgia. When they arrived at the Confederate position the tall man called to an officer: —

"This is my rear guard," said he. "See that he is cared for." Then to little Billy, "When this affair blows over, brush up and call on General Jeb Stuart. He needs a courier, and you are the man."

As there was no sign of a fight the next day, little Billy went to General Stuart's

LITTLE BILLY TROTTED BY HIS SIDE

headquarters and was ushered in. That famous fighter, who happened to be the officer who had noticed him the day before, took him by the arm and introduced him to his staff, and told how he had found him serving a gun after the entire brigade had begun to retreat.

This was the beginning. Little Billy became a courier, then an aid, and when the war closed he was in command of a regiment. His recklessness as a fighter had given a sort of romantic color to his name, so that the newspaper correspondents found nothing more popular than an anecdote about Colonel Cochran.

His fame had preceded him to Hillsborough, and he had a queer feeling when the older citizens, men who had once awed him by their pride and their fine presence, took off their hats as they greeted him. The most demonstrative among these was Major Goolsby.

" You are to come right to my house, Colonel. You belong to us, you know." This was Major Goolsby's greeting, as he clung to Colonel Cochran's hand. " It will be a great surprise to Mary. She 'll never know you in the round world.   Why, you've grown to be a six-footer."

So there was nothing for Colonel Cochran to do but to go to the Goolsby place, a fine house built on a hill beyond the old church. The major wanted to give his daughter a surprise, and so he carried Colonel Cochran into the parlor, and then told Miss Mary that one of her friends had called to see her.

The young lady went skipping into the parlor, and then paused with a frightened air, as she saw a six-foot man in faded uniform rise to meet her.

"Miss Mary," said Colonel Cochran, holding out his hand.

"Are you" — She paused, grew white and then red, and suddenly turned and ran out of the room, nearly upsetting the major, who was standing near the door.

"Why, what on earth's the matter?" he cried.   "Well, if this don't beat —   Did she know you, Colonel?"

"I'm afraid she did," replied the colonel grimly.

The major tiptoed to his daughter's room, opened the door softly, and found her on her knees by her bed, crying.   Thereupon he

tiptoed back again, and said to Colonel Cochran, " It 's all right. She 's crying."

The colonel smiled dryly. " If I make the
women cry, what will the children do when
they see me ! "

The major laid his hand affectionately on
Cochran's arm. " Don't you fret," he said.
" Just wait."

And so wonderful are the ways of women,
that when Miss Mary came out again, she
greeted the colonel cordially, and was as gay
as a lark. And nothing would do but he
must fight his battles over again, which he
did with great spirit when he saw her fine
eyes kindling with enthusiasm, and her lips
trembling from sheer sympathy.

Strange to say, nobody knew what it all
meant but the old cook, who stood in the
doorway leading from the dining-room to
the kitchen and watched her young mistress.
She went back in the kitchen and said to her
husband : —

" Ef you want ter see how folks does when
dey er in love, go ter de door dar an' look at
dat ar chile er our'n."

The old man looked in, watched Miss Mary
a moment, and then looked hard at Colonel
Cochran.

"I dunno so much 'bout de gal," he said, when he went back, "but dat ar man got mo' in his eye dan what his tongue want ter tell."

And it was so; and, being so, the whole story is told.

A BABY IN THE SIEGE

I

THE war correspondents have had their say about the siege of Atlanta, and some of their remarks figure forth as history. They have presented the matter with technical diagrams, and in language flying beyond the reach of idiom into the regions of rhetoric; and the artists have followed close behind with illuminated crayons, turning the Chattahoochee Hills crosswise the horizon, and giving the muddy river a tendency to wash itself in the Pacific Ocean. These are but the tassels and embroideries that history decorates herself with in order to attract attention, and they are inevitable; for experience must serve a long and an arduous apprenticeship to life before it discovers that a fact is more imposing in its simplicity than in any other dress.

The imposing fact about the siege of Atlanta is that the besieged came to regard it as a very tame affair. It is natural, too, that this should have been so, for the lines of defense were two or three miles from the centre of the city, and the lines of the besiegers were almost as far again. The bombardment was not such an affair as a lively imagination might conjure up, being casual and desultory. The streets were thronged day after day with soldiers and civilians, and even women and children were not lacking to lend liveliness to the scene. Business seemed to thrive, and the ordinary forms of gayety went forward with the zest, if not the frequency, characteristic of the piping times of peace.

It seemed that the confusion — the feeling of present or impending danger — had lifted from the population that sense of responsibility that lends an air of sobriety and sedateness to communities that are blessed with peace. Man's crust of civilization is not by any means as thick as he pretends to believe, and war has the knack of thrusting its long sword through in unexpected places, stripping off the disguise, and exposing the whole shallow scheme.

While Atlanta was enjoying itself in a

reckless way, in spite of its portentous surroundings, the outer lines of defense were
kept busy. The big guns and the little guns
were engaged in a rattling controversy, an
incessant dispute, which died away in one
quarter only to be renewed in another. This
was all very satisfactory, but while it was
going on, what must have been the feelings
of the inner lines of defense? The outer
lines had their morning, noon, and evening
frays, and Atlanta had its frolics, but the
inner lines lay still and stupid. Here were
the reserves — the fiery and dapper little
State cadets, fretting and fuming because
they were not ordered to the front with the
veterans. Here were Joe Brown's " melish,"
to be hereafter the victims of the wild mistake at Griswoldsville; and here were the
conscripts that had been seasoning themselves at the camp of instruction at Adairs-
ville, until Johnston's army — performing its
celebrated feat of retiring and sweeping the
ground clean as it went — fell upon and
absorbed them, giving them an unexpected
taste of active service.

Naturally, the inner lines were discontented.
The shells that went Atlantaward flew harm-

lessly over their heads, and the main business
of war going forward in the outer ditches
came to them like the echo of the toy artil-
lery that the children prank with on holidays.
The monotony was all but unbearable, and
the pert and fearless little cadets began to
break it by " running the blockade." They
had an occasional mishap, but their example
was contagious among those who had a spirit
of enterprise and were fond of an adventure
that had a spice of danger in it. The new
and jaunty uniform of the cadets seemed to
carry good luck with it, for those who wore
it went unchallenged about the town at all
hours of the day and night; whereas the rag-
tag and bobtail, who had no such neat and
conspicuous toggery, were frequently put to
it to escape arrest and detention.

Captain Mosely, who commanded the conscript contingent, was not surprised, therefore, when, on the occasion of a visit to the
city, he saw his drill sergeant, Private Chadwick, sauntering along the street arrayed in
the uniform of the cadets. The suit was a
misfit. The jacket was too short in the waist,
and the trousers were too short in the legs,
but Chadwick slouched along in happy un-

consciousness of the figure he was cutting.
The truth is, no one noticed him except his
captain. The people who passed him on the
street, and whom he passed, were much too
busy to be critical. There was hardly a
spectacle so singular as to have the charm of
novelty to them.

In point of fact, there was at that moment,
not a hundred feet in front of Private Chadwick, a curious creature in the similitude of
a man, capering about in the middle of the
street, waving its arms and jabbering away
with a volubility and an incoherence that
struck painfully on the ear. And yet hundreds of people passed the spectacle by without so much as turning their heads. But a
few paused to watch the antics of the monstrosity, and among them was Private Chadwick. Captain Mosely also paused a little
distance away, and gazed curiously at the
cringing and writhing figure in the street.
A closer inspection showed that what appeared to be a monstrosity was merely antic
exaggeration, the contortions of a remark-
ably agile hunchback.

Captain Mosely watched the capers of the
hunchback with an interest that seemed to

breed familiarity. The long and limber legs, the long and muscular arms, where had he seen them before? The hunchback moved from side to side, gesticulating and jabbering like one possessed. Some of the spectators tossed money to him, and some tobacco. These gifts he seized and stowed away with the quickness of a monkey. Suddenly, as he was whirling around in idiotic frenzy, his eyes met those of Captain Mosely. As quick as a flash the hunchback's demeanor changed. His arms dropped to his side, his head, with its mass of wild and tangled hair, fell forward on his breast, and he sidled off down the street, the crowd readily making way for him.

Private Chadwick, who had been watching these manœuvres with almost breathless interest, observed the change that came over the hunchback, and looked around to find the cause of it. His eye fell on Captain Mosely, and he brought his right hand down on the palm of his left with a resounding whack.

" I know'd it ! " he exclaimed breathlessly, as he reached the captain's side.

" You knew what ? "

" Why, I know'd that imp of Satan the minnit I laid eyes on him. I know'd him as quick as he did you."

" Who is he ? "

" Why, good Lord, Cap! don't you know the chap that tuck you in on Sugar Mountain when we went after Spurlock? The man that shot Lovejoy? Don't you know Danny Lemmons? "

For answer Captain Mosely gave a long, low whistle of astonishment.

" An' now he's here playin' crazy. I'd like to know what he's up to, ding his hide ! "

" He's a spy," said Captain Mosely. " He was a Union man on Sugar Mountain. He commanded the bushwhackers. He has slipped through the lines. We must n't let him slip back again. He's a dangerous character. I want you to follow him. He must be arrested. Report to the provost marshal ; you know where his headquarters are. I'll leave instructions there for you."

Chadwick had been trying to keep an eye on the hunchback while talking with his captain, but it was by the merest chance that he saw him turn out of Alabama Street into

Whitehall.   He was going, as Chadwick expressed it, " in a half-canter," waving his
arms and jabbering, and the people were
giving him as much room on the sidewalk as
he wanted.   Private Chadwick walked as
rapidly as he could without attracting attention.   His instinct told him that if he ran or
even appeared to be in too great a hurry he
would presently be arrested ; so he went forward easily but swiftly ; his slouching gait
being well calculated to deceive the eyes of
those who might be moved to regard him
attentively.

But at the corner of Whitehall Street he
was delayed by a file of soldiers conveying a
squad of forlorn prisoners, captured in some
sally or skirmish on the outer lines.   Disentangling himself from the small rabble that
surrounded and accompanied the soldiers and
their prisoners, Chadwick pressed forward
again.   Looking far down Whitehall he saw
the hunchback whisk into Mitchell Street.
He hastened forward, but thereafter he was
compelled to rely wholly on his own judgment, for when he reached the corner of
Mitchell, the hunchback had disappeared.
At the outset, therefore, Chadwick had a

problem before him. Did the hunchback
turn back down Forsyth Street? Did he go
out Mitchell, or did he turn down Peters
Street? Chadwick asked a few of the people whom he met if they had seen the hunchback, but he received unsatisfactory replies.

He therefore turned into Peters Street,
which at that time led into the most disre-
putable part of the town. It led through
"Snake Nation," where crime had its headquarters, and then outward and onward
through green fields and forests until it lost
itself in the red trenches that war had dug.
Private Chadwick followed the street somewhat aimlessly, knowing that only an accident would enable him to find the hunchback. As he crossed the railroad, a shrill
voice railed out at him; it may have carried
a curse, it may have borne an invitation; he
did not wait to see. On the hill-top beyond,
he paused. Here Peters Street became once
more the public road, and here Private Chadwick commanded a fine view of the town and
the country beyond. As he stood hesitating,
he heard the voice of a woman calling him.
He would have shrunk from it as from the
voice of Snake Nation, but this voice pronounced his name.

He turned and saw a woman standing at the gate of a neat-looking cottage, a hundred feet back from the street. With her hair half-falling down, and her sleeves rolled up, this woman did not present a pretty picture at first sight; but, within hearing of Snake Nation, a face that wore the stamp of innocence was a thing of beauty. Private Chadwick saw it and felt it, and though the gesture with which he tipped his hat was awkward, it was quick and sincere.

"I 'mos' know you 've done fergot me," she said, as Chadwick went toward her. "But I 'd a know'd you if I 'd a seed you in Texas."

There was something pathetic in her eagerness to be recognized, yet her attitude was not one of expectation. Chadwick looked at her and shook his head slowly.

"No 'm. I disremember if I 've ever seed you. But, Lord! I 've been so tore up an' twisted aroun' sence this fuss begun, that I would n't know my own sister if she wuz to meet me in a strange place. You may be her, for all I know."

The woman smiled at the deftly put compliment.

"No, my goodness! I ain't your sister.

I wisht I wuz right now, I'd feel lots better.
No! Don't you remember that Christmas
on Sugar Mountain when Israel Spurlock an'
Polly Powers wuz married?"

"Why, yes 'm!" exclaimed Chadwick,
"I 've been a-thinkin' 'bout that all day
long."

"Well, I wuz right thar!"

"Now, you don't say! You ain't Cassy
— Cassy " —

"Cassy Tatum! Yes, siree! The very
gal!" She laughed, as though well pleased
that Chadwick should remember her first
name.

"Well — well — well!" said Chadwick.

"Yes, I married right along after that, an'
you can't guess who to?"

Chadwick scratched his head and pretended
to be trying to guess. By this time, Cassy
had led him into the house by the back entrance, and placed a chair for him in a little
room that was apparently her own. A baby
lay sleeping on the bed. Chadwick gazed at
it suspiciously as he seated himself in the
chair she placed for him. He felt out of
place.

"Oh, you 'd never guess it while the sun,

moon, an' stars shine," continued Cassy. "I married Danny Lemmons!"

"The great kingdom come!" exclaimed Chadwick, leaping from his chair. "The humpback man? Is he anywheres aroun' here? Ef he is, don't tell me — don't tell me! He'd never forgive you while the worl' stan's."

"What's he got agin you?" inquired Mrs. Lemmons.

"Not anything, ma'am, that I knows on," replied Chadwick, sitting down again.

"How I come to marry him I'll never tell you," said Cassy, seating herself on the side of the bed. "But you know how gals is. They don't know their own mind ef they've got one. Pap was in the war fightin' fer sesaysion, an' Maw wuz dead, an' thar I wuz a-livin' roun' from family to family, spinnin' an' weavin', an' waitin' on the sick. I tell you now, a gal that's got to live from han' to mouth thataway, an' be a dependin' on Tom, Dick, an' Harry an' the'r wives — that gal hain't in no gyarden of Eden — now, you may say what you please! Well, jest about that time, here come this here creetur you call Danny Lemmons. He pestered me mighty nigh to death. I could n't take two steps away from the house but what he 'd jump out of the bushes an' ast me to have 'im. An' a whole passel of people up an' tol' me I 'd better marry 'im. They 'low'd a cripple man wuz better 'n no man. Well, they aggervated me tell I married 'im."

Cassy paused here, picking imaginary thrums and ravelings from her apron. Chadwick fumbled with his hat and looked gravely at a sun-spot as round as a dollar dancing on the floor.

"I married him," she went on, "an' I jumped out of the fryin'-pan right spang in the fire. I tell you, he 's the Devil — claws an' all. He led me a dog's life. Jealous! Fidgety! Mean! Low-minded! Nasty! — Shucks! I could n't begin to tell you about that creetur ef I wuz to set here an' talk a week. It got so that I could n't no more live wi' him than I could live in a pot er bilin' water. So when the army come along, I tuck my baby an' come away. He vowed day in an' day out that ef I ever run off he 'd foller me up an' git the baby thar, an' take it off in the woods an' make 'way wi' it."

At this point the baby in question joined

the conversation with some remarks in its own peculiar language, and Cassy lifted it from the bed, a squirming bundle of red fists and keen squalls, and, turning her chair away from Chadwick, proceeded to silence it with the old-fashioned argument that healthy mothers know so well how to use. It was a bundle of such doubtful shape that Chadwick had his suspicions aroused.

"The young un's all right, ain't it?" he ventured. "It don't take atter the daddy, I reckon?"

For answer Cassy bent over the baby, laughing and cooing.

"Did 'e nassy ol' man sink mammy's itty bitty pudnum pie have a hump on 'e fweet itty bitty back? Nyassum did sink so! Mammy's itty bitty pudnum pie be mad in de weckly."

Chadwick, listening with something of a sheepish air, understood from this philological discourse that any person who suggested or intimated that the young Lemmons was shapen or misshapen on the pattern of the senior Lemmons was an unnatural and a perverse slanderer. Cassy looked over her shoulder at him and laughed. In a few moments she placed the baby on the bed.

"Well," said Chadwick, shuffling his feet about on the floor uneasily, "you may as well primp up an' look your best, bekaze it hain't been a half-hour sence I seed Danny Lemmons a-caperin' about in town yander."

The color fled from the woman's face, leaving it white as a sheet. The blue veins in her temples shone ghastly through the skin.

"I hope you ain't afeard of 'im?" inquired Chadwick, with a pitying glance.

"Afeard! Yes, I 'm afeard to do murder. I 'm afeard to have his blood on me!" She spoke in a husky whisper. Her eyes glittered and her lips were drawn and dry. As she reached for her chair, her hands shook. After she sat down, her fingers opened and shut convulsively. "I 've done dreampt about it," she went on, trying to clear her throat, "an' it 's obleege to be. Sev'm times has it come to me in my sleep that I 've got his blood on my han's. Hit wuz as plain as the nose on your face. I seed it an' felt it. How it come thar, my dreams hain't tole me, but I know in reason hit 's bekaze I killt 'im. Well, ef it 's got to come, I wisht it 'ud make 'aste an' come, an' be done wi' it."

She went to a little cupboard in one corner

of the room, turned the wooden button that
kept the door shut, and drew forth a carpen-
ter's hatchet. The blue steel of the blade
shone brightly. It was brand new.

"That little thing," she said, holding it
up, "cost sev'm dollars and a half. But, la!
I reckon it's wuth the money." She lifted
her apron, showing a small wire bent in the
shape of a hook, and suspended from her
belt. On this wire she hung the hatchet,
the hook fitting into the slit or notch on the
inner side of the blade.

"Well," exclaimed Chadwick admiringly,
"that's the fust time I ever know'd what a
notch in a hatchet wuz fer!"

"Let a woman 'lone fer that!" replied
Cassy, making an effort to laugh.

"I don't reckon Danny Lemmons 'll likely
fin' you here," said Chadwick after a while.

"Who — him! Why, he's the imp of the
Ole Boy. Ef he's in town, he kin shet his
eyes tight an' walk right straight here. The
human bein' don't live that kin fool Danny
Lemmons. I reckon maybe I could take the
baby an' hide out in the woods; but them
ole folks in the house thar, they tuck me in
when I did n't have a mouffle to eat ner a

place to lay my head, an' now they 're in
trouble I hain't a-gwine to sneak off an' leave
'em — I hain't a-gwine to do it. They 're
both ole an' trimbly. The ole man says he 's
got a pile er money hid aroun' here some'rs,
but he 's done gone an' fergot wharbouts he
put it at, an' he jes vows he won't go off an'
leave it."

She spoke slowly, and paused every now
and then to pick at her apron, as though re-
flecting over matters that had no part in her
conversation.

"I declare to gracious!" she continued,
"it 's pitiful to see them two ole creeturs go
moanin' an' mumblin' aroun', a-pokin' in
cracks an' in the holes in the groun' a-huntin'
fer the'r money. They 've ripped up the'r
bed-ticks an' tore up the floor a time or two.
They hain't got nothin' to live fer 'less'n it 's
the money."

Chadwick took his leave as soon as he could
do so without breaking the thread of Cassy's
discourse. He left her talking volubly to
the baby, which had jumped in its sleep and
woke screaming with fright.

"I reckon it dreampt it seed its daddy,"
said Chadwick, as he bowed himself out.

II

Meanwhile Danny Lemmons was carrying out plans of his own. He was a spy without knowing what a serious venture he was engaged in. He had been roaming around in the Federal lines for a fortnight, playing his fiddle, and cutting up his queer antics. One night, after playing a selection of jigs and reels for a group of young officers attached to General Slocum's staff, he said he was going into Atlanta after his baby.

"You 'll never go," said one of the officers.

"I 'll go or bust," replied Danny Lemmons.

"If you go you 'll stay," remarked another officer. "I believe you 're a Johnny, anyhow."

"I 'll go, and I 'll come back right here, an' I 'll fetch my baby back."

"Bah! Bring us some papers. Ransack Joe Johnston's headquarters. Stuff a map under your jacket. Bring us something to show you 've been in Atlanta. Anybody can skirmish around here and steal a baby, but not one man in a thousand can go through

the lines and ransack the headquarters of the
Johnnies and bring back documents to show
for it."

"I'm the man! Jest hol' my fiddle till I
git back!" exclaimed Danny Lemmons.

How the hunchback passed the Confederate lines it would be impossible to say. He
was as alert as any flying creature, as cunning as any creeping thing, as crafty as
patience and practice can make a man. He
reached Atlanta and made himself as much
at home in the streets as any of the little
arabs that flitted from corner to corner.
He saw Captain Mosely, knew him, and was
anxious to avoid him, not because he appre-
ciated the danger of his position, but because he could not successfully play the part
of an imbecile under Mosely's eyes.

He went rapidly down Whitehall Street,
keeping up the pretence of idiocy, but when
he turned and went into Forsyth, he dropped
the character altogether, and became once
more the Danny Lemmons of Sugar Mountain, — queer but shrewd. He inquired the
way to headquarters. The soldier whom he
asked directed him to the provost-marshal's
office, which was not far from where the

Kimball House now stands. He made no haste to get there, loitering as he went along, and examining whatever was new or strange with the curiosity of a countryman.

The result was that when he reached the provost-marshal's office, that official was preparing to send out and arrest him. Captain Mosely had preceded him by half an hour. The moment he entered Danny Lemmons knew that something was wrong, and, quick as a flash, he assumed the character of a " loony." The transition was so quick that it was unobserved by two keen-eyed men who fixed their attention on him as soon as he entered the door. He paused and gazed at them with a deprecating grin.

" Is this place whar they conscript them what wants to jine the war? " he asked.

The provost-marshal, a man with a tremendous mustache and beetling eyebrows, stared at him savagely, but made no reply.

" Oh, yes, hit is ! " exclaimed Danny Lemmons, " bekaze they tol' me down the road that you-all 'd let me jine the war."

" You are a spy ! " said the officer fiercely.

" Lord, yes ! Wuss 'n that, I reckon. I kin run an' jump, an' rastle. Whoopee, yes !

You ain't never seed me rastle. Shucks! I kin tie one han' behin' me an' put your back in the dirt. Yes-sir-ree!" He stuck his tongue out of the corner of his mouth and stood blinking at the officer.

The two men who were standing near, one tall and muscular and the other short and fat, exchanged glances and tried their best to keep their faces straight.

"When did you leave the Yankee army?" the officer asked.

"Las' night!" responded Danny Lemmons. "Lord, yes! I follered 'em down from Sugar Mountain, tryin' to see what devilment they wuz up to. When I wanted to jine in the war, they 'low'd I wuz crazy in the head an' unbefittin' in the body."

It was a bold stroke, but it was effectual. The fierce look of the officer faded into one of astonishment.

"How did you get through the lines?" he asked.

"I walked," replied Danny Lemmons; "I jest had to walk. Them fellers tuck my creetur away from me."

"Go in that room there and wait till I call you," said the officer.

" Is that whar they jine inter the war ? " asked the hunchback.

" Yes ; I 'll attend to you directly." The officer stepped to the door and shut it, and turned to the two men who had been listening to the conversation. " What do you think of him, boys ? "

The tall man, whose name was Blandford, was picking his teeth. The short, fat man, whose name was Deomateri, was busily engaged in polishing his finger-nails. They had served as scouts with Morgan, and later with Forrest. Mr. Blandford passed his hand through his long black hair and shook his head. Mr. Deomateri put his knife in his pocket, kicked his heels against the floor one after the other, and remarked : —

" If he is n't an idiot, he is the smartest man in this town."

" I started to say so," said Mr. Blandford, " but it takes a mighty spraddle-legged ' if ' to reach that far."

" Well, I 'll tell you," exclaimed the officer, " he has n't got sense enough to know how to tell a lie. I 'll keep him here until Mosely or his man comes, and then I 'll give him a drink and turn him loose."

As this seemed to dispose of the matter, neither Blandford nor Deomateri made any response. The clerks in the office were busy writing out reports and filling out blanks of various kinds, and to these for a time the officer in charge devoted his attention.

The room in which Danny Lemmons had been placed was the provost-marshal's private office. On his desk was a rough map of the inner defenses of Atlanta. In the pigeonholes were a number of papers of more or less importance. In the farther end of the room was a door. It was locked, and the key gone, but in one of the pigeon-holes was a large brass key. Danny Lemmons noted all these things with inward satisfaction. He took the key, unlocked the door, and saw that it led into an alley-way. Then he replaced the key in the pigeon-hole, leaving the door unlocked. He waited five or ten minutes, and then stuck his head into the outer office, exclaiming : —

"Don't you all run off an' leave me by myse'f, bekaze I hain't usen to it."

The clerks laughed, and even Mr. Blandford smiled sadly, but there was no other response. Danny Lemmons shut the door, seized the map, and as many papers as he could conveniently stuff under his jacket and in his pockets, opened the back-door noiselessly, locked it again, threw the key away, and turned swiftly into Pryor Street.

After a while Chadwick made his appearance. He went in and modestly inquired if Captain Mosely had been there. The provost-marshal, who was at that moment talking to Blandford and Deomateri about their experience with Morgan, recognized Chadwick as the person who had been sent in pursuit of the spy.

" Did you catch your man ? " he inquired.

" Ketch nothin'," responded Chadwick. " A creetur-company could n't ketch him."

" Well, we 've caught him ! "

" Where'bouts is he ? " inquired Chadwick.

" In my room there."

" In there by hisself ? "

" Yes."

" Well, sir," exclaimed Chadwick excitedly, " I 'll bet you a thrip agin a bushel of chestnuts that he ain't in there."

" What do you know about him ? " inquired Mr. Blandford.

" Bless you, man ! I seed his capers in Sugar Mountain."

" Go in there and see if he 's the man you are hunting for."

Chadwick went to the door, opened it, and glanced casually around the empty room.

" Oh, yes ! He 's the man I 'm huntin' fer," he said as he turned away.

" How do you know ? " asked Deomateri, observing an expression of humorous disgust on Chadwick's face.

" Bekaze he ain't in there, by jing ! "

The provost-marshal rushed into the room, followed by Blandford, Deomateri, and the whole army of clerks. He saw that his desk had been rifled of important papers, and he sank in a chair, pale and trembling, and gasping for breath.

" Gentlemen," said Blandford to the clerks, " get back to your work. There is nothing to excite you." Then he closed the door and turned to the officer. " My friend, you will demoralize your office, and destroy all discipline. Brace up and give your backbone a chance to do its work."

" I am ruined," cried the officer. " Ruined ! That miserable thief has stolen the papers that

I ought to have sent to headquarters yesterday."

"Well, you nee' n't to worry about it,"
remarked Chadwick dryly, "bekaze Danny
Lemmons has fooled lots smarter folks 'n
you."

III

But for Blandford and Deomateri, a great
uproar would have been made in the provost-
marshal's office. That functionary sat in his
chair and cried "Ruined!" until he had been
fortified with two or three hearty slugs of
whiskey, and then the blood began to flow
in his veins and he took courage. In fact
he became bloodthirsty. He walked the floor
and waved his arms, and swore that he would
crush Danny Lemmons when he caught him.
He would hardly remain quiet long enough
to agree to any rational plan for the recap-
ture of the hunchback, but he finally con-
sented to let Chadwick have his saddle-horse,
Blandford and Deomateri having horses of
their own.

The three were soon in the saddle, and
now it was Chadwick who undertook to conduct the expedition. By his direction, Mr.

Deomateri was to ride out Peters Street, Mr. Blandford out Whitehall, while he himself was to ride out Pryor and turn into Whitehall Street, some distance out. At the junction of Whitehall and Peters they were to meet and decide on their future course of action. This plan was faithfully carried out, but it came to nothing.

At the point where they met the two thoroughfares had ceased to be streets, and merged into a public road, with a growth of timber-oak and pine on each side.

"Why do we come here?" inquired Deomateri. Blandford merely shook his head. He had dismounted and was leaning against his horse, making a picturesque figure in the green wood.

"Well," responded Chadwick, "we might jest as well be here as to be anywhere, accordin' to my notions. This road is open plum to Jonesboro an' furder. We 've been keepin' it open. The Yanks are bent aroun' the town like a hoss-shoe, an' this road runs right betwixt the p'ints where their lines don't jine."

"That 's so," remarked Blandford, regarding Chadwick with some interest.

"Well, then, we ain't got nothin' to do wi' how Danny Lemmons got in. He's slicker 'n sin, an' he mought 'a' run the picket lines at night; but shore as shootin', he can't run 'em in the daytime. Now, how 'll he git out?"

"Perhaps he has already passed here," Deomateri suggested.

"Well, sir," said Chadwick, "he's come to town on business, an' he 'll try to attend to it." Then Chadwick told his companions about his adventure with Mrs. Lemmons and the baby.

"By George, Deo!" exclaimed Blandford, swinging himself into his saddle, "this begins to look like sport."

"For the baby?" inquired Deomateri.

"For all hands," said Blandford gayly.

"But ef Mizzes Lemmons lays her eyes on Mister Lemmons," remarked Chadwick, "the baby 'll lack a daddy, an' the lack 'll be no loss."

Thereupon, the three men turned their horses' heads into Peters Street and rode toward the hill where Chadwick had found Mrs. Lemmons. They rode leisurely, watching on all sides for the hunchback. When

they reached the point where McDaniel
Street now crosses Peters, they saw a woman
coming toward them waving her arms wildly,
and shouting something they could not hear.

"Ef I ain't mighty much mistaken," said
Chadwick, "that's the lady we've been
talkin' about. Yes, sir!" he exclaimed, as
she came nearer, "that's her, certain and
shore! That hellian has gone an' got the
baby!" He spurred his horse forward to
meet the woman, who, as soon as she saw
him, screamed out: —

"You told him, you sneakin' wretch! You
told him wher' my baby wuz! You did —
you did — you did!"

In the extremity of her excitement she
would have laid her hands on Chadwick, but
his horse shied, and kept him out of her
reach.

"What's this? What's this?" exclaimed
Blandford.

"Oh, I'm distracted!" cried Cassy, breaking down. "My baby's gone! That slink
of Satan has took an' run off wi' my poor
little baby!" she turned to Chadwick and
then to the others. "Oh, ef you've got
any pity in you, run and overtake him. Jes'

ketch 'm an' hol' 'im tell I can git my han's on 'im."

"Which way did he go?" asked Bland-ford.

"He went right up dat away!" exclaimed a negro woman excitedly. She pointed across the railroad. "He come lopin' 'long here, an' he went right up dat away. I seed 'im. I wuz right at 'im. Yasser. Right up dat away." She was both excited and indig-nant. "He look mo' like de Devil dan any white man I ever is see. An' de baby wuz cryin' like it heart done broke!"

"Oh, Lord 'a' mercy, what shall I do?" cried Cassy, wringing her hands.

"'T ain't been long, nuther," said the negro woman, "'kaze I been stan'in' right here waitin'. I des know'd sump'n n'er wuz gwine ter happen. I des know'd it. Why n't you all run on an' ketch 'im? I boun' ef I had a hoss an' could ride straddle I'd ketch 'im."

"Oh, what shall I do?" cried Cassy.

What is now McDaniel Street was not then laid off. It was a short cut through a cow pasture, running through an open country, dotted here and there with clumps of pine

and scrub oak. Through this the horsemen
rode at a swinging gallop, followed at some
distance, as they could observe, by Cassy, the
negro woman, and a few stragglers, whose
curiosity had been turned into sympathetic
interest. Chadwick bore toward the left
calkin of the line that he had described as a
horseshoe, and in a little while his companions
heard him shout and saw him wave his hand.
They swerved to the right and rode toward
him, their horses running easily. As soon
as they caught sight of the fugitive, Blandford rode at full speed until he had passed
the hunchback, and then turned and rode toward him, holding in his right hand a cavalry
pistol that sparkled in the sun.

The hunchback saw that escape was impossible, and he made no further attempt. He
ceased to run and sat down at the foot of a
huge pine, making a vain effort to soothe the
frantic baby, which had screamed until its
cries sounded like those of some wild animal
in mortal agony. This and the sinister aspect
of the hunchback so wrought upon Blandford that he leaped from his horse and would
have brained the creature on the spot, but
for the intervention of Deomateri, who was
in time to seize his arm.

" Watch out, Blandford ! " cried Deoma-teri in great good-humor; " don't scare the baby. If it lets out another link it will go into spasms. Come here, chicksy," he said to the baby. " Poor little thing ! Hushaby, now ! " He tried in vain to quiet the child, but it would not be quieted. He walked up and down with it, clucked to it, tried to give it his watch to play with, dandled it in his hands, but all to no purpose. It continued its hoarse and gasping cries.

Meanwhile, Chadwick and Blandford were giving attention to Danny Lemmons. They searched him from head to foot, and took from him every scrap of paper they could find on his person. Blandford did the search-ing, and he was not at all gentle in his meth-ods. The hunchback was captured, but not conquered.

" Good God A'mighty, gentermen ! can't a man come an' git his own baby atter his wife 's run off wi' some un else ? How you know she did n't tell me to take an' take it home to Sugar Mountain ? Dad blast you ! Ef you 'll jest gi' me a fair showin' I kin whip arry one on you ! I 'm a great min' to spit in your face ! "

Thus he raved as Blandford searched him, and even after his hands had been securely tied with a tether that had hung at Deomateri's saddle. Meanwhile the baby refused to be comforted. It seemed to be nearly exhausted, and the hoarse and unnatural sounds it made were more pitiable than its natural cries would have been. At last Chadwick offered to take it. To his astonishment it held out its little hands to him, and immediately ceased its frantic efforts to cry as soon as it found itself in his arms, though it continued to moan and sob a little. But the child was no longer afraid, for it looked up in Chadwick's face and tried to smile as it nestled against his shoulder.

The problem of the baby temporarily solved, the three soldiers would have made toward the city with their prisoner, but here a fresh difficulty presented itself. The hunchback refused to budge. He had ceased his threats and curses, and was now ominously quiet. If he had been stone-blind and deaf he could not have more completely ignored the orders to get up and move on.

" Break off a hickory lim' an' frail h—ll

out'n 'im," said Chadwick. "That's the way I use to do when my ole steer lay down in the road."

But Deomateri shook his head. For sundry reasons this mode of moving the hunchback was not to be thought of. While they were holding what Chadwick called a council of war, Danny Lemmons's wife came in sight, followed by the negro woman who had been the means of the capture of the hunchback.

"Well," remarked Chadwick, — anticipation in his tone, — "yander comes Miss Cassy herself. I reckon maybe she'll up an' tell us how to make the creetur' move; an' ef I ain't mighty much mistaken she'll whirl in an' he'p us."

At this the hunchback showed signs of uneasiness. He twisted himself around, as if to see where his wife was. Failing in this, he gathered his long legs under him and rose to his feet. He saw the woman and then glanced furtively around as if to find some avenue of escape.

"Gentermen!" he cried, "you-all'll have to keep Cassy off'n me, bekaze she's plum ravin' deestracted when she gits mad." His voice was a whine, and anxiety had taken the place of craftiness in his countenance.

The woman strode forward steadily, but not hurriedly. Her face was pale, and there was a drawn and pinched expression about her mouth that might have been mistaken for grief or fear. Chadwick pressed toward her with the baby, as though proud of the opportunity to deliver it into her arms. But she passed by him with an impatient gesture, in spite of the renewed whimpering of the child at sight of her; and the negro woman came forward and took it instead.

The hunchback would have made a barricade of Blandford, but that blunt soldier seized him by his arm and brought him face to face with his wife.

" You mean, sneakin', thievin' houn' !" she cried, gazing at him and breathing hard. Then she untied her bonnet, which had fallen on her shoulders, and threw it on the ground, her hair falling loose as she did so. Still catching her breath in little gasps, she began to roll up her sleeves, showing an arm as hard and as firm as that of a man.

" Oh, no !" exclaimed Blandford, perceiving what she would be at. " None of that,

ma'am. Don't scratch him. We want him
to look as pretty as possible."

"Mister!" she cried, flinging her head
back and turning to Blandford, "don't git
me stirred up. You seed what he wuz tryin'
to do, but you don't nigh know what he kin
do. Ontie him, an' he kin whip arry one of
you, fair fist an' skull, rush an' scramble."
Her tone was both argumentative and appeal-
ing. As she spoke a shell went spinning and
singing overhead. The hunchback dodged
involuntarily, but the woman remained un-
moved. "I tell you, now," she went on,
"you don't know him. You can't carry him
to town ef it wuz to save the world. He'd
hamstring your creeturs an' git away. You
think he's cripple, an' he does look cripple,
but the man don't live that kin out-do him.
You think I want to take the inturn on him,
but I don't. I ain't nothin' but a woman,
but me an' him is got a score to settle. Ontie him, ef he ain't done ontied hisself, an'
give him a knife or a pistol or anything. I
don't want nothin' but my naked han's."
Her bosom rose and fell convulsively and her
hands refused to remain at rest.

"Don't do it, gentermen!" exclaimed the
hunchback. "She'll kill me."

The tragic features of the situation escaped Blandford and Deomateri, but the simple mind of Chadwick recognized them, —
recognized, in fact, nothing else.

" I think," said Blandford, winking at
Deomateri, " that we 'd better untie this chap
until he and his wife settle this family quarrel. What do you think about it ? "

" Oh, by all means let the family quarrel
be settled ! " remarked Deomateri in a matter-of-fact way.

The result of this grim humor could hardly
have been foreseen. In some way the hunchback had worked his hands loose from the
thong that bound them, and he made a desperate dash for liberty. The woman was
after him in a moment. As she ran, she
drew forth from under her apron the hatchet
that Chadwick had seen her conceal there.
She was hardly a match for the hunchback
in a foot-race, but passion, hatred, the venom
that had supplanted anxiety for her child,
lent swiftness to her feet, and the soldiers,
who stood watching as if paralyzed, expected
every moment to see her bury the hatchet in
the man's deformity. She poised her glittering weapon to strike, but at that moment her

foot slipped and she fell to the ground. Then there was a zooning sound in the air, a thud, and a deafening roar. A shell had burst, as it seemed, full upon pursuer and pursued.

The soldiers, watching, saw the shell strike and felt the concussion shake the ground at their very feet. They saw a volume of dust and turf spout violently upward. When this had subsided they rode forward to view the scene. The woman, unhurt, sat on the ground, half-laughing and half-crying. Not far away lay Danny Lemmons, torn, shattered, and lifeless.

" You all thought," said Cassy simply, "that I wuz atter him by myself. But I know'd all the time the Almighty wuz wi' me." She rose, seized the baby, and hugged it tightly to her bosom, where it lay laughing and cooing.

THE BABY'S FORTUNE

I

THE random shells flung into Atlanta during the siege by your Uncle Tecumseh's gunners were sometimes very freakish. The history of that period, written, of course, by those who have small knowledge of the facts, proceeds on the supposition that the town was in a state of terror, and that every time the population heard a shell zooning through the air it scuttled off to its cellars and bombproofs, or to whatever holes it had to hide in. This doubtless occurred during the first day or two of the siege, but human nature has the knack of getting on friendly terms with danger. As the Rev. Sam Jones would remark, those who hourly defy the wrath of heaven are not likely for long at a time to remain in awe of random shells.

Yet the freaks of these random shells were very queer. One of the missiles (to mention one instance out of many) went tumbling down Alabama Street, turned into Whitehall, following the grade, and rolled through the iron lamp-post that stands in front of the old James's Bank building. It was moving along so leisurely that a negro lounging near the corner tried to stop it with his foot. He was carried off with a broken leg. The lamp-post stands there to this day, having been thoughtfully preserved as a relic that might be of interest, and if you give it a careful glance as you pass, you 'll see the jagged hole grinning at you with open-mouthed familiarity.

A family living on Forsyth Street, near where that thoroughfare crosses Mitchell, saw a weary-looking Confederate sauntering by and thoughtfully invited him in to share a pot of genuine vegetable soup, — a very rare delicacy in those days. It chanced that the soldier was Private Chadwick, and he was prompt to accept the proffered hospitality. Morever, he was politer about it than any other private would have been.

Private Chadwick, being the guest, was served first, but, just as the plate of soup was placed before him, a shell came tearing through the dining-room, entering at one end and going out at the other, grazing the ceiling in its passage and bringing down a shower of plastering, dust, and trash. Chadwick was almost as quick as the shell. He snatched his hat from his knee, and when his hosts had recovered from their momentary alarm they saw him sitting bolt upright in his chair using his head covering as an umbrella to shield his soup from the shower that fell from the shattered ceiling.

"Howdy and good-by," he said. "You might 'a' sp'iled my dinner, but you ranged too high to sp'ile my appetite."

"I can see why you are holding your hat over your plate, and I'm sorry I did n't have something of the kind to hold over mine," remarked the lady who had invited him in ; "but I can't imagine why you are sitting so straight in your chair."

"Well, ma'am," replied Private Chadwick, "seein' as how you 've been so kind, I 'll tell you the honest truth. I was afeared if I humped too much over my plate that the next shell 'd take me to be the twin of Danny Lemmons."

Naturally this aroused the curiosity of the ladies — there were three of them — and nothing would do but Chadwick must tell that tragic story. When it was concluded, one of the ladies inquired if Danny Lemmons had a twin brother.

"No 'm, not that I know of," said Chadwick, laughing at the agility with which the feminine mind can leave tragedy and fly back to inconsequential trifles; "but a shell ain't got time to choose betwixt folks that favor."

You 've heard the story of Danny Lemmons and Cassy Tatum, and so it is unnecessary to repeat the details. They are all true enough, but so antique is the war that they strike the modern ear as lightly as if they had been filched from a manuscript found in the pocket of a stranded play-actor. It is enough to say here that Danny Lemmons was a hunchback — a mountaineer — who married Cassy Tatum, and who, when Cassy left him, followed her to Atlanta, making his way through the Federal and Confederate lines. He had stolen Cassy's baby — if a man can be said to steal his own child — and was on his way back to the Federal lines, pursued by his wife, by Private Chadwick, and one or two other soldiers, when he was killed by the explosion of a shell.

That story was not as old when Private
Chadwick told it over his soup as it is now.
Indeed, it was as new as any event that happened the day before yesterday can be. Private Chadwick told the story as it happened,
and he was sure he was telling all of it, but
if he could have joined the ladies at their
table a week later he would have been able
to add some facts that would have caused his
small audience to wonder at the mysterious
ways of Providence, as, indeed, all of us must
wonder when we pause and take the time
and the trouble to think about the matter,
even in regard to the most trivial and ordinary events.

II

When Cassy Tatum (she declared over and
over again that she never did, and never
could have the stomach to call herself Mrs.
Lemmons) left her husband and went to Atlanta, she took up her abode with an old
couple, who lived in a small ramshackle house
that sat on a hill overlooking Peters Street.
This hill was called Castleberry's Hill a few
years ago, whatever it may be called now,
and, before it was graded down to suit the

convenience of contractors who were greedy
for jobs, was the most elevated spot in Atlanta, and the most picturesque, too, for that
matter, for a fine growth of timber crowned
the summit.

At night the lights of the town twinkled,
and Cassy Tatum, sitting on the front steps,
after everything had been put to rights, and
the old folks had gone to bed, could hear the
cracked and noisy laughter of the women
who lived in the shanties that were scattered
about at the foot of the hill. The place
where these shanties were grouped was called
Snake Nation, and was proud of the name.
Snake Nation slept soundly all day, but at
night — well, old Babylon has its echoes and
imitations in the newest town that ever had a
corporation line run around it at equal dis-
tances from the police court.

" What I hear at night makes me sick, and
what I see in the daytime makes me sorry,"
remarked Cassy Tatum to Mrs. Shacklett
shortly after she had taken up her abode in
the small house that has been described.

" You don't have to hear 'em, and you
don't have to see 'em," remarked Mrs. Shacklett, in her squeaky voice. " Don't bother

'em and they 'll not bother you ; you may depend on that."

" Well, if they don't pester me tell I pester them," said Cassy, " they 'll never so much as know that I 'm a-livin'."

Mrs. Shacklett was very old, but time, that had played havoc with her youth, had in no wise disturbed the fluency of her tongue. Her voice was cracked and squeaky, but that, she said, was asthma and not age. She wore a white cap, that covered her head and ears, and the edges that framed her face were fluted and ruffled. A narrow band of blue ribbon, tied in a bow on the top of the cap, ran down under the fluting and was tied under her chin. She always wore a cape over her shoulders, but beyond this her frock was prim and plain, and the cape was as prim as the frock.

Mrs. Shacklett was eighty-seven years old, so she said, and this fact gave a sort of historic dignity to her presence, where otherwise dignity would have been sadly lacking, for her head shook as with a tremor when she talked, and the uncertainty of old age had taken charge of all her movements. Her mind was fairly good, but it seemed to hesitate, fluttering and hovering now and then, as if on the point of deserting the weak and worn body that had been its tenement for so long.

And no wonder. Born near the beginning of one epoch-making war, she was on the point of seeing another brought to an end. The republic wanted but twelve years to round out its century. Hers lacked but thirteen to complete it. A historian eager for facts that give warmth and color to history might have gathered from her lips an account of many remarkable events and episodes that time has given over to oblivion. Of recent and passing events her memory took small account, but of matters relating to the past she could talk by the hour, and with a fluency that was out of all proportion to her ability to deal with the events of the day.

Mr. Shacklett, her husband, was not so old by several years, and he was better preserved physically, but his mind was quite as feeble, and his memory more unstable, if such a thing could be. If he stayed out of bed a quarter of an hour after taking his toddy at night, he betrayed an almost uncontrollable

tendency to shed tears over the price of wool
hats and the scarcity of tea and coffee. At
such times it was pathetic to hear his wife
try to soothe and console him.

"Cover up and go to sleep, honey, and
you 'll soon disremember all about it," she
would say. "That 's the way I do. The
war can't last always, nohow."

"Can't it? How do you know it can't?
Hey? It 'll outlast me. You mark my
words." In half a minute he 'd be asleep
and snoring as loud as the feeble muscles
of his chest would permit.

It was with this time-worn and childish
couple that Cassy Tatum took up her abode,
when, with her baby on her arm, she ran
away from her husband. She had come into
Atlanta on the Western & Atlantic Railroad, and, in wandering about, searching for
a lodging, chanced to come upon this house.
Though it sat high on Castleberry's Hill, it
was too small to be conspicuous, and so she
knocked at the door. She afterward declared
that Providence sent her there, for when she
arrived the old couple were in quite a pre-
dicament. A negro woman who had long
ministered to their simple wants had just

died, and Cassy found them sitting by their cheerless hearth, unable even to kindle a fire.

She did not hear their feeble response to her knocking, but boldly opened the door and walked in, expecting and hoping to find the house vacant. Her surprise at seeing the old people sitting there was so great that she uttered an exclamation, and this bred in the minds of Mr. and Mrs. Shacklett suspicions that they were long in recovering from.

"I declare! you gi' me sech a turn that a little more an' I'd 'a' drapped the baby."

"You thought we was dead, did you? Hey?" inquired Mr. Shacklett with as near an approach to sarcasm as he could bring to voice and face. "You thought we was dead, and you'd come foraging aroun' to see what you could pick up and tote off. You did, did you? Hey? Well, we ain't dead, by grabs, and nowheres nigh it, I hope. You hear that, don't you? Hey?"

The thought that they had been mistaken for dead people, when, as a matter of fact, they were so very much alive, caused such an energetic flame of indignation to burn in Mr. Shacklett's bosom, that he rose from his chair, and, holding by the chimney-jamb, pre-

tended to be hunting for his pipe, which, as
a matter of fact, was on the floor beside him.
He realized this after a little, but in his agitation he found great difficulty in getting
into his seat again, and would have fallen
had Cassy not made a step forward and
caught him with her free hand.

Mr. Shacklett was not at all mollified by
this timely aid, but kept his anger glowing.

"You see we ain't dead, don't you? Hey?
'T ain't all the time that I'm shaky this way.
It's only because our nigger's dead. She
was a good nigger, — a right good nigger.
We raised her from a baby. *She's* dead,
but we ain't, by grabs! One time a man
come in the door there. He was lots bigger 'n
you are, but we did n't want him about, and
I had to get my gun and shoot him. *He's*
dead, but we ain't. No, by grabs. We don't
look like we're dead, do we? Hey?"

All this time Cassy Tatum stood with her
baby on her arm, staring at the old people
with open-mouthed wonder, not knowing what
to say or do, and unable to frame any excuse
for her intrusion that she thought likely to
appeal to their childish understanding. But
she caught a humorous twinkle in Mrs. Shack-

lett's eye, and was on the point of saying something, when the old lady spoke.

"Don't mind him," she said. "He never shot anybody. Why, Marty would n't harm a flea."

"Oh, I would n't, would I? Hey?" he cried peevishly. "Who made you so wise? Hey? How do you know but what I shot a man whiles you was asleep and had him drug off? How do you know but what I done it? Hey?" Mr. Shacklett turned half around in his chair and glared at his wife. "Tell me that — hey?"

"Why, honey, I would n't 'a' believed it if I'd 'a' seen it — much less when I did n't. You'll make this good woman here believe that a parcel of murderers is harbored in this house, and then she'll go out and set the law on us."

This rather cooled Mr. Shacklett's indignation, but it still smouldered and smoked, so to say.

"Much I care for the law," he said, trying to snap thumb and middle finger, a trick he failed to compass, though he made three trials. "Ain't we got no prop'ty rights? Hey? Must we set down here and be run over and trompled on? Hey? You may if you want to, but not while the breath of life lasts will I set down here and be run over and trompled on."

"Why, honey, who's a-trying to run over and tromple on you?" Mrs. Shacklett inquired.

"Hey? Did you ax me who?" cried Mr. Shacklett. "Scores and scores of folks if they was n't afeard. But I dar' 'em to so much as try it. I jest dar' 'em to!"

With that he settled himself more comfortably in his chair, and closed his eyes, as if he were willing to give scores and scores of folks all the opportunity they wanted if they had any idea of running over and trampling on him. As Mr. Shacklett said nothing more, Cassy Tatum thought proper to explain her intrusion.

"The Lord knows I'm sorry I come in your door," she said, "an' I'd go right out, but I'd be worried mighty nigh to death ef I went off leavin' you-all believin' that I thess walked in here 'cause you're both ol' an' cripple."

Mr. Shacklett fired up again at this suggestion. "Crippled? Who told you we was crippled ? Hey ? You may thank your stars if you ain't no more crippled than what I am. You hear that, don't you ? Hey ? "

Cassy paid no attention to him, but addressed herself to Mrs. Shacklett. " I tell you now, I'm new to this town, bran' new. It hain't been two hours sence I landed here, an' this is the first door I've knocked at. I knocked a dozen times, an' I stood thar waitin' to hear somebody say, ' Go off,' or ' Come in,' an' when I did n't hear nothin', I says to myself, says I, ' I'll thess go in anyhow, an' rest myself, an' fix the baby up, an' maybe thar's a well in the yard whar I kin git a drink of water.' I never no more 'spected to see you-all a-settin' here than I 'spected to fly. Hit took me back so I did n't know what to say. I hain't had sech a turn in I dunno when."

" If you want water," said Mrs. Shacklett, " you'll find a bucket out there on the shelf and a well in the yard. We ain't had nobody to draw us none sence they come after our dead nigger. I tell you I was mighty sorry to lose the gyirl. She was worth twenty thousand dollars if she was worth a cent."

Mr. Shacklett turned half around in his

chair. " Hey ?   Twenty thousand dollars ? Not in *our* money."

" Hush, honey ! I said paper-money," remarked his wife soothingly.

" Hey ? not good paper-money."

Seeing no end of such a dispute as this, Cassy deposited her baby unceremoniously on the floor and went out after the water.

The child kicked its pink feet from under its skirts, turned its head toward Mrs. Shacklett, and laughed cutely.   The old lady nodded her head pleasantly and chirruped as well as she could.

Mr. Shacklett, hearing a noise he could not understand, called out for information. " Hey ?   What 's that ?   What did you say ? Hey ? "   Receiving no answer, he turned his head and saw the baby sprawling on the floor.   Instantly he became very much excited.   " Run and call her back !   What do you mean by setting flat in that cheer and letting her run off and leave that young un here ?   Hey ?   Ain't you gwine to jump up and call her back ?   Hey ?   Do you want me to go ?   Tell me that — hey ?   If I do she 'll rue it."

He was making a painful effort to rise

from his chair when Cassy reëntered the room smiling and bringing a tin dipperful of fresh water.

"Humph !" he grunted, and sank in his seat again.

"I reckon you think I 've been gone a mighty long time, but I had to rench out the bucket an' the gourd too, — they was so full er dirt an' dust," Cassy explained. "I allers said I 'd never let no nigger fool wi' nothin' I had to put to my mouth, an' I 'll say it ag'in."

"They 're not the cleanest in the world," remarked Mrs. Shacklett, taking the dipper in her trembling hand. "Have you drank?"

"No 'm," said Cassy. "Atter you is manners." She still held the handle of the dipper gently, but firmly, and guided it to Mrs. Shacklett's lips.

Mr. Shacklett heard this last remark and turned his head and stared at Cassy. And somehow the expression of displeasure and suspicion cleared away from his face. "I 'll have some, too, if you please," he said.

"I would n't slight you fer the world," replied Cassy, and went after another supply of water.

Mr. Shacklett leaned sidewise as far as was safe for him, and touched his wife on the arm. She looked at him, and he nodded solemnly in the direction Cassy had gone.

" What now ? " she asked.

" What 's she up to now ? Tell me that ? Hey ? "

" She 's gone after some water for you."

" Humph ! " grunted old Mr. Shacklett. " You 'll find out before you 're much older."

Once more Cassy came in, bringing the water, and Mr. Shacklett drank to his heart's content. Then Cassy gave the baby some water. Of course it had to strangle itself, as babies will do, but instead of crying over it, the child merely laughed and wanted to get on the floor again, where, flat on its back, it promptly gave itself up to the contemplation of the problem that its chubby fingers presented when all ten were held tip to tip close to its wondering eyes.

" That 's a right down pretty baby," remarked Mrs. Shacklett.

" I dunner so much about the purty part," replied Cassy with modest pride, " but he 's the best baby that ever was born. Why, he hain't no more trouble than nothin' in the world."

The child, as if understanding that it was
the subject of comment, dropped the study
of its fingers, caught the eye of its mother,
kicked its pink feet in the air, and fairly
squealed in its enthusiastic delight at being
able to sprawl about on the floor after its
long imprisonment in Cassy's arms.

"I thess wish to goodness you'd look at
'im!" exclaimed Cassy. "Hain't he thess
too sweet to live!" Then she switched from
vigorous mountain English to a lingo that
the baby could better understand and appreciate. "Nyassum is mammy's fweetnum pudnum pie, — de besses shilluns of all um shilluns. Nyassum is!"

"Hey?" inquired Mr. Shacklett. Receiving no answer, he found one for himself.
"Humph!"

At this high praise so beautifully bestowed,
the baby kicked and crowed and had a regular frolic. Then it suddenly discovered that
it needed more stimulating food than it had
found in the tin dipper, and Cassy, seating
herself in a chair, promptly satisfied the just
demand. And in the midst of it all, the
baby went fast to sleep, making a pretty picture as it lay happy in its mother's arms.

Mrs. Shacklett, whose age had not robbed her of the maternal instinct that is so deeply implanted in a woman's breast, looked all around the room as if remembering something, and suddenly remarked : —

" Lay him on the bed in the next room. Nobody sleeps in there."

" Hey ? " said Mr. Shacklett, and then, " Humph ! "

" Ef you reely mean it, an' think it won't put you out the least little bit in the world," suggested Cassy. The tone of her voice was serious, and there was a touch of sadness in it which the ear of Mrs. Shacklett did not fail to catch.

" Lay him in there on the bed," she repeated.

" Hey ? " inquired old Mr. Shacklett. " Humph ! "

" Ef you only know'd how mighty much I 'm obleeged to you, I 'd feel better," replied Cassy, the tears coming to her eyes.

She carried the child into the adjoining room, placed it on the bed, darkened the windows as well as she could, and went back to where the old people were sitting.

" Now, hain't there nothin' I kin do ?

Hain't there nothin' I kin put to rights?"
she inquired.

"Nothing I'd like to ask you to do,"
replied Mrs. Shacklett, shaking her head.
"We ain't got no claim on you."

"Why, hain't you human, an' hain't I
human? What more do you want than
that?" There was a touch of wonder in
Cassy's voice.

But Mrs. Shacklett shook her head doubtfully. Fortunately for all concerned, Mr.
Shacklett roused himself.

"I ain't had a bite of breakfast yet. Now
when are you going to have dinner? Tell
me that. Hey?"

"We've had nobody to cook for us sence
our nigger died," Mrs. Shacklett explained.
"I hated mightily to give her up. She was
worth two thousand dollars and she did
everything for us."

Cassy opened wide her eyes. "Well, for
the Lord's sake! No bre'kfus' an' mighty
little prospec' of dinner! No wonder you
hain't able to walk. It's a sin an' a shame
you did n't tell me about it when I walked
in the door. Why, I b'lieve in my soul you
two poor ol' creeturs'd set thar an' starve

before you 'd ax me to whirl in an' warm somethin' for you. I 'll not wait to be axed. Thess show me whar the things is an' I 'll have you a snack cooked before you can run aroun' the house."

" Hey ? " inquired Mr. Shacklett. " Is dinner ready ? Hey ? Don't I smell meat a-frying somewhere ? Hey ? "

" Don't be worried, honey," said Mrs. Shacklett. Then she turned to Cassy. " If you 'll give me your hand and fetch my chair for me, I 'll go in the cook-room and show you where everything is, the best I can."

" Did n't I tell you I smell meat a-frying? Hey ? " cried Mr. Shacklett as his wife went out, bearing on Cassy's strong arm.

The larder was pretty well stocked, as Cassy discovered, but Mrs. Shacklett found an insuperable obstacle to all their plans.

" There 's no wood ! " she exclaimed despairingly.

" Why, I seed plenty in the yard while ago," said Cassy.

" Yes, child, but it 's not cut."

Cassy laughed. " Not cut ? Well, ef I could n't cut wood as good as any man, I ruther think I 'd feel ashamed of myse'f."

So she found the ax, cut and split two
sticks of wood, and soon had a fire on the
kitchen hearth. The rest was easy. Cassy's
cooking would hardly have passed muster at
Delmonico's or any of the fashionable hotels,
but for the time and the occasion it was just
as good as there was any use for. And, wonderful to relate, Mrs. Shacklett, after much
hunting and fumbling with keys, drew forth
a package of genuine coffee, and grudgingly
measured out enough for three cups of the
fragrant beverage.

Cassy picked up two or three grains and
examined them with an interest that partook
of awe. " The land's sake ! " she cried ;
" why, hit 's the ginnywine coffee ! I hain't
seed none in so long tell the sight 's good for
sore eyes. I min' thess as well as if it 't was
yestiday the day an' hour an' the time an'
place whar I last laid eyes on ginnywine coffee." She held the green grains in her hand
and put them to her nose, but fire had not
yet released their fragrance.

" Can you parch it ? " Mrs. Shacklett
asked.

" Thess watch me," said Cassy somewhat
boastfully. " You need n't put in more 'n

three grains fer me," she went on. "Hit's too skace an' too good to be wasted on common folks."

After dinner Mr. Shacklett and his wife were much spryer and in a better humor than they had been on Cassy's arrival. Mr. Shacklett himself felt so much improved in mind and body that he ventured to walk out on the primitive porch, where he stood and gazed abroad in quite a patriarchal way, clearing his throat and pulling down his vest with an attempt at stateliness that would have been comic but for its feebleness.

It was settled in the most natural way in the world that Cassy should remain as long as she found it convenient to make her home there. In fact it was settled by Cassy herself. Before the day was over she had made herself indispensable to the old people. She looked after their bodily comfort with a deftness that they were strangers to, and her thoughtfulness was so forward that it outran and forestalled their desires.

A few days after she had been caring for the old people, she remarked that she had perhaps pestered them long enough.

"What's that?" cried old Mr. Shacklett. "Hey?"

"I knew that would be the way of it," said Mrs. Shacklett, and then she fumbled about until she found her handkerchief, and held it to her face, crying softly. This settled the matter so far as Cassy was concerned. She knelt on the floor beside Mrs. Shacklett and petted and consoled her as if she had been a child.

Matters went on smoothly until Cassy's husband, Danny Lemmons, slipped in one day and stole her baby. The result of that performance is too well known in history to be repeated here. Cassy pursued her husband and came back a widow, but she wore no weeds.

There was only one thing that worried the old people. For years they had been saving and hiding all the gold and silver coin they could lay hands on, and according to their account, told to Cassy in confidence, they had accumulated a considerable store. When their negro girl fell ill, the old people, fearing that she had discovered the hiding-place and would reveal the secret to some of her colored friends who came to visit her, removed their hoard to a new place of concealment. The girl lingered for a week and then suddenly died.

The event was so unexpected to Mr. and
Mrs. Shacklett, and threw them into such a
state of doubt and confusion, that they were
not able to remember where they had hid the
money.

They had many harmless disputes and spats
about the matter, and they hunted and hunted,
and poked about in the cracks of the chimney, and made Cassy lift up the big flat
stones in the hearths, and wandered about in
the yard, until it made the young woman
uneasy.

"I declare to gracious!" she would exclaim, "you-all gi' me the all-overs ever' minnit in the day wi' your scratchin' in the ashes
and pokin' in the cracks. You 'll fall over
the pots an' kittles some of these days and
cripple yourself."

Mrs. Shacklett had often boasted that she
was a Sandedge, and she made no concealment of her belief that the Sandedges were
higher in the social scale than the Shackletts.
Mr. Shacklett could remember this, even if
he had forgotten where the money had been
hid. Indeed, his mind dwelt upon it.

"You ought to know where we put the
money. You was there; you helped to do

it. If the Sandedges is so mighty much better than the Shackletts, why n't you mind
where we put the money? Hey? Tell me
that. You 're a Sandedge, and I ain't nothing but a plain Shacklett. 'T ain't no
trouble for me to forget, but how can a
Sandedge forget? Hey? Tell me that.
When it comes down to hard sense I reckon
the Shackletts is just as good as the Sandedges."

But all this did no good. The old people failed to find their precious store. They
sat and tried to trace their movements on the
day they had carried the money to its new
place of concealment, but they never could
agree. The death of the negro was the only
event they could clearly remember. Each exclaimed, many times a day: "Oh, I know!"
as if a flash of memory had revealed to them
the place, but it always ended in nothing.
Cassy soon became accustomed to the constant talking and hunting for hidden money,
and finally came to the conclusion that the
old people were the victims of a strange delu-
sion. She compared it in her mind to the
game of hide-the-switch which the children
play. At the last, she paid no more atten-

tion to the matter than if the old couple had
been a pair of toddling infants fretting over
some imaginary trouble.

III

Now it happened that while Private Chadwick was enjoying his soup under the gentle
auspices of the ladies who had invited him to
be their guest, his comrades in the trenches
and round about had received some news
that seemed to them to be very bad indeed.
It was in the shape of a rumor merely, but
among soldiers a rumor is merely the fore-
runner of facts. The news was to the effect
that General Johnston was about to be removed and General Hood put in his place.
The news had not yet appeared in the newspapers, and it had reached the soldiers before
it came to the ears of their officers. How,
nobody knows. The commander of a brigade
in Virginia made the rounds of his camp
one night. He saw considerable bustle among
the troops—fires burning and rations cooking.
Inquiring the cause, he was told that the
brigade would receive orders to march before
sunrise the next morning. The brigadier
laughed at this, thinking it was a joke on

the men, but when he returned to his headquarters he found a courier awaiting him
with orders for his brigade to move at dawn.

In the same way, General Johnston's removal was well known to the private soldiers
before the newspapers had printed the information. The news was not very well received,
for, in spite of the fact that they had been
retreating from Dalton to Atlanta, the men
were well enough acquainted with the tactics
of war to know that these retreats were mas-
terly, and they felt that their general was
gathering all his resources well in hand for
a decisive battle at the proper moment.

General Hood, as the successor of General
Johnston, knew what was expected of him by
the political generals and the military editors.
He was a gallant man and a hard fighter, and
he lost no time in showing these qualities.
But the responsibility that had been thrust
upon him was too great for him. He did
the best he could; he hurled himself against
General Sherman and inaugurated the series
of battles around Atlanta that has made the
city and the region round about historic
ground. Finally, he swung his army loose
from the town and went hurrying toward

Nashville, followed by General Thomas, while Sherman took possession of the South's supply-centre and prepared for his leisurely and unopposed march across the State to Savannah.

When the city was evacuated Private Chadwick found himself among the last of the straggling Confederates who were leaving. He found himself, indeed, with the little squad of riflemen commanded by Jack Kilpatrick, captain of the sharpshooters. The line of retreat led along Whitehall and Peters Streets. Chadwick turned into Peters as much by accident as by design, and was of two minds whether to cut across and go into Whitehall, or whether to go on as he had started. But a thought of Cassy Tatum decided him, and so he kept on the way he was going. Jack Kilpatrick accompanied him for old acquaintance's sake, sending some of his dozen men along Whitehall. They talked of old times as they rode along.

"Jack, I allers use to think you was the purtiest boy I ever laid eyes on," remarked Chadwick.

"Is that so?" Kilpatrick asked dubiously. He was slim and trim, and his features were very delicately moulded.

" Yes," replied Chadwick, " and if you was to shave off what little mustache you 've got, blamed if you would n't make a right-down good-looking woman. And you 've got a hand not much bigger 'n a nine-year-old boy. I reckon that 's the reason you draw so fine a bead sech a long ways off."

Kilpatrick smiled boyishly, and, as if to show what a nice girl he could be, threw a leg over the pommel of his saddle and rode sidewise. Far before them they could see clouds of dust rising slowly. Behind them and a little to their left they could hear the Federal guns feeling of the town, and occasionally a shell more venomous than the rest flew over their heads, crying as shrilly as if it had life. This was particularly the case when they came to Castleberry's Hill, which was a more conspicuous eminence then than it is now. Occasionally one of the missiles would strike the brow of the hill and fly shrieking off, or bury itself in the red clay with a queer fluttering sound.

As they came to the brow of the hill, Chadwick saw Cassy Tatum standing on the porch of the house where she lived. He waved his hand and asked her if she intended to remain. Mistaking his gesture, or not understanding his words, she came running along the pathway.

"Howdy?" said Chadwick; "why ain't you refugeein' wi' the rest?"

"I declare I dunno," she replied, with a laugh that was more than half pathetic. "I oughter, I reckon. Some of the Shack-letts's kinnery come by in a carryall soon this mornin' an' tuck 'em away, whether or no. I like to 'a' cried, they went on so. They didn't want to go one bit, an' they holler'd an' went on so that it made me feel right down sorry."

"What 'll you do? Why n't you go wi' 'em?" inquired Chadwick.

"Well, I had sev'm good reasons," replied Cassy, trying hard to joke, "an' all sev'm of 'em was that the folks did n' ax me. It looked mighty funny to me that they 'd let the poor ol' creeturs live here all this time at the mercy of the world, as you may say, an' then come an' snatch 'em up an' bundle 'em off that-away."

"Did they ever find their money?" Chadwick asked.

"Not a thrip of it," said Cassy. "That 's

the reason they went on so when the'r folks come atter 'em. Ef they did n't have no money they thought mighty hard they had it."

At that moment a shell came hurtling through the air. The *pang* of it sounded so near that Cassy dodged, and even the troopers glanced quickly upward. Then there was a crashing sound close at hand. Those who had their eyes turned toward the house — and Cassy was one of them — saw shingles fly from the roof, saw the top of the chimney sink out of sight, and saw a part of the roof itself sway and fall in. Cassy stood for an instant paralyzed, and then flinging her arms wildly, and yet helplessly, above her head, sprang toward the house with a scream of anguish.

"My baby! my baby!" she cried. "Oh, my poor little baby!"

Chadwick and Kilpatrick and their comrades sprang after her. As she reached the house one of the walls that had been pushed outward by the falling roof cracked loudly and seemed to be about to fall. Chadwick would have dragged Cassy out of the way, but she shook his hand off furiously, seized the wall by one of the gaping edges, and pulled it down. Then she rushed at the roof itelf, seized the ends of two of the rafters, and made as if she would overturn the whole affair.

" Wait ! " commanded Kilpatrick. " If the young un's under there you'll fetch the whole roof down on him."

This brought Cassy to her senses, and when a woman is clothed and in her right mind she knows by instinct that the best she can do is to cry. Cassy tried to do this now ; but her eyes were dry, and all the sound that her parched throat and trembling lips could utter was a low and continuous moan so pitiful that it wrung the hearts of the rough soldiers.

To add to the strain and suspense of the occasion, a smothered, wailing cry was heard somewhere in the midst of the ruins. At this Cassy, instead of making another effort to tear away the roof by main strength, as Chadwick expected her to do, fell flat on the ground with a heart-rending shriek of despair and lay there quivering and moaning.

In the midst of all this, Kilpatrick had the forethought to cast his eye occasionally on the portion of the street that lay beyond the railroad. He now saw a small squad of horsemen in blue riding down the incline. He ran to his horse, and his companions, with the exception of Chadwick, did the same. As for the private, he had made up his mind in a flash that he would rather undergo the diet and discipline of Elmira prison than desert Cassy at that moment.

But he had misunderstood Kilpatrick's intentions. Instead of mounting his horse and riding away, the boyish-looking sharpshooter whipped a field-glass from the case that hung on the saddle, and proceeded to carefully inspect the approaching Federals, who were moving cautiously. The inspection seemed to satisfy him, for he closed the glass, went out into the open ground, and waved his handkerchief so as to attract the attention of the horsemen in blue. They stopped, and their horses huddled together in the road as if they were engaged in consultation. Then one of them, a tall man on a powerful sorrel, detached himself from the group and came riding up the hill at an easy canter, his rifle glittering as it lay across his bridle arm ready for instant service.

" Well, dag-gone your skin, Johnny! What are you doin' here this time er day ? Hain't

you the same measly chap that tried to duck
me in the Chattymahoochee when we stuck
up a white flag an' went in washin'? Why'n
the world did n't you do what I told you —
go home to your mammy an' let grown men
fight it out? You're a good shot though,
dag-goned ef you ain't!" He spoke with a
strong Georgia accent, but was from Indiana.

The two men had faced each other on the
vedette line for so many weeks that they had
become acquainted. In fact, they were very
friendly. Once when the "Chattymahoochee" (as the tall Indianian facetiously called
that stream) divided the opposing armies, the
advance line of each went in bathing together every day, and they grew so friendly
that the Confederate generals issued a pro-
hibitory order.

Briefly Kilpatrick explained the situation
to the Federal sharpshooter, and by this time
his companions were on the ground.

The force was sufficiently large now to lift
the roof (which was small, and old, and frail),
and turn it over. The scheme was dangerous if the baby happened to be alive, but it
was the best that could be done, and it was
carefully done.

Cassy still lay upon the ground moaning
pitifully and clutching convulsively at the
tussocks that came in contact with her fingers. The spectacle that the fallen roof had
hid caused the men to utter exclamations of
wonder. Mistaking the purport of these,
Cassy Tatum writhed on the ground in an
agony of grief, and refused to answer when
Private Chadwick called her.

The sight that met the eyes of the men
was enough to carry them away with astonishment. The baby, unhurt, lay on the floor
in the midst of hundreds of gold and silver
pieces, and was trying to rub the dust out of
its eyes.

"Dag-gone my skin!" exclaimed the tall
Indianian; "that baby's pyore grit!" Then
he added, with a chuckle, "Liter'ly kiver'd
with it."

Chadwick went to Cassy, and, stooping
over, laid his hand on her shoulder, saying
gently: "Jest come an' look at him, Cassy!"

Mistaking his tone and intention, she
writhed away from his hand, crying out:
"Oh, kill me! kill me before I kill myself.
Oh, please make haste! Oh, me! He was all
I had in the worl'!"

"What's the matter?" asked the tall Indianian.

"She thinks the baby's dead," replied Chadwick.

"Dag-gone it!" laughed the Indianian; "why n't she git up an' see?"

The laugh startled Cassy so, that she sat up and looked around, throwing her hair behind her shoulders and making an instinctive effort to tidy up.

"What's the matter?" she moaned. "What's he laughin' at?"

"I reckon it's because you're worse hurt than the baby is," responded Chadwick.

"Where is he?" she cried. "Oh, don't le' me go there ef he's dead er mangled! Please, mister, don't le' me go where he is ef he's mashed!"

"All a-settin', ma'am!" said the Federal sharpshooter. "Jest walk this way."

At that moment the baby began to cry, and Cassy leaped toward it with a mother-cry that thrilled the soldiers. She snatched the child from the floor and hugged it so closely to her bosom that it had to kick and fight for air and freedom. Then she began to cry, and in a few moments was calm and apparently happy, but there was a haggard and drawn look in her face that no one had ever seen there before. Chadwick, observing this, turned to Kilpatrick and remarked : —

"If she ain't lost twenty pound in the last quarter of an hour I'm the biggest liar that ever drawed breath." This was an exaggeration, perhaps, and yet it was descriptive too.

"You see what the Yankee shell fetched you, ma'am," said the Federal sharpshooter.

For the first time Cassy saw the gold and silver pieces that were strewn about. "The land er the livin'!" she exclaimed. "That's them poor ol' creeturs' money." She looked at it in a dejected, dispirited way. "You-all kin take it," she went on, speaking to the Federals. "Take it an' welcome ef you'll thess le' me alone. My baby's money enough for me."

"It's dag-goned invitin'," replied the Indianian, laughing, "but you'll have to excuse us this time. It might be a pick-up ef we caught a passel er Johnnies with it — but that money there belongs to the baby, if it belongs to anybody. Would you mind loanin' me your apron a minnit?"

Cassy untied her apron with one hand,

and threw it to the Federal sharpshooter, and in a few minutes he and the rest of the men had picked up all the coins they could find and tied them in the apron, which was a stout piece of checked homespun. The general estimate was that the money amounted to two or three thousand dollars.

Then came what seemed to be the most important question of all. Should Cassy go with the Confederates or remain behind with the Federals?

" You 'll have to make up your mind in three flirts of a chipmunk's tail," remarked the Indianian. " The cavalry 'll be along in less 'n no time."

" I don't see how I kin go," said Cassy doubtfully.

" Ride behind me," suggested Kilpatrick.

" But what about my baby?"

" Oh, I 'll look after that bundle," said Private Chadwick. Another man could carry the money; and so it was all arranged.

" Don't I look it?" laughed Cassy, when she had mounted behind Kilpatrick.

" Yes 'm, you do," bluntly replied the Indianian. " Set square on the hoss ef you can, an' don't squeeze the feller too tight.

He's nothin' but a young thing." Whereupon both Cassy and Kilpatrick blushed, and
even Chadwick seemed to be somewhat dis-
concerted.

So they rode away, and when, far out
Peters Street, Cassy chanced to glance back
to Castleberry's Hill, she saw that it was
crowded with a swarm of cavalrymen. But
somehow she felt safe. She seemed to know
that they would come no farther, for a time
at least. She and her escort traveled as
rapidly as they could, and Cassy, her baby,
and the money were soon safe from pursuit.

Mr. and Mrs. Shacklett were never heard
of again by either Chadwick or Cassy Tatum.
After the war these two married and settled
in Atlanta, and one day Cassy heard that
some one had been digging the night before
on Castleberry's Hill for a box of gold that
had been buried there during the war. Chadwick laughed over the report, but Mrs. Chadwick saw no joke in it. She was combing
her son's hair at the time, and she stooped
and kissed him.

AN AMBUSCADE

I

It befell that in the first scuffle that occurred between the Federals and Confederates somewhere in the neighborhood of
Jonesboro, when Sherman was preparing to
swing loose from his base at Atlanta, Jack
Kilpatrick, commanding a squad of sharpshooters, was seriously wounded. It was all
his own fault, too. He was acting outside
his regular duties. Some excited colonel
called for a courier to send an unnecessary
message to an imaginary regiment. Kilpatrick, seeing no courier at hand, rode forward
and offered his services.

Mounted on his black mare, he made it a
point to expose himself. He could n't help it
for the life of him. It was in his blood. So,
instead of going to the rear, he galloped out
between the lines. A big Irishman on the
Federal side, whose name was O'Halloran,
leveled his rifle at the horseman. Then he

lifted his eyes from the sights and took another look at the venturesome rider.

" 'T is the young Johnny, or Oi 'm a naygur ! " he exclaimed. Then he drew a long breath. " Oi was in wan of tetchin' the traygur."

But there were other marksmen farther up the line who were not nice in such matters. There was a rattling fire of musketry. Plato, Kilpatrick's body servant, saw his young master reel in the saddle as the reins fell loose from the hand that held them — saw him reel again as the mare turned of her own accord and brought her rider whirling back to the point of departure — where he fell fainting in the arms of his own men.

Kilpatrick had taken many chances before and escaped unscathed ; but this time a bullet went tearing through his shoulder, entering obliquely, and going out at the collarbone under his chin. He was promptly carried to the rear by his men, followed by Plato, leading the black mare. A surgeon dressed the wound hastily, remarking that it was a pity the young man could n't be carried where he might get the benefit of careful nursing.

"I kin kyar 'im home, suh," said Plato. "'T ain't so mighty fur ter whar my young marster live at."

"How far?" asked the surgeon.

"In de neighborhoods er forty mile, suh," replied Plato.

The surgeon shook his head. "He can't ride horseback. But he 'll die if he 's left here."

"I wuz layin' off fer ter borry a buggy some'rs," remarked Plato.

The surgeon considered the matter. "Well, get it," he said presently, "and be quick about it. I 'll pad him up for traveling the best I can. It's one chance in ten thousand. But he 's young and strong, and the one chance is his."

Plato sprang on the black mare, and in less than half an hour had returned with a two-seated buggy.

"That 's the very thing," said the surgeon.

The rear seat was taken out, the cushions of both seats were placed on the bottom, and over these a hospital mattress and some blankets were spread. On these the wounded man was placed, and then the surgeon deftly packed a dozen layers of cotton batting under the shattered shoulder. Altogether Jack was made as comfortable as a badly wounded man could be under the circumstances.

"It is now ten o'clock," said the surgeon, looking at his watch. "You ought to have him in his own bed by six this afternoon. Kill the horse on level ground, but bring it to life in the rough places. You know what I mean."

"If he hurts that mare," young Kilpatrick declared, with as much energy as he could command, "I'll see him about it when I get well."

"I wish ter de Lord you could git up an' see me 'bout it now," remarked Plato with unction. "Kaze dish yer filly is sho got ter pick up 'er foots an' put 'em down agin dis day ef she ain't never done it befo'."

Whereupon he climbed back into the buggy, looked around at his young master to see that everything was all right, and then gave the mare the word. Though the spirited animal had been broken to harness by Plato himself, she had been under the saddle so long that this new position fretted her. She was peevish as a woman, Plato said.

The harness chafed her, the shafts worried her, and the rattle of the buggy disturbed her. She wobbled from one side of the road to the other, and went about this unusual business as awkwardly as a colt. Finally Plato stopped her in the road and cut the blinders from the bridle. This was a great relief to the high-strung creature. She could now see what was going on in front, behind, and on both sides. She gave a snort of satisfaction and settled down to work with a will that pleased the negro immensely.

Plato knew every foot of the road, having often traveled it at night, and so the only stops that were made were when the wounded man wanted water, which was to be had from the roadside springs. The journey was made without incident, and Plato, while driving rapidly, had driven so carefully that when he reached home his young master was fast asleep. And the mare, while tired, was in fine condition, only her rations of food and supply of water had to be cut short until after she had thoroughly cooled off.

Plato had hardly got out of sight of the smoke of the firing before the Confederates fell back before the great odds before them and moved aside from Sherman's path. They were not in a panic, but the pressure was too heavy, and when they retired they were compelled to leave some of their wounded in a field hospital in charge of the surgeon who had sent Jack Kilpatrick home. The enemy's skirmishers promptly moved up to the position vacated by the Confederates. Among the foremost was a big soldier who went directly to the rude shelters that had been rigged up to accommodate the wounded. He went through each and examined the faces of the wounded.

"What the devil are you after?" asked the surgeon in a tone in which curiosity and irritability were strangely mixed.

"'T is nothin' but a slip of a lad Oi 'm lookan for, sor," replied the big soldier with extraordinary politeness, considering the time and occasion.

"There are no wounded Yanks here," the surgeon explained, smiling pleasantly as he glanced at the puzzled, good-natured face of the Irishman.

"'T is a Johnny lad Oi 'm lookan for, — a b'y not bigger 'n me two fists. Oi seen um gallopin' on a black horse, an' I seen um

stagger whin a dirty blacksmith in the line
give it to um in the shoulder, — the black-
guard that he was ! "

" Oh ! " exclaimed the surgeon ; " that was
Jack Kilpatrick."

" The same, sor."

" How did you come to know Kilpatrick ? "

" Sharpshootin', sor. We had the divvle's
own time thryin' to ploog aych ither bechune
the two eyes. But we wuz chums, sor, betwixt the lines. Oi sez to meself, sez Oi,
' Oi 'll be lookan afther the lad, whin we
brush the Johnnies away, an' maybe fetch
'im a docther.' Is he clane done for, sor ? "

" He 'll need a doctor before he gets one,
I 'm thinking," remarked the surgeon, and
then he told how Jack Kilpatrick had been
sent home.

The big Irishman seemed better satisfied,
and pushed forward with the advancing lines.

II

Plato was a very wise negro, considering
his opportunities, and as he sat on the edge
of the veranda next day, near the window of
his young master's room, he shook his head
and wondered whether he had acted for the

best in coming home, — whether it would n't
have been better if his young master had
been left to take his chances with the rest in
the rude field hospitals.

For it was perfectly clear to Plato that the
home people were thoroughly demoralized.
" Ole miss," — this was Jack's mother, a
woman of as clear a head and as steady a
hand as anybody in the world, a woman of
unfailing resources, as it seemed to her friends
and dependents, — was now as nervous and
as fidgety and as helpless as any other woman. " Young mistiss," — this was Jack's
sister Flora, a girl with as much fire and
courage as are given to women, — was in a
state of collapse.   Now, if it had been somebody else's son, somebody else's brother, who
had been brought to their house wounded,
these ladies would have been entirely equal
to the occasion.   But it was Jack, of all per-
sons in the world ; it was the son, the
brother.   Courage fled like a shadow, and
all resources were dissipated as if they had
been so much vapor.

The wounded man had slept fairly well
during the night, but in the early hours of
morning his fever began to rise, as was to be

expected, and then he became delirious. He
talked and laughed and rattled away with his
jokes, — he was noted for his dry humor, —
and occasionally he paused to take breath and
groan. And all that the resourceful Mrs.
Kilpatrick and the courageous Flora could
do was to sit and gaze at each other and wipe
their overflowing eyes with trembling hands.

Plato was sent to the village, nine miles
away, for the family doctor, but he returned
with a note from that fat and amiable old
gentleman, saying that he had just been informed that the entire Federal army was
marching to surround the village, and, as for
him, he proposed to stay and defend his
family. This news went to Aunt Candace,
the plantation nurse, in short order. Plato
was her son, and he felt called on to tell her
about it.

Aunt Candace made no comment whatever.
She knocked the ashes out of her pipe, leaned
it in a corner of the fireplace, tightened up
her head handkerchief, and waddled off to
the big house. Plato knew by the way his
mammy looked that there would be a fuss,
and he hung back, pretending that he had
some business at the horse lot.

" Whar you gwine ? " asked Aunt Candace, seeing he was not coming.

" I 'm des gwine "—

" Youer des gwine 'long wid me, dat 's whar you des gwine.   An' you better come on.   Ef I lay my han' on you, you 'll feel it, mon."

"Yassum, I 'm comin'," replied Plato.   He was very polite when he knew his mammy had her dander up.

Aunt Candace marched into the big house with an air of proprietorship.

" Wharbouts is dat chile ? " she asked in a tone that a stranger would have described as vicious.

" He 's in here, Candace," replied Mrs. Kilpatrick gently.

Candace went into the room and stood by the bedside.   The weather was chilly, and she placed her cold hand on Jack's burning brow.   Instantly he stopped talking and seemed to sleep.

" God knows, honey," she said ; " dey 'd set here an' let de green flies blow you befo' dey 'd git up out 'n der cheers an' he'p you."

Mrs. Kilpatrick and Flora forgot their grief for a moment and stared at Aunt Candace

with speechless indignation. This was just
what the old negro wanted them to do.

"Plato ! " she cried, "take de ax an' run
down ter de branch an' git me yo' double
han'ful er dogwood bark, — not de outside;
I want de skin on de inside. An' I want
some red-oak bark, — a hatfull. An' don't
you be gone long, needer. Keze ef I hafter
holler at you, I 'll jump on you an' gi' you a
frailin'. Now, ef you don't believe it, you
des try me."

But Plato did believe it, and he went hurrying off as rapidly as he used to go when he
was a boy.

"Whar dat house gal ? " asked Aunt Candace abruptly.

"I 'll call her," said Flora; but the girl
that moment appeared at the door.

"Whar you been, you lazy wench ! " cried
Aunt Candace. "Go git me a pan er col'
water an' a clean towel; I don't keer ef it 's
a rag, ef it 's a clean rag." Then she turned
her attention to Jack. "God knows, honey,
ef you can't git nobody else ter do nothin'
fer you, ol' Candace 'll do it. She 's nussed
you befo' an' she 'll do it again."

Aunt Candace's words and manner were

calculated and intended to exasperate her old mistress and her young mistress.

"If you think I intend to submit to your impudence"— Mrs. Kilpatrick began with as much dignity as she could command under the circumstances. But Aunt Candace was equal to the emergency. Before her mistress could say what she intended, the old negress rose from the bedside, her eyes blazing with wrath.

"Whose imperdence? Whose imperdence? Ef I felt dat away, I 'd 'a' sot down yander an' nussed my own sickness an' let dis chile die. He 's yo' chile; he ain't none er mine; an' yit youer settin' dar hol'in yo' han's an' wipin' yo' eyes, whiles de fever fair bu'nin' 'im up.

"He ain't none er my chile, yit ef he ain't got none er my blood in 'im, it 's kaze nigger milk don't turn to blood. I don't keer what you say; I don't keer what you do; you can't skeer me, an' you can't drive me. I 'll see you bofe in torment, an' go dar myself befo' I 'll set down an' see Jack Kilpatrick lay dar an die! You hear dat, don't you? Now, go on an' do what you gwine ter do!"

Here was defiance, revolt, insurrection, and riot, and yet somehow Mrs. Kilpatrick and Flora felt relieved when the explosion came. Aunt Candace was very much in earnest, but it needed something of the kind to rouse mother and daughter from the stupor of helpless grief. They began to move about and set things to rights, and in a little while all their faculties came back to them. The house girl returned with cold water and a towel, and Aunt Candace, entirely recovered from her outburst of anger, said to Flora : —

" Ef you want ter do sump'n, honey, set on de side er de bed here an' fol' dis towel up an' dip it in de water an' wring it out an' lay it on yo' brer's forrerd. Hol' yo' han' on it, an' soon ez you feel it gittin' warm, dip it in de water an' wring it out an' put it back agin. An' make dat gal change de water off an' on."

With that Aunt Candace waddled out into the kitchen, where she busied herself making preparations for the decoctions she intended to brew from the red oak and dogwood bark which Plato had been sent after.

To those in the house Plato seemed to be making a good long stay at the branch, but

Plato was doing the best he could. He had so much confidence in his mammy's skill and experience, and was so anxious in behalf of his young master, that he took pains in selecting the trees from which he was to chop the bark. And then he was very particular as to the quality of the bark; and, in order that there might be no mistake about it, he chipped off a larger supply than was necessary. This took time, and when he was ready to start back to the big house he heard his mammy calling him, and there was a certain vital emphasis in her remarks that caused him to return in a run.

In fact, Aunt Candace had infused new energy into everybody about the place. The little negroes that usually swarmed about the yard prudently went to play in the barn, but they were careful not to make a noise that would prevent them from hearing her voice if Aunt Candace should chance to want one of them to run on an errand. The plantation medicine chest was ransacked in search of something, Mrs. Kilpatrick and her daughter knew not what. At any rate the search was a relief. They no longer sat supinely in the midst of their grief. They made little journeys to the kitchen, where Aunt Candace was brewing her simples, and she watched them out of the corner of her eye.

" S'posen he'd 'a' got kilt dead," she re-remarked; " what'd you 'a' done den? Better go 'long an' set down an' nuss yo'se'ves. I'll nuss Jack Kilpatrick. An' 't won't be de fust time I've nuss'd 'im all by myse'f needer."

Scolding and domineering, Aunt Candace went ahead with her brewing, and in a little while had a crock of dogwood-bark tea ready, as well as a red-oak bark poultice. Her remedies were simple, but she had the greatest faith in them. She applied the poultice to the wound on the shattered collar-bone, and compelled Jack to drink a tumbler-ful of the dogwood-bark tea. The dose was a heroic one, and bitter in proportion. To a certain extent both remedies were efficacious. The poultice was a cooling astringent, and the tea allayed the fever, — for somewhere in the dogwood-tree, between root and blossom, there lies the active principle of quinine. Jack fell into a deep sleep, from which he was only aroused by one of those remarkable events that could have occurred in no country but the American republic.

III

When Plato started back to the house from the spring branch, where he had been chopping the red-oak and dogwood bark, he was in such a hurry that he forgot his axe, and when he wanted it again, a few hours afterwards, he hunted all over the yard for it, until he suddenly remembered where he had left it. He started after it, but as he was going down the spring branch he heard a clatter in the road to the left, and, looking in that direction, saw two Federal cavalrymen galloping by.

"Ah-yi!" he exclaimed, as if by that means he could find vent for surprise, and slipped behind a tree. The day was raw and drizzly, and there was no movement on the plantation. The negroes were in their cabins, the horses were in their stable, the mules were standing quietly under the long shed in the lot, and even the sheep that were in the ginhouse pasture were huddled together under shelter, nibbling at a pile of waste cotton seed. The riders were couriers, and Plato, observing them, saw that they did not pursue the road to the village, but turned off squarely to the right. For Sherman had already begun his famous march to the sea. He had begun it, indeed, before the little skirmish in which Jack Kilpatrick had been wounded, and, though Plato had no knowledge of the fact, he traveled with his young master for fifteen miles between the parallel lines of the advancing army, Slocum's corps being one of the lines and Howard's corps another.

Ignorant of this fact, Plato was very much surprised to see the Federals riding by. "Dey er pursuin' right on atter us," he remarked aloud. "A little mo' en' dey 'd 'a' cotch us, sho. An' dey may ketch us yit. Kaze Marse Jack can't hide out, an' I know mighty well I ain't gwine nowhar whiles Marse Jack got ter stay." He turned back and went to the big house, but once there he remembered his axe and started after it again.

He found it where he had left it. He picked it up and flung it across his shoulder. As he raised his head he saw a big Federal soldier sitting on a horse fifty yards away, watching him intently. "Name er Gawd!" he exclaimed. He stared at the soldier, undecided whether to run or to stand where he was. Then he saw the soldier beckoning to him, and he made a great pretense of hurrying forward.

" 'T is the name of the place Oi 'm afther," said the soldier.

" Suh?" exclaimed Plato.

" Who lives in the house ferninst us?"

" Ole Miss an' Miss Floe," replied Plato.

" Ah, to the divvle wit' ye!" exclaimed the soldier impatiently. " 'T is the name Oi 'm axin' ye."

" Dis de Kilpatrick place, suh."

" Where 's the wounded Johnny?"

" Who? Marse Jack?" inquired Plato cautiously. " What make you ax dat? Marse Jack ain't never hurted you, is he?"

" Is he killt intirely?" the soldier persisted, misled by the serious aspect of the negro's countenance.

" How you know he been hurted?" Plato asked.

" Oi seen 'im whin the ball pasted 'im," replied the soldier, with a careless toss of his head. " Where 've ye tuck 'im?"

" What you gwine do wid 'im when you fin' 'im? You ain't gwine ter take 'im ter prison ner nothin' er dat kin', is you?"

" Listen at the gab av 'im!" exclaimed

the soldier impatiently. " Is the Johnny dead ? "

" Who ? Marse Jack ? No, suh. He hurted mighty bad, but he ain't daid yit. Ain't you one er dem ar gentermens what I seed tradin' wid Marse Jack an' de yuthers out dar twix de camps ? "

" Upon me soul, ye 're a long time makin' that out. Oi 'm that same peddler."

Plato's honest face broadened into a grin. " Marse Jack up dar at de house," he said in a confidential tone. " Ef his min' done come back I speck he 'd be mo' dan glad ter see you. But I 'm skeer'd ter kyar' you up dar, kaze I dunner what ole Miss, an' Miss Floe, an' mammy 'll say."

" Trust me for that same," remarked the soldier. " Take me down this fince, will ye, an' tell 'em at the house that private O'Halloran, av the sharpshooters, has taken the liberty for to call on the lad."

The negro proceeded to make a gap in the worm fence, remarking as he did so : " I be bless' ef I don't b'lieve dat ar nag what you er settin' on is Marse 'Lisha Perryman's saddle-hoss."

" Like as not," said private O'Halloran calmly.

" Mon! won't he rip an' r'ar when he miss dat ar hoss? Ef 't wuz me, an' I had tooken dat ar hoss, I 'd be gallopin' out'n de county by dis time. Kaze Marse 'Lisha is de mos' servigrous white man in deze parts. He mighty nigh ez servigrous ez ol' marster use ter be in his primy days. I 'm tellin' you de naked trufe, mon! "

Private O'Halloran laughed by way of reply, as he rode through the gap Plato had made in the fence.

" Oi 'll go up an' put me two eyes on 'im," said O'Halloran, as he turned his horse's head towards the house, " an' see the look av 'im be the toime the Twintieth Army Corps comes trudgin' by."

" Yasser," replied Plato, taking another critical view of the steed the big Irishman was riding. Then he laughed.

" Fwhat 's the joke?" inquired O'Halloran.

" 'T ain't no joke ef you 'll hear my horn," said Plato. " I wuz des thinkin' how Marse 'Lisha Perryman gwine ter cut up when he fin' out his saddle-hoss been rid off. I dun- ner whever he 'll kill a Yankee er a nigger, er whever he 'll go out an' shoot a steer. He the most servigrous man *I* ever see, an' he sho did like dat ar hoss. You er de onliest white man what been straddle un 'im ceppin' Marse 'Lisha. I ain't gwine to be nowhars 'roun' when he come huntin' dat hoss."

The horse evidently knew all about the Kilpatrick place, for he went directly to the hitching-post and there stopped. As O'Halloran dismounted, Plato took the halter strap, dexterously fastened it to the ring in the post, and promptly disappeared. He evidently had no idea of being made an interested party in the scene that he supposed would take place when the big Irishman loomed up before the astonished gaze of his mistress and her daughter.

But the scene he anticipated did not occur. It is the unexpected that happens, and it happened in this instance. O'Halloran went to the door that Plato had indicated, removed his waterproof coat, shook off the shining rain mist, and laid it on a convenient bench seat. Then he took off his hat, roached back his hair, and knocked confidently at the door. He was quite a presentable figure as he stood there, considering all the circumstances. His look of expectation had a genial smile for its basis, and there was a large spark of humor glistening in his fine black eyes.

It chanced that Aunt Candace came to the door in response to the summons. She opened it wide with a frown on her face, but when she saw the Federal soldier looming up she threw up her hands with a loud cry.

" My Gawd ! Dey got us ! Dey got us ! " Then recovering herself somewhat, she planted herself in the doorway. " G'way fum here ! G'way fum here, I tell you ! Dey ain't nobody on de place but wimmen an' childern, nohow ! Go on off, man ! Don't you hear me ? "

" Aisy, aisy ! Will ye be aisy, now ? " said O'Halloran, when he could get in a word edgewise. " Where's the lady ? "

" What you want wid her ? " cried Aunt Candace. " G'way fum here ! " She stood like a tiger at bay.

At that moment Mrs. Kilpatrick appeared in the hallway. The sight of the soldier in blue paralyzed all her faculties except memory of the fact that her son lay wounded not forty feet away. Making a supreme effort at self-control, she stood before the big Irishman with white face and clasped hands. Something in her attitude touched the soldier. He bent low before her.

"No harm to you, mum, beggin' your pardon. Oi says to a nagur in passin', 'Whose iligant place is this?' 'The Kilpathrick place,' says he. 'Upon me sowl,' says Oi, ''t will be no harm for to call in an' see the b'y.' How is he, mum?"

"Do you know my son?" Her voice was so harsh and strained that she hardly recognized it. The big Irishman had no need to answer. The door through which the lady had entered the hall was thrown open, and a weak voice called out: —

"If that is O'Halloran, let him come in."

"'T is that same," replied the Federal soldier with a smile. But he waited for the lady to lead the way, and then followed her. On the bed lay Jack Kilpatrick, and near the fireplace stood his sister Flora, statuesque and scornful. O'Halloran bowed to her as politely as he knew how, but her lip curled disdainfully. An expression of perplexity crept into the honest, smiling face of the Irishman; but this quickly changed into one of genuine pleasure when he caught sight of young Kilpatrick's face.

"Why, ye 're as snug as a bug in a rug!" exclaimed O'Halloran cheerily. "Which paw

shall Oi squeeze? The lift? Well, 't is
nearest the gizzard. Ah! but 't was a close
shave ye had, me b'y. Oi seen ye comin'
betwixt the lines, an' says Oi, ' Fwhat the
divvle ails the lad?' 'T was the very word
Oi said. Oi seen ye roll in the saddle, an'
thin Oi put me rifle to me shoulder. Says
Oi, ' If the nag runs wild an' the lad falls
an' his fut hangs, Oi'll fetch the craycher
down.' But divvle a run — beggin' pardin
of the ladies. An' so ye're here, me b'y,
more worried than hurt!"

Jack Kilpatrick was really glad to see his
friend, the enemy, and said so as heartily as
he could. O'Halloran drew a chair by the
bed, and, in the midst of his talk, which was
as cheerful as he could make it, studied the
young Confederate's condition. He made the
wounded man fill his lungs with air several
times, and placed his ear close to the expand-
ing chest. Then he sat twirling his thumbs
and looking at the bed-quilt, which was home-
made and of a curious pattern. Finally he
turned to Mrs. Kilpatrick with a more serious air than he had yet displayed.

"He wants a surgeon, mum. 'T is an
aisy case wit' a surgeon standin' 'roun' an'

puckerin' his forrerd; Oi 've seen 'em do 't many 's the toime. Wan surgeon in the nick av toime is like to do more good than forty docthers at a funer'l."

" We can get no surgeon; that is out of the question," said the lady curtly and positively.

Once more O'Halloran fell to studying the pattern of the quilt. He even went so far as to count the pieces in one of the figures. Flora and her mother resented this as a piece of unnecessary impertinence, and moved restlessly about the room.

" That is what they call the broken stove lid," explained Jack, seeing the big Irishman's apparent interest in the quilt pattern.

" Now is that so?" said O'Halloran. " Upon me sowl it looks as if the whole chimley had tumbled down on top av it. Faith! Oi have it!" he exclaimed with a laugh. " Oi 'll rope in the chap that drinched me the same as if Oi was a sick horse. 'T will be somethin' traymenjous, upon me sowl! He 's a bloomin' pillmaker from wistern New York."

The big Irishman paused and hugged himself with his Samson-like arms as he bent over with laughter.

" Bedad, 't will be the joke of the day ! " he exclaimed. " 'T is all laid out as plain as the nose on me face. D' ye mind this now, me b'y : 'T is no Kilpatrick ye are, for ye 've thried to kill me many's the odd time. Ye 're from Hornellsville, — mind that now ; upon me sowl, 't is the nub av the whole bloomin' business."

" Where 's Hornellsville ? " asked Jack.

" In York State, bedad. Ye 're Cap'n Jarvis, av Hornellsville. Ye know the Finches an' the Purvises, but ye 're too wake for to argy till he fixes ye foine an' doses ye."

Mrs. Kilpatrick uttered a protest that would have been indignant, but for her apprehensions in regard to Jack.

" He 's a darlin' of a surgeon, mum," explained O'Halloran. " 'T is a business he knows loike a book. Nayther is he bad lookin'. The loikes av him is hard for to come up wit' in the Twintieth Army Corps — clane as a pache an' smilin' as a basket av chips. 'T will be no harm to him for to fix an' dose ye. Two days av fixin' will put ye right, an' then he kin ketch his rijmint."

" Scoop him up and fetch him in," said Jack, and to this the mother and daughter made no serious objection, bitter as their prejudices were.

Among his own belongings O'Halloran was carrying the haversack of his captain, in which he knew there was a coat. This he took out, carried into the house, and hung on the back of a chair near Jack's bed. Then he mounted his horse and rode to the big gate, where he knew the Twentieth Corps would shortly pass.

He was just in time, too, for a party of foragers was engaged in gathering up the horses, mules, and cattle that were on the place. These he dispersed in a twinkling, by explaining that the ladies of the house were engaged in caring for a Federal captain, who had been compelled by his wounds to seek refuge there. This explanation O'Halloran made to all the would-be foragers who came that way, with the result that the stock on the place remained unmolested. In a little while the Twentieth Army Corps began to march by, and many an acquaintance saluted the big Irishman as he sat serenely on his borrowed horse near the entrance to the wide avenue. The troops going by supposed as a matter of course that he had been stationed there.

III

To Mrs. Kilpatrick and her daughter, watching this vast procession from behind the curtains of the windows, the spectacle was by no means an enchanting one. Their belief in the righteousness of the Southern cause amounted to a passion ; it was almost a part of their religion, and they prayed for its success with a fervor impossible to describe. It was a cause for which they were prepared to make any sacrifice, and it is no wonder that they watched the army go by with pallid and grief-stricken faces. Their despair would have been of a blacker hue if they had not remembered that, away off in Virginia, Robert Lee was mustering his army against the hosts that were opposing him.

The spectacle of this army in blue marching by was so strange — so impossible, in fact — that their amazement would not have been materially increased if the whole vast array had been lifted in air by a gust of wind, to dissolve and disappear in the swaying and whirling mist.

Presently they saw O'Halloran spur his horse toward the moving files, and touch his cap by way of salute. Then another horseman, after some delay, detached himself from the ranks, joined the big Irishman, and the two came up the avenue together. Mrs. Kilpatrick, by an instinct rather than an impulse of hospitality, prepared to go to the door to receive them, pausing in Jack's room to see that everything was ship-shape. As the two came up the broad, high steps, and delayed a moment on the veranda to remove their waterproofs, Flora, peeping from behind the red curtains in the parlor, saw that the surgeon was both young and stalwart. His brown hair was cut short, and the fierce curl of his mustache was relieved by a pair of gold spectacles, that gave a benign and somewhat ministerial air to features that were otherwise firm and soldier-like. He was not as tall as the Irishman, — few men in all that army were, — but he bore himself more easily and gracefully.

When O'Halloran knocked at the door, Mrs. Kilpatrick opened it without a moment's delay.

"'T is the surgeon, mum, to see the captain."

"Good morning, madam. Dr. Pruden.

The man here tells me that Captain Jarvis of a New York regiment lies wounded in this house." He held his cap in his hand, and his bearing was all that was affable and polite.

" Come in, sir," said the lady, inclining her head slightly.

He stepped into the hallway, O'Halloran following with a broad grin on his face that disappeared as by magic whenever the surgeon glanced in his direction. Mrs. Kilpatrick led the way to Jack's room, to which Flora had flitted when the knock came at the door. Dr. Pruden acknowledged her presence with a bow and then turned his attention to his patient.

" I 'm sorry to see you on your back, Captain Jarvis," he said sympathetically. " And yet, with such quarters and such nurses, I dare say you are better off than the rest of us."

" Yes — well off," replied Jack in a weak voice that was not borrowed for the occasion. In fact, the surgeon had not arrived any too soon. The wounded man had grown feebler, and his condition was not helped by an occasional fit of coughing that racked his whole body and threatened to tear his wounds open afresh.

Dr. Pruden wiped his hands on a towel that chanced to be hanging on a chair near by, and then proceeded to examine into the wounded man's condition.

" You may thank your stars, young man," he said after a while, " that these ladies were charitable enough to forget the color of your coat there and give you the shelter and the care and attention that were absolutely necessary."

The note of unaffected gratitude in the young surgeon's voice was so simple and genuine that Flora felt a momentary pang of regret that he should have been made the victim of the Irishman's crafty scheme. But the pang was only momentary ; for what the Irishman did he had done for Jack's sake, and that was a sufficient excuse. And yet the knowledge that the surgeon had been deceived made both mother and daughter more considerate in their demeanor — more genial in their attitude — than they could otherwise have been.

O'Halloran stood watching the ladies and the surgeon with a quizzical expression, keeping his hand in the neighborhood of his mouth to screen his smiles. Finally he seemed to discover that he could not safely remain and maintain his dignity.

"Oi 'll be goin', captain," he said to Jack. "The ladies 'll look afther yure belongin's. Termorrer whin the rear guard comes by maybe ye 'll be well enough for to be lifted in the ambulance I brung ye in."

"What amuses you?" inquired the surgeon, seeing the Irishman trying to suppress a laugh.

"Upon me word, sor, Oi was thinkin' av the drinch ye give me whin Oi was ailin'. Says Oi: 'Ef 't is as bitter to the captain here as 't was to me, he 'll be on his feet in a jiffy.'"

Whereupon O'Halloran turned on his heel and went out, closing the door gently after him.

Dr. Pruden went to work with a will. He smiled at the big poultice that Aunt Candace had applied to the wound made by the bullet in its exit, but found that the inflammation had been controlled by it. Then with the aid of the fair Flora, who offered her assistance, he proceeded to deal with the wound on the shoulder, which he found to be in a much more serious condition.

He had no need to probe the wound, but saw at once that, while it was a painful and dangerous hurt, no vital part had been touched. To Flora, who asked many questions in a tone of unaffected concern, he explained that the cough was caused by inflammation of the lung tissues, which would pass away as the wound healed. He said that it would be necessary for him to give the wound only one more dressing, which could be done the next morning, if the ladies could put up with his presence for that length of time; or, if they preferred, he could call an ambulance and have the wounded man carried along with the army, though that would be both awkward and dangerous. The condition of the lungs, he said, was such that the slightest exposure might result in pleurisy or pneumonia.

Both the ladies protested so earnestly against the removal of the wounded man that Dr. Pruden inwardly abused himself for having formed the idea that Southern women had violent prejudices against the Yankees. During the discussion Aunt Candace had come in. She knew nothing of the scheme that O'Halloran had employed to secure the services of a surgeon for her young master. When she heard the suggestion that Jack could be placed in an ambulance and carried along with the army she pricked up her ears.

" Which army you gwine take him 'long wid? De Yankee army?" she exclaimed. " Huh! ef you do you'll hafter kyar' me wid 'im."

" Are you wounded, too?" Dr. Pruden inquired humorously.

" No, I ain't; but I won't answer fer dem what try ter take dat boy fum und' dis roof." She turned and stared at her mistress and young mistress as if she had never seen them before. Then she raised her fat arms above her head and allowed them to drop helplessly by her side, muttering, " Gawd knows, you ain't no mo' de same folks dan ef you'd 'a' been moulded outer new dirt."

And after that she watched Mrs. Kilpatrick and Flora closely, and listened intently to every word they said, and shook her head, and muttered to herself. To Plato she made haste to give out her version of the puzzle that the situation presented.

" You kin talk much ez you please 'bout

de Kilpatrick blood, but hit done run'd out."

"How come?" Plato inquired.

"Ain't you got no eyes in yo' haid? Can't you see what gwine on right spang und' yo' nose? Ef mistiss an' Miss Floe ain't done gone ravin' 'stracted, den I done los' what little min' I had. You make me b'lieve dat ole miss 'd set up dar in de house an' let any Yankee dat's ever been born'd talk 'bout takin 'yo' Marse Jack off wid de army, an' dat, too, when he layin' dar flat er his back wid a hole thoo 'im dat you kin mighty nigh run yo' han' in? Uh-uh! uh-uh! you nee' 'n' tell me! Ole miss would a riz up an' slew'd 'im — dat what she'd 'a' done."

Plato scratched his head and ruminated over the puzzle.

"Did mistiss an' young mistiss bofe say dey want Marse Jack tuck off wid de army des like he is?"

"Dee ain't say it right out in black an' white, but dey sot dar an' let dat ar Yankee talk 'bout it widout so much ez battin' der eyes. An' Miss Floe, — *she* sot dar an' make out she want ter laugh. I could 'a' slapped

her, an' little mo' an' I'd 'a' done it, too."
Aunt Candace's anger was almost venomous.

"Well, I tell you now," responded Plato,
"I seed some mighty quare doin's up yander
endurin' de war." He nodded his head towards Atlanta. "Dey wuz one time when a
river run'd right 'twixt de lines, an' it got so
dat mighty nigh eve'y day de Yankees an' our
boys 'd go in washin' an' play in de water
dar des like a passel er chillun. Marse Jack
wuz in dar eve'y chance he got, an' him an'
dat ar big Yankee what wuz in de house —
he up yander watchin' de stock right now —
dey 'd git ter projickin' an' tryin' ter duck one
an'er, an' I tuck notice dat de big Yankee
allers let Marse Jack do de duckin'. 'Fo' dat,
dey 'd meet twixt de lines when dey wa'n't no
rumpus gwine on, an' dey 'd swap an' trade
an' laugh an' talk an' take on like dey been
raised wid one an'er."

"Huh! Much he look like bein' raised
wid Marse Jack!" snorted Aunt Candace.

"Maybe he de one what want ter take
Marse Jack off wid de army," suggested
Plato, pursuing the subject. "Ef he is you
nee' n' ter let dat worry you, kaze he 'll be
safe wid dat big Yankee, sho."

" No, he won't needer ! " exclaimed Aunt Candace.

" How come ? " asked her son.

" Kaze he ain't gwine, dat's how come ! "

Plato shook his head significantly, as if his mammy's decision settled the whole matter. Still he was puzzled at the alleged willingness of his mistress and Miss Floe to allow Jack to be carried off by the Yankee army.

Dr. Pruden, the surgeon, was also worried with a problem he could not fathom, and puzzled by a great many things he could not understand. The problem was not very serious, as matters go in time of war, but it was very interesting. Why should these Southern ladies, who, his instinct told him, had very bitter prejudices against the Northern people, and especially against the Union soldiers, betray such interest in Captain Jarvis of New York ? And not interest only, but genuine solicitude, that they sought in vain to conceal ? The surgeon was a young man, not more than twenty-five or thirty years old, but he had knocked about a good deal, and, as he said to himself, he was no fool. In fact, he had a pretty good knowledge of human nature, and a reasonably quick eye for " symptoms."

He cared nothing whatever for such prejudices as the ladies surely had. They were
natural and inevitable. They belonged to
the order of things. They were to be expected. It was their absence in the case of
Captain Jarvis that worried him. He could
see that the seprejudices were in full bloom,
so far as he was concerned, and that his presence was tolerated only because he could be
of some possible service to Jarvis.

While dressing Jack's wounded shoulder,
which, under the circumstances, was a tedious
operation, Dr. Pruden noticed what beautiful
hands Flora had. She was helping him the
best she could, and in that way her hands
were very much in evidence. He observed,
too, that these beautiful hands had a knack
of stroking the wounded man's hair, and once
he saw such an unmistakable caress expressed
in the pressure of the fingers that he glanced
quickly at her face. The surgeon's glance
was so frankly inquisitive that Flora blushed
in spite of herself; and it was the rosiest of
blushes, too, for she instinctively knew that
the man suspected her to be desperately in
love with a Yankee captain after the acquaintance of only a few hours. Then she

was angry because she blushed, and was so
disturbed and distressed withal that Dr. Pruden, discovering these signs of mental per-
turbation, was vexed with himself for being
the involuntary cause of it.

But he was none the less satisfied that he
had surprised and discovered the young woman's secret; and he wondered that it should
be so, weaving with his wonderment the pret-
tiest little romance imaginable. It was such
a queer little romance, too, that he could not
repress a smile as he bent over Jack's broken
shoulder and deftly applied the bandages.
Flora saw the smile and with a woman's
intuition read its meaning. Whereupon,
with ready tact, she transferred her anger.
She made the surgeon, instead of herself, the
object of it, so that when Jack's wounds
had been properly dressed, Dr. Pruden found
that the young lady's haughtiness toward
him was in significant contrast to the tender
solicitude she felt for the supposed Captain
Jarvis.

The surgeon paid small attention to this,
as he told himself, and yet it was not a pleasant. experience. The careful way in which
Flora avoided his glances gave him an oppor-

tunity to study her face, and the more he
studied it the more it impressed him. He
thought to himself with a sigh that Jarvis
would be a lucky fellow should his little romance turn out happily.

He would have been glad to talk with
Jarvis, but that was out of the question now;
to-morrow would do as well. So he sat in
the library and smoked his pipe, finding
some very good tobacco in an old cigar-box
on the table, and heard the Twentieth Army
Corps go tramping by, the noise the troops
made harmonizing well with the dull roar of
the November wind as its gusts went through
the tree-tops outside. Strangely enough, it
all seemed to emanate from the flames in the
fireplace. After a while, he leaned his head
against the cushion on the back of his chair
and closed his eyes.

When he opened them again night was
falling. On one side of the fireplace Plato
sat prone on the floor. On the other side
sat O'Halloran. Plato was nodding, his head
falling from side to side. The big Irishman
was leaning forward, gazing into the fire, his
elbows on his knees and his chin on his
hands.

" What time is it ? " the surgeon asked.

" 'T is long past yure dinner hour, sor," replied O'Halloran, straightening himself.

Plato aroused himself, drew a pine knot from some place of concealment, and threw it on the glowing bank of coals.

" Mistiss say yo' vittles wuz ter be kep' warm in de dinin'-room, suh," said Plato. " Dey ringded de dinner bell all 'roun' you, an' mistiss come in ter ax you ter have some dinner, but she 'low you wuz sleepin' so soun' she di'n' want ter wake you up."

" Well," replied Dr. Pruden, " a bite of something would n't hurt, that 's a fact. I 'll go in and see how Jarvis is, while you have it fixed for me."

A candle in the hall showed the surgeon the way to his patient's room. There was no need for the surgeon to go there, for Jack was still asleep. The candle had been placed on the floor to keep the light from shining in the wounded man's face, and the room was darker on that account ; but it was not too dark for the surgeon to see as he entered the room that Flora was sitting over against the bed. And, if he was not mistaken, she had been holding Jarvis's hand, for he saw her make a quick movement as he entered, and the patient stirred slightly. This seemed to confirm all his inferences, and increased his wonder that such a complication could arise here in the very heart of rebeldom, as it were. He seated himself by the bed and laid his hand on the patient's forehead.

"How long have you been awake, Jarvis?" he asked presently.

"Not long," replied Jack. "How did you know I was awake?"

"Why, I heard you swallow," replied Dr. Pruden.

Jack tried to laugh, but he found that his chest was very sore, and the laugh ended in a groan.

"Don't try to laugh, and don't talk," said the surgeon, in a professional tone, "You are out of danger now, and you ought to be forever grateful to your nurse."

"You mean old Aunt Candace?" suggested Jack, with dry humor.

Dr. Pruden stared at his patient with wide open eyes. "I'm surprised at you, Jarvis," he said, in a tone of rebuke. "I mean Miss Kilpatrick, of course. Go to sleep now; your head is still in a flighty condition."

Whereupon Dr. Pruden went from the room into the library again. Soon he was summoned to the dining-room, where, contrary to his expectations, he found Mrs. Kilpatrick presiding at the table. Naturally they fell into a conversation about the war, but both restrained their prejudices, and the talk turned out to be so pleasant — though there were critical moments that had to be bridged over with silence — that Dr. Pruden thought he had never seen a more charming or a more gracious hostess.

IV

At early dawn the next morning, O'Halloran, piloted by Plato, went into Jack's room, took his captain's coat from the back of the chair where he had placed it, folded it up neatly and tucked it under his waterproof. Jack stirred uneasily and then awoke. Plato and the Irishman looked like huge shadows. Aunt Candace, seated in a rocking-chair before the fireplace, snored as gently as she could under the circumstances.

"What is the matter?" asked Jack. He felt so much better that he wanted to sit up in bed, but found that his shoulder was too sore.

" 'T is but a whim of mine for to come an' kiss me hand to ye, me b'y. The naygur here says that a squad av Johnnies wint past this half hour. So Oi says to a man Oi know, ' O'Halloran, we 'll while away the toime with a canter acrost the country.' The naygur knows the way, me b'y, an' 't will take 'im not more 'n a hour for to put me betwixt the trottin' Johnnies an' the stragglers."

" What about the other fellow, — this doctor ? " asked Jack.

" Oi misdoubt but he 'll board along wid ye," remarked the big Irishman with a broad grin. " 'T will be a nate way fer to pay 'im his fay, Oi dunno ! Molly ! but Oi hould the taste o' his phaysic in me goozle down to this blissed day an' hour ! "

He patted Jack affectionately on the head, and with " God bless you, me b'y ! " went from the room, followed by Plato.

Outside the house Plato turned to the big Irishman. " Boss, you gwine ter walk ? "

" An' lade me horse ? 'T is not in me bones to do that same."

" You — you — you sholy ain't gwine ter take Marse 'Lisha Perryman's saddle-hoss, is you, boss ? "

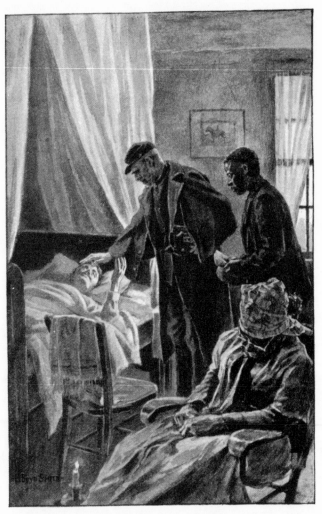

"GOD BLESS YOU, ME B'Y!"

"Not in the laste, ye booger. 'T is the horse that will be takin' me."

"Well, de Lawd knows I don't want ter be nowhars 'roun' in deze diggins when Marse 'Lisha fin' out dat dat horse done been took an' tooken."

Plato said nothing more, but he shook his head significantly many times, while he was helping the big Irishman saddle Mr. Perryman's favorite horse. In a short while they were on their way, and, by traveling along the plantation by-ways — paths known to the negroes and to the cattle — O'Halloran soon came up with the rear guard of the Twentieth Army Corps.

Meanwhile, after breakfast, Surgeon Pruden dressed Jack's wound again and then began to make his preparations to rejoin the army. He called for the big Irishman, and was a little uneasy when he learned that O'Halloran had left before sunrise. Nevertheless, he went on with his preparations, and was ready to take his departure, waiting only for Mrs. Kilpatrick to come into the library where he stood with Flora to tell them farewell together, when he heard the clatter of hoofs on the graveled avenue. Looking from the win-

dow he saw a squad of Confederate cavalrymen galloping toward the house. At their
head rode a man in citizen's clothes, — a man
past middle age, but with a fierce military air.
Flora saw them at the same moment, and the
color left her cheek. She knew the man in
citizen's clothes for Mr. Perryman, their
neighbor, who had a great reputation for
ferocity in that section. Mr. Perryman had
missed his horse, and had been told by some
of his negroes that the man who had taken
him had stopped over night at the Kilpatrick
place. He was a widower who had been
casting fond eyes on Flora for some time, and
now thought to render her an important service and give her cause for lively gratitude by
ridding her of the presence of the Yankee soldier, if he were still in possession of the house,
or, if he had escaped, to attract her admiration
by leading the Confederates to her rescue.

Surgeon Pruden drummed a brief tattoo on
the windowpane, and then threw back his
head with a contemptuous laugh.

"I see!" he exclaimed. "My comrade
and myself have been drawn into an ambuscade. I thank you, Miss Kilpatrick, for this
revelation of Southern hospitality."

"Into an ambuscade!" cried Flora, her color returning.

"Why, certainly! into a trap! I have but one favor to ask of you, Miss Kilpatrick. Let them take me and leave my comrade. Surely he can do you no harm!"

"They will not take you," she said with a calmness he thought assumed.

"Will they not? It will be their fault then. If I could escape by raising my finger — so — I would scorn to do it. Not if I knew they would furnish you a spectacle by hanging me to the nearest tree."

She looked at him so hard, and such a singular light blazed in her eyes that he could not fathom her thoughts.

"What do you take me for?" she cried.

"For a Southern lady loyal to her friends," he replied, in a tone bitingly sarcastic. "Call them in! But stay — you shall be spared that trouble. I will go to them. I ask only that my comrade be not disturbed."

He started for the door, but she was before him. She reached it just as Mr. Perryman knocked, and opened it at once.

"Good morning, Mr. Perryman," said Flora.

Mr. Perryman took off his hat and was in the act of politely responding to the salute, as was his habit, when, glancing over Flora's shoulder, he saw Surgeon Pruden staring serenely at him through gold spectacles. Thus, instead of saying "Good morning, Miss Flora; I hope you are well this morning," as was his habit, Mr. Perryman cried out : —

" There's that scoundrel now! Surround the house, men! Look to the windows! I'll take care of the door! Watch the side window yonder!"

Mr. Perryman was so far carried away by excitement that he failed to hear Flora's voice, which called out to him sharply once or twice. He was somewhat cooled, however, when he saw the surgeon drawing on a pair of heavy worsted gloves instead of trying to escape. And at last Flora got his ear.

" Mr. Perryman, this gentleman is our guest. Dr. Pruden, this is our good neighbor, Mr. Perryman. Under the circumstances, his excitement is excusable."

The surgeon acknowledged his new acquaintance with a bow, but Mr. Perryman's surprise gave him no opportunity to respond.

"Why, my God! the man's a Yankee! Your guest! I know you are mistaken. Why, he's the fellow that stole my horse!"

"My horse is in the stable," remarked the surgeon coolly, yet reddening a little under the charge. "If he is yours, you can have him."

"I know how it is, Miss Flora," Mr. Perryman insisted. "You're a woman, and you don't want to see this Yankee dealt with."

"I'm a woman, Mr. Perryman; but I am beginning to believe you are not as much of a man as I once thought you were. This gentleman has saved my brother's life. He is more than our guest; he is our benefactor."

Mr. Perryman stood dumbfounded. As the phrase goes, his comb fell. His mustachios ceased to bristle. The surgeon on his side was as much surprised as Mr. Perryman. He turned to Flora with a puzzled expression on his face — and the look he gave her was sufficient to prevent Mr. Perryman from throwing away his suspicions.

"Do you mean Jack?"

"Certainly, Mr. Perryman. I have no brother but Jack."

" When and where did you save Jack Kilpatrick's life?" asked Mr. Perryman, turning
to Dr. Pruden abruptly.

" I'm sure I could n't tell you," replied
the surgeon placidly.   He was engaged in
wiping his spectacles, but turned to Flora.

" Is the wounded man your brother, Miss
Kilpatrick?"

" Certainly," she answered.

" I'm glad of it," he said simply.

" You'd better be glad!" exclaimed Mr.
Perryman.

The surgeon threw his right hand upward.
" Nonsense, man!   I'd be glad if I had to
be shot or hanged in half an hour."

" Come in and see Jack, Mr. Perryman,"
said Flora, with such a change in her voice
and attitude that both men looked at her.

Mr. Perryman stepped into the hallway,
and Flora led the way to Jack's room.

After that no explanation was necessary.
Mr. Perryman talked to Jack with tears in
his eyes, for behind his savage temper he
carried a warm heart.   He and Jack had been
companions in many a foxhunt and on many
a frolic, and there was a real friendship between the two.

Finally Mr. Perryman turned to Dr. Pruden. "I'm mighty glad to meet you, sir, and I hope you'll allow me to shake your hand. You've been caught in a trap, but I hope you'll find bigger and better bait in it than is often found in such places."

Just then there was a knock at the door. The captain of the cavalry squad wanted to know what was going on, and why the Yankee prisoner was n't brought out. The state of affairs was made known to him briefly.

"That satisfies me, I reckon, but I ain't certain that it 'll satisfy my men."

"What command do they belong to?" asked Mr. Perryman.

"Wheeler's cavalry."

"Aunt Candace! Aunt Candace!" cried Flora. "Give Wheeler's cavalry a drink of buttermilk and let them go!"

The hit was as palpable as it was daring, for the men of this command were known far and wide as the Buttermilk Rangers.

It need hardly be said that Surgeon Pruden had a very comfortable time in that neighborhood. Within the course of a few months the war was over, and he was free to go home; but in 1866 he came South and settled in Atlanta. Then, to make a long story short, he married Flora Kilpatrick. At the wedding, Mr. Perryman, irreconcilable as he was, nudged Dr. Pruden in the ribs and winked.

"What 'd I tell you about the bait in the trap?"

THE CAUSE OF THE DIFFICULTY

I

IF you are a reader of the newspapers you saw the account they printed the other day in regard to the murder of a young woman by Toog Parmalee, in the neighborhood of " Hatcher's Ford." You could n't have missed it. The night editors dished it up as a great sensation, spreading it out under startling black headlines.

The account said that two young ladies — sisters — were walking along the road, when they saw Toog Parmalee come out of the bushes with a pistol in his hand. He had been courting one of them for two or three years, and when she now saw him coming she turned and fled in the opposite direction, while the other sister, not knowing what to think or how to act, stood still. In this way she probably saved her own life, for Toog passed her by in pursuit of the flying girl, who was overtaken and shot in cold blood. These harrowing details were spread out with great particularity in the newspapers, and the verdict, made up by those who furnished the details, was that Parmalee was stark crazy.

The only fact given in the account was that Parmalee had killed his sweetheart, and this could have been made clear in much less space than a column of reading matter occupies, for Hatcher's Ford is fifty miles from the settlement where the affair occurred. That settlement is known as Hatch's Clearing, because, as Mrs. Pruett says, nobody by the name of Hatch ever lived there, or on any clearing on that side of Tray Mountain, and as for the other side — well, that was in another part of the county altogether.

So much for the first mistake; and now for the second. Was Toog Parmalee crazy? There's no need for you to take the word of an outsider on that subject, but before you make up your mind go and ask Mrs. Pruett. It is a tiresome journey, to be sure, but it is always worth the trouble to find out the truth. You may go to Clarksville from Atlanta, but at Clarksville you'll have to hire a buggy, and, although the road is a long one, it is very interesting. It would be well to take a companion with you, if your horse is skittish, for it will be necessary to open a great many big gates as you go along. All the farms are under fence in this particular region, and the gates are a necessity.

Though the road to Hatch's Clearing is a long and winding one, you can't miss your way. You turn into it suddenly and unexpectedly twelve miles from Clarksville, and after that there is no need of making inquiries, for there are no cross-roads and no "forks" to embarrass you. There's only one trouble about it. You ascend the mountain by such a gentle grade that when you reach the top you refuse to believe you are on the summit at all. This lack of belief is helped mightily by the fact that the mountain itself is such a big affair.

Presently you will hear a cowbell jingling somewhere in the distance, and ten to one you will meet a ten-year-old boy in the road, his breeches hanging by one suspender and an old wool hat flopping on the back of his head. The boy will conduct you cheerfully if not gayly along the road, and in a little while you will hear the hens cackling in Mrs. Pruett's horse lot. This will give the lad an excuse to run on ahead of you. He will exclaim, with as much energy as his plaintive voice can command: —

"Oh, Lordy! them plegged dogs is done run the ole dominicker hen off'n the nest."

Whereupon he will start to running and pretend to go to the horse lot. But it is all a pretense, for when you come in sight of the house you will see three or four, maybe a half-dozen, white-headed children on the fence watching for you, and if you have said a kind word to the boy who volunteered to be your guide, Mrs. Pruett herself will be standing on the porch, the right arm stretched across her ample bosom, so that the hand may serve as a rest for the elbow of the left arm, which is bent so that the reed stem of her beloved pipe may be held on a level with her good-humored mouth. You will have time to notice, as your horse ascends the incline that leads to the big gate, that the house is a very comfortable one for the mountains, neatly weather-boarded and compactly built, with four rooms and a " shed," which serves as a dining-room and a kitchen. Two boxwood plants stand sentinel inside the gate, and are, perhaps, the largest you have ever seen.

There is also a ragged hedge of privet, which seems to lack thrift.

Mrs. Pruett will turn first to the right and then to the left. Seeing no one but the children, she will call out, in a penetrating, but not unpleasant, voice : —

"Where on the face of the yeth is Sary's Tom?" Forth from the house will come the boy you met on the road. "Can't you move?" Mrs. Pruett will say. "Yander's the stranger a-wonderin' an' a-reck'nin' what kind of a place he's come to, an' here's ever'body a-standin' aroun' an' a-star-gazin' an'a-suckin' the'r thumbs. Will you stir 'roun', Tom, er shill I go out an' take the stranger's hoss? Ax 'im to come right in — an', here! you, Mirandy! fetch out that big rockin'-cheer!"

It is safe to say that you will enjoy everything that is set before you; you will not complain even if the meat is fried, for the atmosphere of the mountain fits the appetite to the fare. If Mrs. Pruett likes your looks you will catch her in an attitude of listening for something. Finally, you will hear a shuffling sound in one of the rooms, as if a man were moving about, and then, if it is Mrs. Pruett's "old man" — and she well

knows by the sound — she 'll lift her voice
and call out: " Jerd! what on the face of
the yeth air you doin' in there? You 'll
stumble an' break some er them things in
there thereckly. Why don't you come out
an' show yourse'f? You hain't afeard er
nothin' ner nobody, I hope."

Whereupon Mr. Pruett will come out — a
giant in height, with a slight stoop in his
shoulders and a pleasant smile on his face.
And he will give you a hearty greeting, and
his mild blue eyes will regard you so stead-
fastly that you will wonder why Mrs. Pruett
asked him if he was afraid of anybody. Later,
you will discover that this inquiry is a standing joke with his wife, for Jerd Pruett is
renowned in all that region as the most dangerous man in the mountains when his temper is aroused. Fortunately for him and his
neighbors, he has the patience of Job.

You will find on closer acquaintance with
Jerd Pruett that he is a man of considerable information in a great many directions,
and that he is possessed of a large fund of
common sense. Naturally the talk will drift
to the murder of the young woman by Toog
Parmalee. If you don't mention it, Mrs.

Pruett will, for she has her own ideas in regard to the tragedy.

"What's bred in the bone will come out in the blood," she will say. "Crazy! why Toog Parmalee wer n't no more crazy when he killt Sally Williams than Jerd there — an' much he looks like bein' crazy!"

And then Mrs. Pruett will hark back to old times, and tell a story that has some curious points of interest. It is a long story the way she tells it, but it will bear condensation.

It was in the sixties, as time goes, when noxious influences had culminated in war in this vast nursery of manhood, the American republic. Some of us have already forgotten what the bother was about, never having had very clear ideas as to the occasion of so much desperation. Nevertheless it will be a long time before some of the details and developments are wiped from our memories. As good luck would have it, Tray Mountain was out of the line of march, so to speak. The great trouble encircled it, to be sure, but the noxious vapors were thinner here than elsewhere, so that Tray elbowed his way skyward in perfect peace and security and would hardly have known that the war was going on but for one event which came like an explosion on the quiet neighborhood. The echo of the explosion, Mrs. Pruett claims, was not heard until Toog Parmalee's pistol went off close to his sweetheart's bosom — and that was only the other day.

Now, the war began gently enough and went along easily enough so far as Tray Mountain was concerned. Its sunsets were not more golden nor its wonderful dawns rosier on that account. The thunders that shook Manassas, and Malvern Hill, and Gettysburg, gave forth no sounds in the crags of Tray. If the truth must be told, there are no crags nearer than those of Yonah, or those which lift up and form the chasm of Tallulah, for Tray is a commonplace, drowsy old mountain, and it does nothing but sit warming its sway-back in the sun or cooling it in the rain.

But Tray Mountain had one attraction, if no other, and the name of this attraction was Loorany Parmalee. In a moment of high good humor, Mrs. Pruett remarked that " ef Jerd had any fault in the world it was in bein' too good." Paraphrase this tender tribute, and it would fit Loorany Parmalee to a T. If she had any fault it was in being too handsome. But beauty, it must be borne in mind, is a relative term when you employ it in a descriptive sense. No doubt Loorany would have cut a very unfashionable figure in a group of beautiful girls dressed according to the demands of fashion. She lacked the high color and the lines that are produced by contact with refining influences; but on the mountain, in her own neighborhood, she was a cut or a cut and a half above any of the rest of the girls. Her eyes were black as coals, and latent heat sparkled in their depths. Her features were regular, and yet a little hard, her under-lip being a trifle too thin, but she had the sweetest smile and the whitest teeth ever seen on Tray Mountain. Her figure — well, her figure was what nature made it, and that wise old lady knows how to fashion things when she's let alone and has the right kind of material to work on. She had the leisure as well as the material in Loorany's case, and the result was that in form and in grace the girl belonged to the age that we see in some of the Grecian marbles.

In the right light, and in the foreground

of a boulder, with a roguish streak of sunshine whipping across her black hair, her sunbonnet hanging between her shoulders, her right hand lifted as if listening, her lips half parted, and a saucy smile dancing in her eyes, no artist in our day and time has ever conceived a lovelier picture than Loorany Parmalee made. To find its counterpart, you will have to hark back to the romantic rascals who laid on the color in old times.

Anyhow, Loorany's beauty was known far beyond the cloud-skirted heights of Tray Mountain. Nacoochee, the Vale of the Evening Star, had heard about it, and was curious, and far away on the banks of the Chattahoochee, in the county of Hall, a young man knew of it, and became " restless in the mind," as Mrs. Pruett would say. This young man's name was Hildreth; Hildreth of Hall, he was called, because there was a Hildreth in Habersham.

Now, it would have been better in the end for Hildreth of Hall if he had never heard of Loorany Parmalee, but small blame should be laid at his door on account of his ignorance ; the future was a sealed book to him, as it is to all of us. It was what he knew and

what he did that he is to be blamed for, if
a dead man can be blamed for anything.

It happened in the summer of 1863 that
Hildreth of Hall was visiting Hildreth of
Habersham, — there was some matter of rela-
tionship between them, — and they both concluded to attend the camp-meeting that was
held every year on Taylor's Range, a small
spur that seemed to have been sent down by
Tray to inform the Vale of the Evening Star
that it could spread out no farther in that
direction. Nacoochee was polite and agreeable, and went wandering off westward, where
it stands to-day, the loveliest valley in all the
world. But Taylor's Range so far caught
the infection from the valley as to permit its
top to spread out as level as a table, and on
this table the Christians pitched their rude
tents and built them a rough tabernacle, and
here they held their yearly campmeeting.

To this meeting in 1863 came Hildreth of
Hall and his kinsmen. Hither also came a
number of people from Hatch's Clearing, and
among them Loorany Parmalee. The old
people had come to pray, but the youngsters
had come to frolic, and the gayest of all was
Loorany Parmalee. There were girls from

the villages round about, as well as girls from the valley, and some of these made believe to laugh at Loorany, but the laugh was against them when they saw the boys and young men flocking after her. Mrs. Pruett had more than half promised to keep an eye on Loorany, and she did her best, but how can a pious, maimed lady keep up with a good-looking girl who is at an age when she is less a woman and feels more like one than at any other stage of her existence? Mrs. Pruett tried good-humoredly to put a curb on Loorany, but the lass laughed and shook the bridle off, and no wonder, considering the weakness of human nature. She was beginning to taste the sweets of her first real conquest, for here was Hildreth of Hall, the finest young fellow of the lot, following her about like a dog, and running hither and yon to please her whims and fancies.

It is true that John Wesley Millirons had been casting sheep's eyes at her for several years, hanging around the house on Sunday afternoons and riding with her to church on Sundays; but what of that? Was n't John Wesley almost the same as home folks? And did he ever see the day that he was as polite, or as quick to fetch and carry, or as nimble with his tongue as Hildreth of Hall?

Go along with your talk about solid qualities! Girls must enjoy themselves and have fun, and how can you have the heart to ask them to sit for hours with a chap that mopes or is too bashful to talk fluently, or who looks like he is frightened to death all the time?· It is too much to ask. Girls must have a chance, and if you don't give it to them they will take it.

So Mrs. Pruett watched Loorany gallanting around with Hildreth of Hall, and all the other chaps ready to take his place, except John Wesley Millirons, who sat in the shade and made marks in the sand with a twig. Mrs. Pruett watched all this, and gravely shook her head. And yet the head-shaking was good-humored and lenient. If Mrs. Pruett had been asked at the time why she shook her head she could n't have told. She said afterwards that she knew why she shook her head, and she was inclined to plume herself on her foresight. But you know how people are. If matters had gone on smoothly, or even if Loorany had been like other girls, Mrs. Pruett would have forgotten all about the fact that she shook her head when she saw the lass gallanting around with Hildreth of Hall.

Mrs. Pruett had a "tent" on the camp-ground, a small cabin, roughly, but very comfortably, fixed up, and she stayed the week out. So did Loorany. So did Hildreth of Hall. But along about Wednesday — the meeting had begun on Sunday, — John Wesley Millirons flung his saddle on his mule and made for home. Loorany Parmalee and Hildreth of Hall were sitting in a buggy under a big umbrella, and very close together, when John Wesley went trotting by, his long legs flapping against the sides of the mule. He bowed gravely as he passed, but never turned his head.

"Don't he look it?" laughed Loorany, as he passed out of sight up the road that led to Tray.

II

As may be supposed, John Wesley Millirons was n't feeling very well when he rode off, leaving Loorany sitting close to Hildreth of Hall, under the big umbrella. And yet he was n't feeling very much out of sorts, either. His patience was of that remarkable kind that mountain life breeds, — the kind that belongs to the everlasting hills, the over-hanging sky.

So John Wesley Millirons, as he rode home, laughed to himself at the thought that he was the mountain and Loorany the weather. It was an uncouth thought that could n't be worked out logically, but it pleased John Wesley to hug the idea to his bosom, logic or no logic. And so he carried it home with him and nursed it long and patiently, as an invalid woman in a poorhouse nurses a sick geranium.

After the camp-meeting Hildreth of Hall became a familiar figure on Tray Mountain, especially in the neighborhood of Hatch's Clearing. As the year 1863 was a period of war, you will wonder how such a strapping young fellow as Hildreth of Hall kept out of the Confederate army, since there was such a strenuous demand for food for the guns, big and little. The truth is, it was a puzzle to a good many people about that time, but there was no secret at all about it. The Hildreths, both of Hall and Habersham, had a good deal of political influence. If you think war shuts out politics and politicians you are very much mistaken. On the contrary, it widens their field of operations and thus sharpens their wits. In the confusion and uproar their increased activity escapes attention. Thus it happened that Hildreth of Hall was a commissary. He had a horse and buggy at the expense of the government, and the taxpayers of the country had to pay him well for every trip he made to Tray Mountain.

Under these circumstances, you understand, courting was not only easy and pleasant, but profitable as well, and Hildreth of Hall took due advantage of the situation. He would have made his headquarters at Mrs. Pruett's, but somehow that lady, who was thirty-odd years younger then than she is now, had no fancy for the young man. She politely rejected his overtures, and so he made arrangements to put up at old man Millirons' — of all places in the world. It was such a queer come-off that John Wesley used to go behind the corn-crib and chuckle over it by the hour, especially on Sundays, when he had nothing else to do.

It was plain to everybody, except John

Wesley Millirons, that Loorany was perfectly crazy about Hildreth of Hall, but a good many, impressed by Mrs. Pruett's prejudice against the young man, had their doubts as to whether he was crazy about Loorany. On the other hand, there were just as many, including the majority of the young people, who were certain, as they said, that Hildreth of Hall loved Loorany Parmalee every bit and grain as hard as Loorany loved him. Between the two friendly factions you could hear all the facts in regard to the case and still never get at the rights of it.

Once Mrs. Pruett took John Wesley to task in a kindly fashion. " I never know'd you was so clever, John Wesley, tell I seed you give the road to Hild'eth o' Hall — an' Loorany a-standin' right spang in the middle watin' to see which un 'ud git to 'er fust. Oh, yes, John Wesley, you er e'en about the cleverest feller in the worl'."

" How come, Mis Pruett? " he inquired blandly.

" Why, bekaze you was so quick to give way to that chap from below."

" Shucks ! that feller hain't a-botherin' me," exclaimed John Wesley.

"Oh, I hope not," said Mrs. Pruett; "the Lord knows I do. Fer ef he ain't a-botherin' you, I know mighty well he ain't a-botherin' Loorany. Ef you could 'a' seed 'em a-swingin' in the bullace vine, as I did yistiddy, you would n't 'a thought Loorany was bothered much. Well, not much!" Mrs. Pruett added, sarcastically.

"I seed 'em," remarked John Wesley, chuckling.

"You did?" cried Mrs. Pruett. She was both surprised and indignant.

"Lor', yassum! I thess sot up an' laughed. S' I: 'The feller thinks bekaze he's got his arm 'roun' Loorany that she's done his'n!' I laughed so I was afeared they'd hear me."

Mrs. Pruett said afterwards that her heart jumped into her throat when she heard John Wesley talking in such a strain, for the idea flashed in her mind that he was distracted — and it so impressed her that for one brief moment she was overtaken by fear.

"Well," she said, trying to turn the matter off lightly, "when you see a feller wi' his arm aroun' a gal an' she not doin' any squealin' to speak of, you may know it's not so mighty long tell the weddin'."

"Yassum," responded John Wesley, still chuckling, "it may be so wi' some folks, but not when the gal is Loorany Parmalee. No, ma'am! You thess wait."

"Oh, it hain't no trouble to me to wait," said Mrs. Pruett; "but what 'd I do ef I was a-standin' in your shoes?"

"You 'd make yourse'f comfortuble, thess like I 'm a-doin'," remarked John Wesley.

Mrs. Pruett was so much disturbed that she told her husband about it, and suggested that he look into the matter to the extent of making such inquiries as a man can make. But Jerd shook his head and snapped his big fingers.

"Oh, come now, mother," he said, "it 's uther too soon er it 's too late. An' that hain't all, mother; by the time I git done tendin' to my own business an' yourn, I feel like drappin' off ter sleep."

Matters went on in this way until late in 1863, and then there came a time when Hildreth of Hall ceased to visit Hatch's Clearing. Some said he had been "conscripted into the war," as they called it, and some said he had been appointed to another office that took up his time and attention. But, whatever the cause of his absence was, Loorany seemed to be satisfied. She went about as gay as a lark and as spry as a ground squirrel. John Wesley, too, continued to take things easy. He made no show of elation over the absence of Hildreth of Hall, and never inquired about it. He had never ceased his visits to the Parmalees, but he went no oftener, now that his rival had disappeared from the field, than he had gone before. As Mrs. Pruett remarked, he was the same old John Wesley in fair weather as he was in foul. Patient and willing, and good-humored, for all his seriousness, he went along attending to his own business and helping everybody else who needed help. Thus, in a way, he was very popular, but somehow those who liked him least had a pity for him that was almost contemptuous. John Wesley paid no attention. to such things. He just rocked along, as Mrs. Pruett said.

It was the same when, one day in the spring of 1864, Hildreth of Hall came riding up the mountain driving a pair of handsome horses to a top buggy. He wore a gray uniform, and the coat had a long tail to it, — a sure sign he was an officer of some kind, for Jerd Pruett had seen just such coats worn by the officers in the village below. To be sure, there ought to have been some kind of a mark on the sleeves or shoulders; but no matter about that; nobody but officers could wear long-tailed coats. That point was settled without much argument.

And the buggy was new or had been newly varnished, for the spokes shone in the sun, and the sides of the body glistened like glass. What of that? Well, a good deal, you may be sure; for some people can put two and two together as well as other people, and the folks on the mountain had n't been living for nothing. What of that, indeed! Two fine horses and a shiny top-buggy meant only one thing, and that was a wedding.

Everybody was sure of it but John Wesley Millirons. When Mrs. Pruett twitted him with this overwhelming evidence he had the same old answer ready: " You-all thess wait."

" Well, we hain't got long to wait," said Mrs. Pruett.

" You reckon?" exclaimed John Wesley, with pretended astonishment. Then he chuckled and went on his way, apparently happy and unconcerned.

Hildreth of Hall remained in the neighborhood about a week, and was with Loorany Parmalee pretty much all the time, except when he was asleep. They took long buggy rides together, and everything seemed to be getting along swimmingly. But one morning early Hildreth of Hall harnessed up his horses with his own hands and went off down the road leading to Clarksville.

It was noticed after that that Loorany was not as gay and as spry as she had been. In fact, the women folks could see that she was not the same girl at all. She used to go and sit in Mrs. Pruett's porch and watch the road, and sometimes her mind would be so far away that she would have to be asked the same question twice before she 'd make any reply. And she had a way of sighing that Mrs. Pruett did n't like at all. You know how peculiar some people are when they are fond of anybody. Well, that was the way with Mrs. Pruett.

III

Nearly two months after Hildreth of Hall went away with his two fine horses and his shiny top-buggy, Tray Mountain got wind of some strange news. The word was that conscript-officers were coming up after some of the men, both old and young, who were of the lawful age. The news was brought by a son of Widow Purvis, Jerd Pruett's sister, who lived within a mile of Clarksville. She had gone to town with butter and eggs to exchange for some factory thread — "spun truck" Mrs. Pruett called it — and she heard it from old man Hathaway, who was a particular friend of Jerd Pruett's.

Word reached the mountain just in time, too, for within thirty-six hours four horsemen came riding along the road and stopped at Mrs. Pruett's. And who should be leading them but Hildreth of Hall! Mrs. Pruett saw this much when she peeped through a crack in the door, and she was so taken aback that you might have knocked her down with a feather. But in an instant she was as mad as fire.

"Hello, Mrs. Pruett!" says Hildreth of Hall. "Where's Jerd?"

"And who may Jerd be?" inquired Mrs. Pruett placidly.

The young man's face fell at this, but he said with a bold voice: —

" Why, don't you know me, Mrs. Pruett?"

" I mought 'a' seed you before, but folks is constant a-comin' an' a-gwine. They pass up the road an' down the road an' then they pass out'n my mind."

" Well, you have n't forgotten me, I know; I 'm Hildreth of Hall."

" Is that so, now? " remarked Mrs. Pruett, with just the faintest show of interest. " It 'pears to me we hyearn you was dead. What's your will and pleasure wi' me, Mr. Hall? "

The unconscious air with which Mrs. Pruett miscalled the young man's name was as effectual as a blow. He lost his composure, and turned almost helplessly to his companions. If he expected sympathy he missed it. One of them laughed loudly and cried out to the others: " We 'll have to call him Blowhard. Why, he declared by everything good and bad that he was just as chummy with these folks as their own kin. And now, right at the beginning, they don't even know his name."

" Where's your husband? " inquired Hildreth of Hall. " If he don't know me he will before the day 's over."

" He may know you better 'n I do," said

Mrs. Pruett, "but I hardly reckon he does, bekaze I 'd mos' likely 'a' hyearn on it."

"Where is he?" insisted the young man.

"Who? my ole man? Oh, him an' a whole passel of the boys took their guns an' went off to'ards Hillman's spur bright an' early this mornin'. They said signs of a b'ar had been seed thar, but I allowed to myse'f that they was thess a-gwine on a frolic."

Mrs. Pruett took off her spectacles, wiped them on her apron, and readjusted them to her head, smiling serenely all the while.

"We may as well go to the Millirons'," remarked Hildreth of Hall.

"I don't care where you go, so you don't lead us into a trap," remarked one of the men.

They turned away from Mrs. Pruett's and rode farther into the settlement. But they soon discovered that Tray Mountain had practically closed its gates against them. The women they saw were as grim and as silent as the mountain. Hildreth of Hall had been telling his companions what a lively place (considering all the circumstances) Hatch's Clearing was, and this added to his embarrassment and increased his irritation. So that you may well believe he was neither gay nor good-humored when, after passing several houses, he came to Millirons', where he had been in the habit of making himself free and familiar.

Everything was as grim and silent as the grave, and John Wesley sat on the fence as grim and as silent as any of the surroundings.

"There's one man, anyway," remarked one of Hildreth's companions. "Be blanked if I don't feel like going up and shaking hands with him — that is, if he's alive." For John Wesley neither turned his head nor stirred.

"How are you, Millirons?" said Hildreth of Hall curtly.

"Purty well," replied John Wesley, without moving.

"We are going to put our horses under the shed yonder and give them a handful of fodder," Hildreth of Hall declared. John Wesley made no reply to this. "Did you hear what I said?" asked the young man, somewhat petulantly.

"I hyearn you," answered John Wesley.

Whereupon Hildreth of Hall spurred his horse through the open lot gate, followed by

his companions. They took off saddles and
bridles, made some halters out of plough
lines, and gave their horses a heavy feed of
fodder. Then they returned to the house,
and found John Wesley sitting where they
had left him, and in precisely the same position.

"Can we get dinner?" asked Hildreth of
Hall.

"I reckon not," replied John Wesley.

"Why?"

"Nobody at home but me an' the tomcat,
an' we 're locked out. Maybe you can git
dinner at Parmalee's when the time comes.
They 're all at home. But it hain't nigh dinner time yit." John Wesley slowly straightened himself out and came off the fence with
an apologetic smile on his face. "Ef these
gentermen here don't mind, I 'd like to have
a word wi' you, sorter private like." He
looked at Hildreth of Hall, still smiling.

For answer, Hildreth of Hall walked to a
mountain oak a hundred feet away, followed
by John Wesley. "What do you want?"

"I s'pose you 've come up to marry the
gal?" suggested John Wesley.

"I have not," replied Hildreth of Hall.

"I mean Loorany Parmalee," said John Wesley, pulling a small piece of bark from the tree.

"It matters not to me who you mean," remarked Hildreth.

"I just wanted to find out," John Wesley went on, fitting the piece of bark between thumb and forefinger as if it were a marble. "I allers allowed you was a d—— dog." The bark flew into the face of Hildreth of Hall and left a stinging red mark there, as John Wesley, with a contemptuous gesture, turned away.

Hildreth's hand flew to his hip pocket.

"Watch out there!" cried one of his companions in a warning tone. "He'll shoot!"

"I reckon not," said John Wesley, without turning his head. "The fact of the business is, gentermen, they won't narry one on you shoot. A bulldog'll fight, but you let him foller a sheep-killin' houn' to the pastur, an' a bench-legged fice can run 'im. You-all may n't believe it, but it's the fact-truth."

But John Wesley would have been shot all the same if the thought had n't flashed on Hildreth's mind that the house was full of armed mountaineers. This stayed his hand — not only stayed his hand, but, apparently, put him in a good humor. He followed John Wesley and said : —

"As you are so brash about it, we 'll go and see the young lady. Come on, boys."

"' What about the horses?" asked one of the men.

"Come on," said Hildreth of Hall in a low voice. "The horses are all right. These chaps don't steal. Come on; that house is full of men."

"I told you you were leading us into a trap," growled one of his companions; "and here we are."

When they were out of sight, John Wesley went into the lot and looked at the horses. He was so much interested in their comfort that he loosed their halters. Then he cast a glance upwards and chuckled. A wasps' nest as big as a man's hat was hanging between two of the rafters, teeming with these irritable insects. John Wesley went outside, climbed up to the top of the shed, counted the clapboards both ways, planted himself above the wasps' nest, and with one quick stamp of the foot knocked a hole in the rotten plank. The noise startled the horses, the wasps swarmed down on them, and the next instant they were going down the road the way they had come, squealing, whickering, kicking, and running like mad.

When they were out of hearing John Wesley went into the house by a back door, got his rifle, and went off through the woods.

Hildreth of Hall and his companions must have had a cool reception at Parmalee's, for in about an hour they came back in some haste. If they were alarmed, that feeling was increased tenfold at finding their horses gone. Their saddles and bridles were where they had left them, but the horses were gone. They held a hurried consultation in the lot, climbed the fence instead of coming out near the house, skirted through the woods, and entered the road near Mrs. Pruett's, moving as rapidly as men can who are not running. A half-mile farther down, the road turned to the left and led through a ravine.

On one bank, hid by the bushes, John Wesley sat with his rifle across his lap, lost in meditation. Occasionally he plucked a rotten twig and crumbled it in his fingers. After a while he heard voices. He raised himself on his right knee and placed his left

foot forward as an additional support. Then
he raised his gun, struck the stock lightly
with the palm of his hand to shake the
powder down, and held himself in readiness.
When the men came in sight Hildreth of
Hall was slightly in advance of the others.

John Wesley slowly raised his rifle and
was about to bring the barrel to a level with
his eyes when he saw a flash of fire on the
opposite bank, and heard the sharp crack of
a rifle. He was so taken by surprise that he
raised himself in the bushes and looked about
him. Hildreth of Hall had tumbled forward
in a heap at the flash, and the other men
jumped over his body and ran like rabbits.
Before the hatful of smoke had lifted to the
level of the tree-tops they were out of hearing.

John Wesley crossed the road and went to
the other side. There he saw Loorany Parmalee leaning against a tree, breathing hard.
At her feet lay a rifle.

" You sp'iled my game," he remarked.

" Is he dead ? " she asked.

" E'en about," he replied. She threw her
head back and breathed hard. John Wesley
picked up the rifle and examined it.

"Was you gwine to kill him?" Loorany asked.

"Well, sorter that away, I reckon."

"Did you have the notion that I'd marry you atterwards?"

"I wa'n't a-gwine to ax you," said John Wesley.

"Will you take me now, jest as I am?"

"Why, I reckon," he replied, in a matter-of-fact tone.

So they went home and left other people to look after Hildreth of Hall.

In course of time a boy was born to Loorany Millirons, and the event made her husband a widower, but the child was never known by any other name than that of Toog Parmalee — and Toog was the chap that shot his sweetheart.

All these things, as Mrs. Pruett said, were the cause of the difficulty you read about in the newspapers the other day. "Thribble the generations," she added, "an' sin's arm is long enough to retch through 'em all."

THE BABY'S CHRISTMAS

I

ROCKVILLE ought to have been a harmonious community if there ever was one.
The same families had been living there for generations, and they had intermarried until everybody was everybody else's cousin.
Those who were no kin at all called one another cousin in public, — such is the force of example and habit. Little children playing with other children would hear them call one another cousin, and so the habit grew until even the few newcomers who took up their abode in Rockville speedily became cousins.

There were different degrees of prosperity in the village before and during the war, but everybody was comfortably well off, so that there was no necessity for drawing social distinctions. Those who were comparatively poor boasted of good blood, and they made as nice cousins as those who were richer.

When the editor of the " Vade Mecum " wished to impress on his subscribers the necessity of settling their accounts, he prefaced his remarks with this statement: " We are a homogeneous people. We are united. What is the interest of one is the interest of all. We must continue to preserve our harmony."

But envy knows no race or clime, and it had taken up its abode among the cousins of Rockville. It was not even rooted out by the disastrous results of the war, which tended to bring each and every cousin down to the same level of hopeless poverty. When, therefore, Colonel Asbury announced in the streets that his wife had concluded to take boarders, and caused to be inserted in the " Vade Mecum " a notice to the effect that " a few select parties " could find accommodations at The Cedars, there were a good many smothered exclamations of affected surprise among the cousins, with no little secret satisfaction that " Cousin Becky T." had at last been compelled to " get off her high horse," — to employ the vernacular of Rockville.

Such an announcement was certainly the next thing to a crash in the social fabric, and while some of the cousins were secretly

pleased, there were others who shook their
heads in sorrow, feeling that a deep and last-
ing humiliation had been visited on the community. For if ever a human being was
seized and possessed by pride of family and
position, that person was Cousin Becky T.
Her pride was reënforced by a will as firm,
and an individuality as strong, as ever woman had; and these characteristics were so
marked that she was never known among her
acquaintances as Mrs. Asbury, but always as
Rebecca Tumlin or "Cousin Rebecca T."
The colonel himself invariably referred to
her, even in his most hilarious moments, as
Rebecca Tumlin. Times were hard indeed
when this gentlewoman could be induced to
throw open to boarders the fine old mansion,
with its massive white pillars standing out
against a background of red brick.

The colonel had three plantations, — one
near Rockville, one in the low country, and
one in the Cherokee region; but in 1868
these possessions were a burden to him to
the extent of the taxes he was compelled to
pay. There was no market for agricultural
lands. The value they might have had was
swallowed up in the poverty and depression

that enveloped everything in the region where war had dropped its litter of furies. Colonel Asbury might have practiced law: he did practice it, in fact; but it was like building a windmill over a dry well.

Cousin Rebecca Tumlin finally solved the problem by announcing that she purposed to take boarders. No one ever knew what it cost her to make that announcement. Envious people suspected the nature of the struggle through which she passed, — the hard and bitter struggle between pride and necessity, — and some of them predicted it would do her good. The colonel, who was proud after his own fashion, and also sympathetic, was shocked at first and then grieved. But he made no remark. Comment was unnecessary. He walked back and forth on the colonnade, and measured many a mile before his agitation was allayed. More than once he went down the long graveled avenue, and turned and gazed fondly at the perspective that carried the eye to the fine old house. It seemed as if he were bidding farewell to the beauty and glory of it all. But he made no complaint. When he grew tired of walking, he went in with the intention of taking down some family pictures that adorned the walls of the wide hall. But his wife had forestalled him. The house, by a few deft changes, had been made as cheerless as the most fastidious boarder could wish.

And so the word went round that Cousin Rebecca Tumlin would be pleased to take boarders. The response was all that she could have desired. The young men — the bachelor storekeepers and their clerks — deserted the rickety old tavern and the smaller boarding-houses, and took up their abode at The Cedars, and soon the house was gay with a company that was profitable if not pleasant.

The advent of boarders — some of them transient traveling - men — opened a new world for Mary Asbury, Cousin Rebecca Tumlin's daughter, and she made the most of it. She followed the example of her father, the colonel, and made herself agreeable to the young men. She made herself especially agreeable to Laban Pierson, the young conductor of the daily train on the little branch railroad that connected Rockville with the outside world. Cousin Rebecca T. held herself severely aloof from her boarders, but her attitude was so serene and graceful, so evidently the natural and correct thing, that it caused no ill-natured comment. Mary was sixteen, and when she sat at the head of the table, her mother was not missed. The young girl's manners were a rare combination of sweetness, grace, and dignity. She was affable, she was thoughtful, and she had a fair share of her father's humor. Above all, she was beautiful. Naturally, therefore, while her mother nursed her pride, and counted the money, Mary beamed on the boarders, and her father drew upon his vast fund of anecdote for their instruction and amusement.

Laban Pierson was not a very brilliant young man, but he was fairly good-looking, and he knew how to make himself agreeable. His train arrived at Rockville at half-past two in the afternoon, and left at five o'clock in the morning, so that he had plenty of time to make himself agreeable to Miss Mary Asbury, and he did so with only a vague notion of what the end would be. Mary made herself agreeable to Laban simply because it was her nature to be pleasant to everybody. As for any other reason, — why, the idea of such a thing! If young Pierson had told himself

that he was courting Mary Asbury, he would
have blushed with alarm. Perhaps he would
have left The Cedars and gone to the old
tavern again. Who knows? Young men
will do very desperate things at certain
stages of their checkered careers.

It was the old story with its own particular
variations. Mary loved Laban, and was too
shy to know what she was about. Laban
loved Mary, and never discovered it until the
disease had become epidemic in his system,
and spread over his heart and mind in every
direction. Neither one of them discovered
it. It was a beautiful dream, too good to be
true, too sweet to last. Finally the discovery
was made by old Aunt Mimy, the cook, who
had never seen Mary and Laban together.
The affair, if it can be called by so imposing
a name, had been going on a year or more,
and Mary was past seventeen, when one afternoon the train failed to arrive on time. The
afternoon wore into evening, and still the
train did not come. Mary had the habit of
sitting in the kitchen with Aunt Mimy when
anything troubled her, and on this particular
afternoon, after waiting an hour for the train,
she went to her old seat near the window.

Aunt Mimy was beating biscuit. Mary looked out of the window toward the depot.

"Train ain't come yit, is she, honey?" asked Aunt Mimy.

"No, not yet," replied Mary. "What can be the matter?"

"Run off de trussle, I speck," said Aunt Mimy.

"O mammy!" cried Mary, starting to her feet; "do you really think so? What have you heard?"

The girl stood with one hand against her bosom, her face pale, and her nether lip trembling. Aunt Mimy regarded her with astonishment for a moment, and then the shrewd old negro jumped to a conclusion. She paused with her arm uplifted.

"Is yo' ma on dat train? Is yo' pa on dat train? What de name er de Lord you got ter do wid dat train?"

She brought the beater down on the pliant dough with a resounding thwack. Mary hid her face in her hands. After a little she went out, leaving Aunt Mimy mumbling and talking to herself.

The cook lost no time in relating this incident to Cousin Rebecca T., and that lady lost

just as little in making plain to her daughter
the folly and futility of interesting herself
in such a person as the young conductor.
Cousin Rebecca T. gave Mary a brief but
picturesque biography of Laban Pierson.
His family belonged to the poor white trash
before the war, and he was no better.
Muddy well, muddy water. He had been a
train-hand, a brakeman, baggage-master, and
what not. The colonel was called in to ver-
ify these biographical details.

Mary's reply to it all was characteristic.
She listened and smiled, and tossed her head.

"What do *I* care about Laban Pierson?
What have *I* to do with his affairs? Ought
I to have jumped for joy when mammy told
me the train had dropped through the tres-
tle?"

The colonel accepted this logic without
question, but Cousin Rebecca T. saw through
it. She was a woman, and had a natural
contempt for logic, especially a woman's
logic. She simply realized that she had
made a mistake. She had gone about the
matter in the wrong way. As for Mary, she
had found out her own secret. She hard-
ened her heart against Aunt Mimy, and when

the old woman sought an explanation, it was readily forthcoming.

"You got me into trouble," said Mary; "you won't get me into any more if I can help it." Aunt Mimy grieved over the situation to such an extent that she made herself disagreeable to everybody, especially to Cousin Rebecca T. She broke dishes, she burned the waffles, she flung the dish-water into the yard, and for a day or two she whipped the little negroes every time she got her hands on them.

Cousin Rebecca T. did not let the matter drop, as she might have done. The colonel used to tell his intimate friends that his wife had a fearful amount of misdirected energy, and the results that it wrought in this particular instance justified the colonel's description. Cousin Rebecca T. went straight to young Laban Pierson, and gave him to understand, without circumlocution or mincing of words, what she thought of any possible notion he had or might have of uniting his fortunes with those of her daughter. As might have been expected, Laban was thunderstruck. He blushed violently, turned pale, stammered, and, in short, acted just as any

other young fellow would act when con-
fronted with his own secret thoughts and desires, hardly acknowledged even to himself.
To Cousin Rebecca T. all this was in the
nature of a confession of guilt, and she con-
gratulated herself on the promptness with
which she had put an end to the whole miserable business. As a matter of fact, she did
what many another hasty-tempered woman
has done before her ; she kindled into flame
a spark that might have expired if let alone.

Young Mr. Pierson promptly took himself
away from The Cedars, and it was not until
after he was gone that the other guests discovered what an interesting companion he
was at table and on the wide veranda. They
began to talk about him and to discuss his
good qualities. He was a clean, manly,
bright, industrious, genial, generous young
fellow. This was the verdict. The colonel,
missing the cigars that Laban was in the
habit of bringing him, and resenting the situation (inflamed, perhaps, by a little too much
toddy), went further, and said that in the
whole course of his career, sir, he had never
seen a finer young man, sir. So that in spite
of the fact that Laban sat at the table no
longer, he was more in evidence than ever.

Affairs went on without a break or a ripple. Occasionally Mary would walk in the direction of the depot in the afternoon, and whenever she saw Laban she made it a point to bow to him, and this salutation he always returned with marked emphasis. But Mary was not happy. She no longer went singing through the house. She was cheerful, but not in the old fashion. No one noticed the change but old Aunt Mimy, and perhaps she would have been blind to it if her conscience had not hurt her. The old woman's conscience was not specially active or sensitive, but her affections were set on Mary, and for many long weeks the girl had hardly deigned to speak to her. Conscience lives next door to the affections. Aunt Mimy rebelled against hers for a long time, but at last it roused her to action.

One afternoon, when dinner had been cleared away, she filled her pipe, adjusted her head-kerchief, and sallied out in the direction of the depot. The wheezy old locomotive was engaged in shifting the cars about, and Conductor Pierson was assisting the brakeman. Aunt Mimy seated herself on the depot platform, smoked her pipe, and patiently waited till the shunting was over. Then she placed herself in Pierson's way. He seemed to be preoccupied, but the old woman did not stand on ceremony.

"Look like our victuals wa'n't good 'nough fer you," she said bluntly.

"Why, this is Aunt Mimy!" He shook hands with her, and asked about her health, and this pleased her very much. He asked about the family, and especially about Miss Mary. When it came to this, Aunt Mimy took her pipe out of her mouth, drew a long breath, and shook her head. She could have given points on the art of pantomime to any strolling company of players. The whole history of the sad case of Mary Asbury was in the lift of her eyebrows, the motions of her head, and in her sorrowful sigh; and Conductor Pierson seemed to be able to read a part of it, for he asked Aunt Mimy into the passenger-coach, and there the two sat and talked until it was time for Aunt Mimy to go home and see about supper.

That night, as Aunt Mimy sat on the kitchen steps smoking her pipe and resting herself, preparatory to going to bed, she saw Mary sitting at her room window looking out into the moonlight. It was not a very beautiful scene that fell under the young girl's eye. There was nothing romantic or picturesque in the view of the back yard, with the kitchen and the comical figure of the fat old cook in the foreground : but when a young girl is in love, it is wonderful what a mellowing influence the moonlight has on the most forbidding scene. It pushes the shadows into strange places, and softens and subdues all that is angular and ugly. Take the moon out of our scheme, and a good deal of our poetry and romance would vanish with it, and even true love would take on a prosiness that it does not now possess.

Aunt Mimy looked at Mary, and felt sorry for her. Mary looked at Aunt Mimy, and felt that she would be glad to be able to despise the old negro if she could. Aunt Mimy spoke to her presently in a subdued, insinuating tone.

"Is dat you, honey?"

"Yes."

"Better fling on yo' cape" —

"I'm not cold."

"An' come down here an' talk wid me."

"I don't feel like talking."

" Been long time sence you felt like talkin'
wid me. Well, dem dat don't talk don't
never hear tell."

She pulled from somewhere under her
apron something white and oblong, dropped
it on the ground purposely, picked it up, and
put it back under her apron. Then she
said : —

" Good-night, honey! I ain't tellin' you
good-night des fer myse'f."

Aunt Mimy's tone was charged with information. Mary vanished from the window,
and came tripping out to the kitchen. Then
followed a whispered conversation between
the cook and the young lady. At something
or other that Aunt Mimy said to her —
some quaint comment, or maybe a happy
piece of intelligence — Mary laughed loudly.
The sound of it reached the ears of Cousin
Rebecca T., who was playing whist. The
colonel was dealing. She slipped away from
the table, peeped through the blinds of the
dining-room, and was just in time to see Aunt
Mimy hand Mary something that had the
appearance of a letter. She returned to the
whist-table, revoked on the first round, and
trumped her partner's trick on the second.

Such a thing had never been heard of before. Her partner shook his head, and buried his face in his cards. Her husband regarded her with amazement. She made no excuse or explanation, but in the next two hands more than made up in brilliant play for the advantage she had lost.

Meanwhile Mary was reading the letter that Laban Pierson had sent her. It was a frank, manly declaration of his love expressed in plain and simple language. He had written, he said, on the impulse of the moment, but he did not propose to engage in a clandestine correspondence. He did not invite or expect a reply, but would always — ah, well, the formula was the same old one that we are all familiar with.

Mary placed the letter where she could feel her heart beat against it, and went to bed happy, and was soon dreaming about Laban Pierson. Cousin Rebecca T. played whist fiercely and won continuously. After the game was over, she went upstairs, stirred a stiff toddy for the colonel, and put him to bed. Then she went into her daughter's room, shading the lamp with her hand so that the light would not arouse Innocence from its happy dreams. She moved as noise-lessly as Lady Macbeth moves in the play, though not with the same intent. She searched everywhere for the letter, and at last found it where a more feminine woman would have hunted for it at first. One corner of this human document was peeping modestly forth from the virgin bosom of Innocence. Deftly, gently, even lovingly, Cousin Rebecca T. lifted the letter from its warm and shy covert.

It was a very simple thing to do, but there were hours and days and years when Cousin Rebecca T. would have given all her possessions to have left the letter nestling in her daughter's bosom ; for, in lifting it out, Innocence was aroused from its sleep and caught Experience in the very act of making a fool of itself. Mary opened her wondering eyes, and found her mother with Laban's letter in her hand. The young lady sat bolt upright in bed. Cousin Rebecca T. was inwardly startled, but outwardly she was as calm as the moonlight that threw its slanting shadows eastward.

" I don't wonder that you blush," she cried, holding up the letter.

"Do you think I am blushing for myself?" asked Mary.

"If you know what shame is, you ought to feel it now," exclaimed her mother.

"I do — I do," said Mary, with rising indignation. "After to-night I shall always be ashamed of myself and of my family."

Cousin Rebecca T., stung by the tone and by this first sign of rebellion, turned upon her daughter; but her anger quickly died away, for she saw in her daughter's eyes her own courage and her own unconquerable will.

The scene did not end there, but the rest of it need not be described here. Innocence has as long a tongue as Experience when it feels itself wronged, and the result of this family quarrel was that Innocence went farther than Experience would have dared to go. When Laban Pierson's train went puffing out of Rockville at five o'clock the next morning, it carried among its few passengers Miss Mary Asbury and old Aunt Mimy. The colonel and Cousin Rebecca T. lost a daughter, and their boarders had to wait a long time for their breakfast or go without.

The next number of the "Vade Mecum"

had a beautifully written account of the marriage of Mary Asbury to Laban Pierson, under the double heading

LOVE LAUGHS AT LOCKSMITHS

A LOCAL ROMANCE WITH A HAPPY ENDING

Cousin Rebecca T. turned up her nose at the newspaper account, but the colonel cut it out and hid it away in his large morocco pocket-book. That night, after he had taken his toddy and was sound asleep, Cousin Rebecca T. took the clipping from its hiding-place, and read it over carefully. Then she put out the light, and sat by the window and cried until far into the night. But she cried so softly that a little bird, sitting on its nest in the honeysuckle vine not two feet away from the lady's grief, did not take its head from under its wing.

II

This was at the beginning of 1870, and about this time Colonel Asbury's fortunes took a decided turn for the better. During the war, in a spirit of speculative recklessness, he had invested thirty thousand dollars in Confederate money in ten thousand acres of land in Texas. He thought so little of the investment then, and afterwards, that he did not take the trouble to pay the taxes. But the purchase of the land was a fortunate stroke for the colonel. In 1870 land-values in Texas were not what they were in Georgia. That vast southwestern empire (as the phrase goes) was just beginning to attract the attention of Northern and foreign capital. Railway promoters, British land syndicates, and native boomers, were combining to develop the material resources of the wonderful State.

In the early part of 1870, a powerful combination of railway promoters determined to build a line straight through the colonel's Texan possessions. His land there increased in value to thirty dollars, and then to forty dollars, an acre, at which figure the colonel was induced to part with his titles. Cousin Rebecca Tumlin thus found herself to be the wife of a very rich man, and her pride at last found something substantial to cling to. The Cedars ceased to be a boarding-house. The old family pictures were brought down from the garret, dusted, and hung in their accustomed places. Great improvements were made in the place, and Cousin Rebecca and the colonel sat down to enjoy life as they thought it ought to be enjoyed.

But something was lacking. Life did not run as pleasantly as before. The dollar that brings content is at such a high premium among the nations of the earth that it can never be made the standard of value. That dollar was not among the four hundred thousand dollars the colonel received for his Texan lands. The old style did not fit the new times. The colonel's old friends did not fall away from him, but they were less friendly and more obsequious. His daughter did not come forward to ask his forgiveness and his blessing. Something was wrong somewhere. The colonel and Cousin Rebecca Tumlin fretted a good deal, and finally concluded to move to Atlanta. So they closed their house in Rockville, and built a mansion in Peachtree Street in the city whose name has come to be identified with all that is progressive in the South.

The building is on the left as you go out Peachtree. You can't mistake it. It is a queer mixture of summer cottage and feudal castle, with a great deal of fussy detail that bewilders the eye, and a serene stretch of

roof broken by a delirious display of scroll-
work. It is Rebecca Tumlin all over; pride
— pride nailed to the grim walls, and vexa-
tion of spirit worked into the ornamentation.
Yet it is a house that easily catches the eye.
It is on a little elevation, and it has about it
a certain suggestion of individuality. On
the dome of the middle gable a smart and
business-like dragon upholds the weather-vane
with his curled and gilded tail.

The colonel prospered steadily. He was
regarded as one of the most successful business men and financiers the South has ever
produced. It is no wonder the Bible parable
gives money the name of "talent." It *is* a
talent. Give it half a chance, and it is the
most active talent that man possesses. It is
always in a state of fermentation; it grows;
it accumulates. At any rate, the colonel
thought so. His capital carried him into the
inner circles of investment and speculation,
and he found himself growing richer and
richer, only vaguely realizing how the result
was brought about.

The receptions at the Asbury mansion were
conceded to be the most fashionable that Atlanta had ever seen; for along in the seventies

Atlanta was merely experimenting with the social instinct. The " smart set " had no kind of organization. Society was engaged in disentangling itself from the furious business energy that has made Atlanta the best-known city in the South. It was at this juncture that Cousin Rebecca T., with her money, her taste, and her ambition to lead, appeared on the scene. She had all the requisites of a leader. Pride is a quickening quality, and it had made of Cousin Rebecca T. a most accomplished woman. There was something attractive and refreshing about her strong individuality. There was a simplicity about her methods that commended her to the social experimenters, who stood in great awe of forms and conventions.

Naturally, therefore, the Asbury mansion was the social centre. The younger set gathered there to be gay, and the married people went there to meet their friends. But many and many a night after the lights were out in the parlors, and the gas was turned low in the hall, Cousin Rebecca T. and the colonel sat and thought about their daughter Mary, each refraining from mentioning her name to the other, — the colonel because he was afraid of irritating his wife, and Cousin Rebecca T. because she was afraid of exhibiting any weakness before her husband. Each, unknown to the other, had set on foot inquiries in regard to the whereabouts of Mary, and the fact that the inquiries elicited no response and no information gave the two old people a more valid excuse for misery than they had ever known.

The trouble was that their inquiries had begun too late. For a few months after her marriage the colonel had kept himself informed about his daughter. He expected her to write to him. He had a vague and unformed notion that in due season Mary would return and ask her mother's forgiveness, and then, if Cousin Rebecca T. showed any hardness of heart, he proposed to put his foot down, and show her that he was not a cipher in the family. The mother, for her part, fully expected that some day when she was going about the house, neither doing nor thinking of anything in particular, her daughter would rush suddenly in upon her and tell her between laughter and tears that there was no happiness away from home. Cousin Rebecca T. had her part all prepared. She would frown at first, and then throw her arms around Mary, and tell her what a naughty girl she had been.

But all this mental preparation was in vain. Weeks, months, and years passed by, but Mary never came. When the colonel and Cousin Rebecca T. woke up to their new prosperity, they were very busily engaged for some time in fitting themselves to it. It was during this period that Mary and her husband disappeared. The colonel heard in a vague way that Laban Pierson had moved to Atlanta, and that from Atlanta he had gone out West. All the rest was mystery.

But it was no mystery to Laban and Mary. For a little while their affairs went along comfortably. Laban became the conductor of a passenger-train on the main line of the Central of Georgia. Then he moved to Atlanta. Afterward he accepted a position on the Louisville and Nashville Railway, and there had the misfortune to lose a leg in a collision. This was the beginning of troubles that seemed to pursue Laban and Mary. Poverty laid its grim hand upon them at every turn. Mary did the best she could. She was indeed a helpmate and a comforter; she was brave and hopeful; yet she would have given up in despair but for old Aunt Mimy, who worked and slaved that her young mistress might be spared the bitterest pangs of poverty. Her faithfulness was without boundary or limit. Day and night she toiled, cooking, washing, and taking care of the toddling baby that had come to share the troubles of Laban and Mary. As soon as Laban could get about on his crutches, he tried to find work; but his efforts were fruitless. The time came when he was ready to say to his wife that he could do no more.

Finally the little family drifted back to Atlanta. Here Laban found employment in a small way as a solicitor of life insurance. He was doing so well in this business that a rival company sought his services, offering to pay a fixed salary instead of commissions. But no sooner had he given notice to his employers that he intended to accept the new position than a complication arose in his accounts. How it happened Laban never knew; he was as innocent as a lamb. The company was a new one, trying to establish a business in the Atlanta territory, and out of the funds he collected he used money to pay expenses incurred in the company's behalf. His vouchers showed it all; he had been careful to put down everything, even to the cost of a postal card. He turned over these vouchers and accounts to his employers. But when it was found that he had entered the service of a rival company, the charge of embezzlement was made against him. He found it impossible to give bonds, and was compelled to go to jail. A young lawyer took his case, and was sure he could clear him when the case came to trial. But meanwhile Laban was in jail, and to Mary this was the end of all things; for a time she was utterly prostrated. She refused to eat or sleep, but sat holding her child to her bosom, and crying over it. This went on for so long a time that Aunt Mimy thought it best to interfere. So she took the two-year-old child from its mother, and made some characteristic observations.

"You ain't gwine ter git Marse Laban out'n jail by settin' dar cryin,' honey. Better git mad an' stir roun', an' hurt somebody's feelin's. Make you feel lots better, kaze I done tried it."

"O mammy! mammy!" moaned Mary.

"Day atter ter-morrer 'll be Chris'mus," Aunt Mimy continued, "an' Marse Laban got ter be here ter dinner. Dey ain't no two ways 'bout dat."

"Oh, what a Christmas!" cried Mary.

"Yes 'm; an' de cake done baked. Don't you fret, honey! De Lord ain't fur f'om whar folks is in trouble. I done notice dat. He may n't be right dar in de nex' room, an' maybe he ain't right roun' de cornder, but he ain't so mighty fur off. Now, I tell you dat."

Whereupon Aunt Mimy, carrying the child, went out of the house into the street, and was so disturbed in mind that she walked on and on with no thought of the distance. After a while she found herself on Peachtree Street, where the baby's attention was attracted by the jingling bells of the street-car horses. In front of one of the large mansions a fine carriage was standing. On the veranda a lady stood drawing on her gloves and giving some parting orders to a servant in the hall. Aunt Mimy knew at once that the lady was her old mistress. But she turned to the negro coachman, who sat on the box stiff and stolid in all the grandeur of a long coat and brass buttons.

" Who live' here ? " she asked.

" Cun-nol Asbe'y," the coachman replied.

" Ain't dat Becky Tumlin yonder ? " inquired Aunt Mimy, with some asperity.

" No, ma'am ; dat is Missus Cun-nol Asbe'y."

" Well, de Lord he'p my soul ! " exclaimed Aunt Mimy.

Then she turned and went back home as fast as she could, talking to herself and the child. Once she looked back, but Cousin Rebecca T. was sitting grandly in the carriage, and the carriage was going rapidly toward the business portion of the city. Cousin Rebecca T. bowed right and left to her acquaintances and smiled pleasantly as the carriage rolled along. She bowed and smiled, but she was thinking about her daughter.

Aunt Mimy hurried home as fast as she could go. She had intended at first to tell Mary of her discovery, but she thought better of it. She had another plan.

" You see me gwine 'long here? " she said, as much to herself as to the baby. " Well, ef I don't fix dat ar white 'oman you kin put me in de calaboose." She stood at the gate of the house Laban had rented, and compared its appearance with the magnificence of the mansion she had just left. The contrast was so startling that all the comment she could make was, " De Lord he'p my soul ! " She took the child in, got its playthings, and then went about her business more briskly than she had gone in many a day. If Mary had not been so deeply engaged in contemplating her troubles, she would have discovered at once that something unusual had occurred. Aunt Mimy was agitated. Her mind was not in her work. She drew a bucket of water from the well when she intended to get wood for the little stove. Occasionally she would pause in her work and stand lost in thought. At last Mary remarked her agitation.

" What is the matter, mammy ? " she asked. " Something has happened."

" Ah, Lord, honey ! 'T ain't happen' yit, but it 's gwine ter happen."

" Well," said Mary, shaking her head, " let it happen. Nothing can hurt me. The worst has already happened."

Aunt Mimy made no audible comment, but went about mumbling and talking to herself. Mary sat rocking and moaning, and the little

child made the most of the situation by toddling from room to room, getting into all
sorts of mischief without let or hindrance.
After a while Aunt Mimy asked : —

"Honey, don't you know whar yo' pa an'
ma is?"

"Yes," said Mary languidly; "they live
in Atlanta."

"Right here in dis town?"

"Yes."

"Whar'bouts?"

"Oh, don't worry me, mammy! I don't
know. They care nothing for me. See how
they have treated Laban!"

"Why n't you hunt 'em up, an' tell 'em
what kinder fix you in? I boun' dey 'd he'p
you out." Mary gazed at Aunt Mimy with
open-eyed wonder. "Write a letter ter yo'
ma. Here's what 'll take it. *I* 'll fin' out
whar she live at."

Mary rose from her chair and took a step
toward Aunt Mimy, not in anger, but by way
of emphasis.

"Mammy," she cried, "don't speak of such
a thing!"

"Humph!" Aunt Mimy grunted; "ef
you ain't de ve'y spi't an' image er Becky

Tumlin, I 'm a saddle-hoss. Proud! consated! Dat ain't no name fer it. De nigger man what I got now ain't much, but ef he wuz in jail I 'd be trottin' roun' right now tryin' ter git 'im out."

The next morning Aunt Mimy was up betimes. She cooked breakfast, and after that meal was over (it need not have been prepared so far as Mary was concerned), she dressed the baby in some of its commonest clothes, and put on its feet a pair of shoes that were worn at the toes. This done, she took the lively youngster in her arms and started out.

" Where are you going?" Mary asked.

" Baby gwine ter walk," Aunt Mimy answered.

" Not in those clothes!" Mary protested.

" Now, honey," exclaimed Aunt Mimy, " does you speck I ain't got no better sense dan ter rig dis baby out, an' his pa down yonder in de dungeons?"

" Oh, what shall I do?" cried Mary, forgetting everything else but her own misery and her husband's disgrace.

" Stay right here, honey, tell I come back. I won't be gone so mighty long. Den you kin take dis precious baby down ter see his pa."

The day was clear and bright, and although it was Christmas, the soft breezes and the invigorating sunshine had the flavor and quality of spring. Aunt Mimy paid no attention to the auspicious weather, but made her way straight to the Asbury mansion on Peachtree Street. On her face there was a frown, and her "head-han'k'cher," which usually sat straight back from her forehead, had an upward tilt that gave her a warlike appearance.

She went up the tiled walk and rang the door-bell. A quadroon girl came to the door; the girl's voice was soft, and her manners gentle, but Aunt Mimy had a strong prejudice against mulattoes, and it came to the surface now.

"Is yo' mist'ess in?" she asked harshly.

"Mis' Asbury is in," said the girl softly.

"Ax her kin I see her."

The girl slipped away from the door, leaving it ajar. The glimpse of the magnificence within angered Aunt Mimy. Presently the girl returned.

"Has you got any message?" she asked.

"No, I ain't. Tell her dat a' ole nigger 'oman fum de country want ter see her."

Cousin Rebecca T. was listening at the farther end of the hall, and thought she recognized the voice. The girl turned away with a smile to deliver the message, but her mistress was standing near. With a wave of her hand, Cousin Rebecca T. dismissed the servant, saw her safely out of hearing, and then opened wide the door.

"Come in, Mimy," she said in a voice as serene as a summer morning; "come into my room. I have n't seen you in a coon's age." She dropped easily into the vernacular of Rockville and the region round about. She took Aunt Mimy somewhat off her guard, but this only served to increase the agitation of the old negro. Cousin Rebecca T. led the way to her back parlor.

"Come in," she said kindly. "How have you been since I saw you last?" She shut the door and caught the thumb-bolt. "Sit in that chair. Now, what have you to tell me?"

Aunt Mimy saw that the thin white hand of her old mistress trembled as she raised it to her hair.

" Wellum," Aunt Mimy replied, " I des tuck er notion I 'd drap by an' say ' Chris'mus Gif'.' You know how we use' ter do down dar at home. I ain't seed you so long, it 's des de same ez sayin' howdy ? "

Cousin Rebecca T. looked hard at the old darky, and drew a long breath.

" Do you mean to say you have nothing to tell me — nothing ? What do you want ? " She would have laid her hand on Aunt Mimy's shoulder, but the old woman shrunk away, exclaiming : —

"God knows dey ain't nothin' here *I* want! *No, ma'am !* "

Cousin Rebecca T. took a step toward her old servant.

" Where is Mary ? " she asked, almost in a whisper.

" She down yander — down dar at de house." Aunt Mimy put the child down, faced Cousin Rebecca T., whose agitation was now extreme, and raised her strong right arm in the air. " I thank my God, I ain't got no chillun ! I thank 'im day an' night. Ef I 'd 'a' had 'em, maybe I 'd 'a' done 'em like you done yone."

" You are impudent," said Cousin Rebecca

T.   The little child had gone to her, and her hand rested on its curly head.

"Wellum," Aunt Mimy rejoined, "ef you want ter call de trufe by some yuther name, let it go at dat."

"Whose child is this?"

"Heh!" the old negro grunted. "He look like he know who he kin ter."

Cousin Rebecca T. took the child in her arms and carried it into her bedroom, closing the door behind her. Aunt Mimy went to the door on tiptoe, and listened silently for a moment. Then she nodded her head vigorously, ejaculating at intervals — "Aha-a-a!" "What I tell you?"   "Ah-yi!"

Cousin Rebecca T. placed the child on the floor and knelt beside it.

"Darling, what is your name?"

"Azzerbewy Tummerlin Pierson," replied the child solemnly.

"Oh, will the Lord ever forgive me?" cried Cousin Rebecca T., falling prone on the floor in her grief and humiliation.

"Yonner mudder!" said the child.

"Where?" exclaimed Cousin Rebecca T., starting up.

"Yonner." The youngster pointed to a

picture of his mother hanging on the wall, an enlarged copy of a photograph taken before she was married. Seeing that the lady was crying, the child went to her, laid its soft face against hers, and gently patted her with one of its pretty hands.

"Mudder c'y — all, *all* 'e time," said the child, by way of consolation.

"Oh, precious baby!" exclaimed Cousin Rebecca T., "she shall never cry any more if I can help it."

"Ah-yi!" responded Aunt Mimy on the other side.

At this juncture the colonel walked into the back parlor. "Well, my dear," he said, "what is the programme to-day? In my opinion — why, this is Mimy! Mimy," — his voice sank to a whisper, — "where is your young mistress?"

"Ah, Lord! you been waitin' a mighty long time 'fo' you ax anybody dat quesh-t'on!"

"Mimy, is she dead?" The ruddy color had fled from his face.

"Go in dar, suh." Aunt Mimy pointed to the door leading into the bedroom.

The colonel found his wife weeping over

the little child, and, being a tender-hearted man, he joined her. As Aunt Mimy said afterward, "Dey went on in dar mo' samer dan ef dey 'd 'a' done got erligion sho 'nough, an' de Lord knows dey needed it mighty bad."

The colonel went on at a great rate over the baby. "Look at the little shoes with holes in them!" he cried. "Look at the torn frock!" Then he fairly blubbered.

In the midst of it all, Aunt Mimy opened the door and walked into the room, calm, cool, and indifferent. Ah, how wonderfully she could play the hypocrite!

"Come on, honey," she said. "Mudder waitin' fer you. I tole 'er we wuz comin' right back. Come ter mammy." The baby ran away from its old nurse, and hid its face in its grandmother's bosom, then sought refuge between its grandfather's knees, and was otherwise as cute and as cunning as babies know so well how to be. But Aunt Mimy was persistent.

"Come on, honey; time ter go. Spile you ter stay here. Too much finery fer po' folks."

"Randall," said Cousin Rebecca T., calling her husband by his first name (something she had not done for years), "order the carriage."

"No, ma'am; *no, ma'am!*" Aunt Mimy cried. "You sha'n't be a-sailin' roun' *my* chile in a fine carriage wid a big nigger man settin' up dar grinnin' — *no, ma'am!* I won't go wid you. I won't show you de way. I'm free, an' I'll die fust. I ain't gwine ter have no fine carriage sailin' roun' dar, and Marse Laban lyin' down town dar in jail."

"In jail!" cried the colonel. "What has he done?"

"Nothin' 't all," said Aunt Mimy. "De folks des put 'im in dar 'ca'se he wuz po'."

"Randall, go and get him out, and bring him here. Take the carriage." In this way Cousin Rebecca settled the trouble about the carriage. Then she went with Aunt Mimy to find her daughter, and the old woman had to walk rapidly to keep up with her. When they came to the door, Aunt Mimy paused and looked at her old mistress, and for the first time felt a little sympathy for her. Cousin Rebecca's hands were trembling, and her lips quivering.

"Des go an' knock at de door," said Aunt Mimy kindly. "De po' chile 's in dar some'r's. I 'm gwine roun'."

She went round the corner of the nouse, and there paused to listen. Cousin Rebecca T. knocked, a little timidly at first, and then a little louder. Mary opened the door, and saw standing there a richly dressed lady crying as if her heart would break. For a moment she was appalled by this appearance of grief incarnate on her threshold, and stood with surprise and pity shining from her eyes.

"My precious child!" cried Cousin Rebecca T., "have you forgotten me?"

"Mother!" exclaimed Mary.

Then Aunt Mimy heard the door close. "Come on, honey," she said to the baby; "I 'll turn you loose in dar wid 'em."

Cousin Rebecca T. took her daughter home, and not long afterward the colonel appeared with Laban, and the baby's Christmas was celebrated in grand style. Aunt Mimy was particularly conspicuous, taking charge of affairs in a high-handed way, and laughing and crying whenever she found herself alone.

"Nummine!" she said to herself, seeing

Mary and Laban and the old folks laughing and carrying on like little children — " Nummine! You 're all here now, an' dat 's doin' mighty well atter so long a time. I b'lieve dat ar aig-nog done flew'd ter der heads. I know mighty well it 's done flew'd ter mine, kaze how come I wanter cry one minute an' laugh de nex' ? "